R.M. Clarke began her career moving into voiceover and wri published in *The Irish Times, Sp* *Pen Anthology* and written for Dublin 2020. Her debut novel, *The Glass Door*, won the 'Discovery' award at the Dalkey Book Festival and The Irish Writers Centre Greenbean Novel Fair 2016. She is editor of and contributor to *The Broken Spiral* anthology in aid of the Dublin Rape Crisis Centre, published in 2017 with the assistance of Dublin UNESCO City of Literature. She was part of the 2018 XBorders:Accord writing project in association with the Irish Writers Centre and Arts Council Northern Ireland. She holds a BA and the Gold Medal in English from Trinity College Dublin. She lives in Wicklow.

First published in 2018 by Dalzell Press.

Dalzell Press
54 Abbey Street
Bangor, N. Ireland
BT20 4JB

© R.M. Clarke 2018

ISBN 978-0-9563864-4-1

Cover design by Baby Duka

The Glass Door

R.M. Clarke

Dear Eóin

Enjoy.

[signature]

Dalzell Press

(a)

'Are you ready?' Dr. Waters asked.

Rosie nodded once and closed her sweaty fingers around the hard thing hidden inside her palm. Its solidness comforted her. She hoped it would stay that way.

Dr. Waters smiled.

'Don't be nervous,' he said.

Rosie swallowed: 'Will it hurt?'

'No.'

He smiled again, a little sadly the second time. He opened his mouth to say something, but seemed to think better of it and with a shake of his head closed his mouth again.

'Ready?'

Her ears were hot. She cleared her throat and felt them pop.

'Ok.'

He tapped the metronome on his desk. Slowly it swung from side to side, each doleful arc punctuated by a click. Rosie wished she could reach inside her chest and hold her heart still.

'Now, Rosie. Relax. Feel where your body connects to the couch. Feel how it supports and holds you. Allow your eyelids to slowly, gently close. Very good. Now, listen to my voice, and only the sound of my voice. Feel your entire body relaxing as I speak ...'

The clicking metronome gathered the couch, Rosie and the man's voice inside its crescent shaped swing.

'Ten, nine, eight, seven, six ...'

The little raven tumbled from Rosie's hand onto the carpet as she felt herself sinking down, down -

'... five, four, three, two ...'

One

Before Rosie was born, her mother sank into a deep depression.

It was 1970: the year of the earthquake, as the people of Ireland called it. Most had not seen the like of such a thing in their lifetimes, being of an island known for its mild winters, wet summers and distinct lack of earthly disasters. In later years - or was that now? - on the chair in Dr. Waters' office, Rosie would remember this winter as clearly as a ringing bell and marvel at her own mind and wonder how -

Small clouds of dust rose from the carpet as fringed lampshades swung and the plates clattered together like cold teeth in the cupboards. Rosie's host, her mother Sandra Cotton, and her mother in turn, Marie, were forced to run for the doorways and spread their arms between the posts, even though the quake amounted to nothing more than a loaded truck's journey down the narrow pass that ran between the rows of houses on their quiet road. But it gave the neighbours plenty to talk about. And when one of the worst winters ever to touch them followed afterward rendering travel impossible, the subject of the earthquake was talked over so much it grew arms and legs and the head of a beast, and was recalled with fond and awful reverence in local minds.

The weather dictated that Sandra, in her condition, was stuck inside. She longed for escape. Ceramic figurines winked at her in stillness from the shelves as weak beams of sunlight caught them, reflecting the snow drenched ground outside the window. The relentless landscape of pure white drove her madder still each day. Every night Sandra prayed for rain. Every morning she longed for sun, for freedom, for clear roads to the ferry port at the coast, where her carriage awaited. But even if she had managed to plough her way through the deep snow drifts to get there, gouging out a path by hand with her protruding stomach leading the way, there would be no way across. The seas were treacherous and all ferry crossings were cancelled.

What she needed, was some sort of sign. The only person she had exchanged words with in almost six months was her mother Marie: widow, homeowner and rhypophobe. Marie dusted and polished with mounting hysteria as her daughter's belly swelled and something altogether new grew within her. Marie was a respected member of the community, a woman called upon for advice in times of disarray, and a stalwart of the Sunday service in the local church. She was renowned for her clear thinking and cutting judgements, and for her own daughter to let herself be taken in by that feckless wanderer of a man ... She would not allow her out. She could not let her be seen.

'You'll stay in your room until that child is born and then we'll be done with it!' Marie had said it the first time Sandra had slunk before her; she'd said it many times since. He had disappeared, the boy. He was as spineless as they came. All words. And he had left her. Gone to England like the rest of them.

But Marie was getting soft since Ned passed on for wasn't that daughter of hers sitting with her dirty feet up on the couch in the living room and the radio that should have been in the kitchen blaring and crackling on the dresser, upsetting the order of her gleaming menagerie?

'You enjoying yourself there Sandra?' Marie asked as she rounded the room with the duster.

'Oh yes,' Sandra replied, tossing her light hair and folding her arms, the child in her still knit into her as well as planted inside of her: 'I am fat, alone, pregnant –'

'Well, you've nobody to blame for it but yourself.'

Marie tried not to say it, but it came spilling out nonetheless.

'– and I've been stuck inside this house with nobody but you to talk to for fucking ages and if my ankles weren't so swollen I would put on shoes and run away!'

'And I'd be glad to see the back of you!'

Rosie-in-process grew restless and the two ends of Sandra's body became book covers and snapped shut. A groan of pain escaped her, but Marie wouldn't have heard a second earthquake above her outrage.

'And you wouldn't heed me would you, and all the warnings I gave you. And where is he?'

'Don't. Please.'

Sandra had still not caught her breath.

'What is it?' Marie noticed at last the deep blue beneath her daughter's eyes and came to her side.

'The baby.'

Sandra was pale, brittle, the inside of an eggshell. Marie felt a strange compulsion to embrace her daughter but fought it.

'I need some air,' Sandra said.

The prospect of fresh light and of things beyond the house and garden thrilled Rosie, within her mother she shivered. Sandra's eyelids fell shut as she closed her arms around her stomach.

'I'll be damned if you do.'

'I'll put on a coat,' Sandra said faintly.

'But you'll be seen –'

If only I could disappear ... Sandra's mouth formed the words silently, but inside they shook Rosie by the ears.

'– And then I'll be damned for sure.'

... or fly.

An image of a man, dark-haired and pale with eyes that cut a path through the water formed before Rosie inside. Her spine tingled.

'And you in that state, looking as you do? Not a coat - not a tent! - would hide that. The answer is no.'

Sandra opened her eyes, returning from a warm thought, a memory. A day when the ground was damp and yielding and the sky danced above her as she looked past the sharp angle of his shoulder. Her aching feet had kissed only wood and tile for months. And each day Marie's disgust was written deeper into the tired lines of her face. Sandra turned her gaze toward the window. How long had it been since she'd tasted the world beyond her front door?

'They're all asking for you, all the time. How's Sandra today, is she over the worst of it, what's the doctor been saying, when can we see her? I'm running out of things to say. They think you're dying.'

Marie laughed, but her eyes remained cold.

'Do you know Mrs. Kennedy didn't even look at me when I went for the milk today and I said hello to her twice. And as for the three of them up the way, the questions they were coming out with. And I don't know how many times they've asked if they could call. What am I to keep telling them? And if you go out they'll know then. They'll all know. And him gone is the worst. They've picked up on that well enough.'

Haven't we all, thought Sandra, still ice-like at the window.

Haven't we all, echoed Rosie.

'If only your father had been around. He'd have known that boy from the moment he looked at him. He would have stopped it, even with you creeping out at night chasing after him. Like a limpet! I should have listened to my brother and sent you over to him in Canada. I might still.'

Sandra looked at her mother then, straight at her, testing. Marie couldn't hold her, and turned away to polish the swans. Sandra moved towards the door. She lifted her coat heavy with dust off the hook. She sneezed.

'What do you think you're doing?' Marie cried, coming at her like a train: 'Have you not listened to a word I've just said?'

But a wild look had come into Sandra's face that caught Marie in the hallway and she knew then that save strapping her own daughter down to a chair until the time came there was nothing she could do to hold her.

What she needed, Sandra thought, as she heaved her way through the snowfall, was some sort of sign. From Him. For Rosie's mother was quite pregnant, that much was certain. Pregnant and alone. Her love was across the sea in London, shoulder to shoulder with so many others who had also left. So few young men had remained in the Wicklow hills where she lived and those that did gasped for air, even though there was plenty of it. And he was gone too: hers. *Theirs* now. He had promised to send money and letters, she had received neither. Sandra told herself - and deep within Rosie cheered these thoughts on with an inexplicable nausea - that no postman coming out from the Dublin city sorting office could battle with conditions like this. But every time she tried the number he had given her, waiting with a growing giddiness for the dial to revolve before she swung in the next digit, for the ringing to stop and a voice to speak, she felt her fingers would tear and bleed. As much as she tried to believe otherwise, she was most definitely alone.

And yet, life went on. Her neighbours still chatted on their doorsteps as though in defiance of the changed world around them. Snow swirled and wind howled and Rosie trembled as her mother battled through the drifts to get to the now severely understocked shop at the mouth of the village down the hill. And there they stood: Mrs. No.4, Mrs. No.5 and Mrs. No.6, arms crossed like nuns, clucking knee-deep about the usual banalities as though nothing had changed in their day-to-day lives and likely never would.

'Temperatures at a record low today,' said Mrs. No.4.

'Heaven help us and Mary down the road was eight inches under this morning. And her Catriona's sick,' said Mrs. No.5.

'Ah that's terrible,' said Mrs. No.4.

'And the laundry was frozen to the line today, stiff as himself's wood,' said Mrs. No.6.

'Thought I'd never hear the like!' cried Mrs. No.4.

Their dirty laughter rose into the air like scattered crows, but dropped back to earth with an almost audible impact as they sensed the approach of Rosie and her mother. Though Rosie could not see them, she knew they were there. She sensed the searing heat of their gaze as though it were an irresistible magnetic draw.

'Hello,' Sandra said as she shuffled past.

Mrs. No.4 went still and Mrs. No.6 smiled sideways at Mrs. No.5. Sandra rounded her shoulders and pulled her coat taut, shielding the curve of her stomach. But she had always been slight. Rosie had not inherited her physique. Sandra focused her attention on moving through the snow. Fresh flakes began to fall. The going was tough. She couldn't move fast enough. Rosie was ashamed. She cursed her father his broad sharp shoulders and the heavy breasted woman who bore him.

Said Mrs. No. 4: 'Oh Sandra, we haven't seen you in Such A Long Time!'

'And aren't you only looking well? So healthy and ... robust,' said Mrs. No. 6.

'Ah, are you off to the shops?' asked Mrs. No. 5. 'Be sure to call in and have a cup with us on your way back. We're only *dying* to hear what you've been up to.'

Sandra shook her head, though whether in dissent or agreement none could tell. Only Rosie knew. Together they continued on their path to the shop and exchanged no messages. The mutterings of the Mrs.' stalked them wraith-like all the way to the shelves.

Sandra's surroundings were becoming more remote to her each day. Rosie felt the restlessness pass to her through the veins and knew that her time was near. As the hours passed Sandra seemed to detach from the polished wood and gleaming of her mother's home. Marie had supported her, kept her out of sight and safe, for that she knew to be grateful. But such care was threaded with shame. It burned in her, a still-hot coal, and in the final weeks of her pregnancy she developed a temperature.

11

In the cold, cold nights that came, buried under piles of itchy blankets and swinging between shivering numbness and wild fevers, Sandra awoke sweating from dreams of fat fingers punching uselessly into the dial holes; no answer, a dead line, a spinning void. He retreated from her endlessly, she would call for him mute as a swan and he would not turn, but shrink away into nothing. In the small hours she spoke into the darkness certain the figure of her dead father sat at the end of her bed silently watching over her, ready to ease her and the unborn child into the next world where with him they could be complete.

'Come. Come, Little Button,' he whispered. 'I wait for you always. I'll have you, I'll take you, just as you are.'

Rosie pleaded with her mother to hold on, persuaded her that the world of the living was the world for them. She did not know what she was doing.

Christmas arrived and life on the island came to a standstill. The snowfall increased. Miraculously, the village public houses stayed open, enjoying record sales that would not be broken decades later in the years of economic boon. Even still, there was plenty to be talked about. The Mrs.' No.4, 5 and 6 needed a new audience for what they had to spill. Soon the pub was feasting on stout and the scandal of the Cottons at No. 11. A few miles north, Rosie sensed her time was near. When The Blizzard came, she was ready.

The roads were now impassable - that was the official line - and as the first contraction struck The Blizzard surged in sympathy with Sandra's pains. Rosie had chosen her moment and there was nothing to be done about it. Marie went running into the night after the waters broke, hammering on neighbours' doors for medical knowledge and help. Sandra faded in and out of consciousness, unsure which of the looming faces before her were really there and whether there was here or anywhere at all. At last, Rosie forced herself stickily into the physical world, aided by the powerful hands of Jane From Next Door, just as it was feared that all was lost.

One (a)

'This is what you were told?' The doctor asked. 'By your mother? Your grandmother?'

'No. This is what I remember,' said Rosie. Her voice was subdued, far away.

He cleared his throat softly: 'Continue.'

Two

It was the main story on the news for weeks. The Blizzard, that is, not the birth. Not many knew of the latter (apart from the whole road) and Marie did her utmost to contain it within the few who did. She kept Jane From Next Door, who had once delivered a local calf, sweet with a bottle of something from the cupboard in the good room. She dropped a few loaves of her soda bread over to Mrs. Kennedy who had come laden with a pile of old sheets and blankets for Sandra to push on just at the moment Marie thought the mess would spread to the legs of the old grandfather clock in the hallway. Despite Marie's efforts, news about the birth got out.

Sandra was grey for days after it and had such weakness in her arms and legs that Marie had to hand feed her in the bed. She winced as the oily broth flecked the white sheets she had so painstakingly preserved over the years, but her daughter's helplessness brought on another sort of pain.

'When babies have the babies but stay the babies that is when the trouble starts,' Marie muttered, hushing her moaning daughter and helping the newborn latch on. Breastfeeding sucked the life out of them. Marie watched their interpretation of it with mild horror. They fed off each other with a religious devotion, the baby pulling hard at the teat, the mother devouring the child with her eyes as though hoping she could reverse the whole thing and disappear inside her. It was the only time in the first days after the birth that Sandra could be roused. Once it was over, the two collapsed into a deep shared sleep. Marie watched them. Sandra was serene, a corpse, and her stillness lulled Marie into a standing slumber. But Rosie jerked violently beside her, and more than once Marie would have to hold her down to stop her from thrashing against her mother or the bars of the cot.

'I'm afraid to say that we're stuck over here too,' was all the comfort Dr. Callaghan could offer when Marie called the surgery in place of a nervous breakdown. 'Until this snow melts I can only assist you over the phone.'

Marie counted the minutes like beads, with a gnawing feeling that she was the only living person left in the house.

Neighbours no longer able to feign ignorance grew bold and called to the door. A stream of visitors kept the doorbell well-oiled. It had been a difficult birth, so the visitors suspended their judgements until Sandra was well enough to take them. And the child itself was a draw. She was beautiful.

'Look at that hair. It's like fire,' said Mrs. Kennedy.

'Her eyes are terrible green though aren't they,' said Mrs. No. 4, bending over the cot to look at her.

'Awful bright,' said Mrs. No. 5.

'Unnatural really,' said Mrs. No. 6.

'And so far away. You know, Sandra, I don't think the child has looked at one of us,' said Mrs. No.4.

'That must worry you,' said Mrs. No. 5.

Sandra kept her gaze upon the canvas of grey outside the window and could not be moved to speak. Rosie ignored them all and silently urged the shadow that hid in the wardrobe not to come out again that night.

'Well she's a good healthy size anyway is what matters,' said Jane From Next Door. After that there was nothing else worth saying, both mother and child had fallen back into a sleep so absolute it would shame the dead.

A week passed. Visitors stopped calling. Number 11 had taken on the sense and feel of a mausoleum. And Marie no longer offered tea.

'Oh Ned,' Marie spoke into the ticking kitchen when the last of the visitors had gone. Their reluctant charity had left her with only a pint of milk, a wedge of Christmas cake, three tins of soup, six eggs and half a loaf of brown to keep all three of them in calories until the melt.

'With the shop empty and the car froze, what am I to do? If only you were here,' she sighed, as his imprint formed on the linen beside her sleeping daughter upstairs.

And time was not on their side. The snow was defiant. When Rosie was nine days old Marie started skipping meals so she had something for Sandra, who lapped at the soup she brought but rarely answered to her name. Marie suppressed her hunger pains with hot water and spoons of sugar, something she usually took great care to avoid. For someone who knew how it was to be comfortable, even a little well-off, she took to the Spartan lifestyle without complaint, though she had nobody to complain to even if she had wanted to. She had exhausted her neighbours' charity. By the close of the first fortnight of Rosie's life, Marie was down to her last few ounces of flour. All that was left of fresh food was an onion and a handful of sprouting potatoes and the milk and eggs had dried up days before. She knew Sandra would not survive for much longer without the doctor or food, and what then was to become of the child? For the first time in her life, Marie found her feet leading her toward what was once Ned's cupboard in the good room, and the solace to be found within it.

That night a shadow hovered over the house and the rooms grew cold. A breeze whispered across Marie's collarbone and the squat glass she had been holding slackened in her grip and tumbled brightly to the floor. She jerked awake. Up above Rosie stirred, and was sure she could see the dark shape of a man crouching low by the bed, singing softly into her mother's ear.

The next morning Sandra woke with life in her cheeks to find that trees had leaves, houses had rooftops made of tiles and blades of grass were green in colour. Another thing she noticed was that the roads were clear. There was no hesitation. Her bags had been packed for months.

Three

When she was three weeks old, Rosie crossed the sea.

Rosie was at home on the waves. It was a portal between the worlds to her, between the old life and the new. An open doorway. Neither here nor there. And for a reason she couldn't grasp then still being shy of a month old, but was with the help of a metronome and a soothing voice closer to grasping now, she felt at ease with the uncertainty of it. The rocking of the boat was soothing to her in the absence of a cot. Something about its doleful swing from side to side was familiar, though she knew that couldn't be right.

She crossed the sea in search of a father she had misplaced along the way, or rather had misplaced her. She heard tell that the waves had stolen him away.

'Have you seen my father?' she asked the dolphins as they plunged in and out beside the boat. The roar of the waves was monstrous and they did not answer. Sandra, restored to an unhealthy vigour in the week that had elapsed between death's door and the sea, gripped her daughter fiercely as though if she lost hold of her she might herself float away.

Once on dry land, where a concrete metropolis bloomed around them in the place of lakes and hills, Rosie and Sandra began the search. They looked in many places for Rosie's father, but he was nowhere to be found.

'Have you tried the _____ house?' Men in heavy boots and bright jackets said.

'Have you tried the _____ house?' Ladies on the street said.

'Have you tried _____'s house?'

'Or _____'s house?'

'Or _____ and _____'s house?'

The more these people talked, the more Sandra's face sagged. Rosie bounced along roads crying out for trees and grass on her mother's chest, her fat feet dangling over hard grey earth. Sandra lit up when Rosie tried to cheer her, but went dull again long before Rosie's smile had faded. It was tiring work searching for her father, even though she didn't have to use her own legs. It went on endlessly. Phone numbers were punched in and dialled, and letters were written and posted. Rosie began to suspect that her father was not a man at all but a ghost.

He was discovered at last on a stool in a building that had the words Free House on the sign outside. And so the mystery of the houses was solved. Rosie had never thought they would find him in a place like that. For one thing, it looked nothing like a house.

As her mother pushed the door open, Rosie knew she had entered into an untouched world. Sandra's steps were slow and tentative, their bodies knew that they were not welcome in this place, something in their scent and shape, something deep within them clashed with the musk of arousal and brutality long soaked in the oxblood carpet. Voices climbed over one another aiming for an indefinable precipice and more clawed from behind to tear the leaders down. Rosie was left with an impression of souls scaling and tumbling down a mountain on an eternal circuit.

'Another round!'

'Who's paying?'

'It's yours –'

'I took care of the last one.'

'My turn's been.'

'Get your hand in your pocket for once.'

'Look at this specimen. Had water on his, now it's a pint. Typical!'

A breeze blew past them from the street and carried their perfume towards the dripping bar. The bodies there stiffened. Talk faltered. The man behind the taps raised his eyebrows: a warning. Slowly the large backs turned towards them and their faces, rich with famine, took them in: every curve, every inch.

Only one remained hunched over, aloof. Sandra took a step forward. The door swung shut behind her. They were closed in. The man behind the bar disappeared into the back room as though washing his hands of what was to come.

Sandra cleared her throat, spoke. A kettle whistled in place of words. She cleared her throat again.

'I'm looking for ___.'

The famine faces looked towards the one unmoved back, panting. His broad shoulders tensed, sharper still. At last, he turned. His dark hair, long like a woman's, fell back as he betrayed himself. His eyes were so blue they could have clothed the morning sky. So blue they could cut a path through the surf. So blue they could have ferried them all the way across the sea. There he was. There he was, before them. Rosie leaned her head back until her neck was almost unhinged and grasped tightly to her mother's sweaty neck. She looked at him. She remembered from some primitive sense the tumbling dark hair, the large hands roughened from work, and that face: forever impressed with the mocking half-smile of a man whom life as far as he believed had chosen to scorn. All of the little parts that made up the whole: dad, daddy, pa, padre, papa, pop. The man who was her father.

Was he one of this shatter of men? Where they were grizzled and beyond repair he was elegant, with a wild untameable quality that was irresistible to Sandra (and most other women, to tell the truth). But they knew him, had his name. And he had theirs. It was more than what Rosie had.

Her father's eyes met her mother's for the first time. They flicked quickly towards Rosie and away, as though the vision of her burned him. Sandra swayed and Rosie felt her grip slacken around her waist.

'Have you anything to say to me, after all this time?' Sandra said to him then, the first words to break their swollen separation. Rosie felt the tremor in her mother's throat beneath her fingers. She closed her hand upon it, trying to catch it, to hold it still.

19

He stood. He was unsteady on his feet, but effortlessly so. He made the occupation of hard drinking look so glamorous. His smile flattened, the gentle curve of it smoothing out, needlelike.

This was significant, Rosie knew. Every memory, every touch and vision she had of her father came to her now vivid and distinct, as though it were happening in real time. It started to rain. Little droplets splashed against her cheeks. But no, she was indoors. Inside the Free House, inside somewhere else. No. It was not raining at all.

'Can you go on?' a voice said.

It could have been any voice but it was definitely not his, for she remembered that. Oh, she remembered that well.

Sandra trembled. Her father's smiling lips parted. The Free House took a collective intake of breath as it awaited his words. Rosie held hers.

He said: 'Sandra. My love. What took you so long?'

His voice. Delicious as syrup and as sweet. He swept her into his arms and in that flickering moment something entirely new. One kiss and Sandra developed amnesia. She melted into him, she seemed to drink in his breath. He ruffled Rosie's red, red hair. It was far too easy. Sandra gave herself up, Rosie hung back. Who was this man after all?

He came and held them then and the smell of him was a thing she would remember always even when all the hard evidence of him had faded from her world. His scent, and his voice. The men at the bar turned away. The man reappeared, pulled down a tap. Talk broke out. The door closed behind them once more, shutting the oxblood carpet in, reuniting mother, daughter and father.

'Daisy, Daisy, give me your answer, do. I'm so crazy over the love of you ...'

On the wet hard street his arm was around them and his hot breath sang in their ears. If it had still been daylight they would have walked toward an orange sun sliding under the horizon. Instead, the squares of light from The Free House windows grew smaller behind them as they stumbled away to find a house they could call their own.

Together at last, the little family set up home in a cold disused building where ice grew on the inside of the windows. Rosie's father dislodged one of them and climbed in and Sandra passed Rosie through to him like a present. She climbed in after him, her frame, slighter still these days, passing through the gap he had made with a grace Rosie could only wonder at. Inside, Sandra's good rearing was wasted. The floor was bare and would burn bald feet. Rosie hovered above it in her father's one armed grip, hoping her toes wouldn't touch its grey-ness and dust. Bright, chaotic writing scarred the walls. Standing in such a place, Sandra looked like a shining vision. Rosie's father assured them it was only temporary.

Sandra got a new job a fortnight later, in a restaurant. This job stood between Sandra and Rosie's father like a mistress. His work boots had worn through and the money Sandra kept lending him for a new pair had a habit of mysteriously disappearing between sunset and sunrise. Securing a new position was impossible without them, yet still they did not appear. Sandra worked long hours, saving money so they could rent a flat with heating. The cold was beginning to creep into all of them. Rosie had developed a cough.

'Are you happy you found me?' her father said to her one private evening. Sandra was doing the late shift.

A bark escaped Rosie's throat. He ignored it and ran his fingers through her hair.

'I said, are you happy?'

Rosie smiled a red smile, gurgled as hard as she could, but could not form the words.

'Where did you get this hair?'

He pulled the scarlet curls straight and held them tight. In five months her hair had grown like wildfire. His smile held his face like a mask and his own hair, jet and brilliant, framed it.

'What has your naughty mother been up to?'

A scraping sound from behind the sofa caught Rosie by the ears then and she was pulled in two directions. The scraping sound was winning. She tracked it as it moved beneath her. Her father tugged at her hair still and his words took the shape of a dissonant melody, it pulsed below the other noise, the more interesting one. A small furred creature shot out and ran across the room. Rosie laughed.

'What is that?'

Her father jumped up and chased it around the room with his foot. He was screaming like a little girl. His boot had murder written all over it. Rosie began to cry then, desperate for the gift of speech.

Don't hurt it, she wanted to say. *I want to keep it.*

The thing escaped. Her father jigged maniacally on the spot making hooting noises like a bronchial wolfhound.

'Fucking disgusting. I'm not staying here anymore. I can't.'

He held his hands out from his body, scared to touch anything, even himself. It was as though he was performing litany.

'I didn't want any of this,' he told Rosie, who struggled to sit upright and fell into a fit of coughing.

'I didn't ask for it.'

He hovered awkwardly in the centre of the room, one leg going in a half-jig, looking towards Rosie, towards the door. He grabbed his leather jacket off the back of the chair beside him and shook it out furiously. Rosie reached her arms up toward him, tiny fists opening and closing like a blinking light.

'I'm just going out for a walk,' he said, the curve of his cheek hidden behind his curtain of hair. He brushed himself down. His pockets chimed like fine bells.

'I won't be too long.'

After a time, the room grew silent and cold. Rosie fell into sleep. She woke again in the blue light of the small hours into the smell of her mother. She struggled, and her chest was tight with phlegm, but Sandra's rhythmic sobbing rocked her back to sleep, the refrain repeating like the revolution of a wheel.

'It's ok-ay, It's ok-ay, It's ok-ay ...'

'It's asthma I'm afraid, quite a bad dose.'

The White Lady pressed against Rosie's chest with something hard-cold and silver. She was called a Doctor. She shook her head. Sandra grabbed Rosie around the middle.

'Do you smoke?' she asked.

'Yes,' said Sandra

'How often?'

Sandra swallowed back a cough.

'Around her?'

Sandra's legs crossed and uncrossed beneath the table, paused. Her foot continued to dance. The Doctor wrote something on a piece of paper then winked at Rosie.

'These sweets will make you better,' she said, handing the slip to Sandra. 'And – '

She produced a large clear balloon from a cabinet behind her.

' – this will help you breathe. And for you, mum,' she said, producing another piece of paper, 'take one before bed every night and you'll feel right as rain again.'

The White Lady looked at mother and child and broke into a smile.

'I know it's late,' she said, 'but I feel a bit like Father Christmas today.'

They had found him, but it didn't take long for them to lose him again. Rosie knew those early memories as a long game of hide and seek, where her mother was always seeking and her father was a master at finding the good hiding places, though he couldn't keep them secret for long. But it didn't stop him trying.

There was happiness in London. It was in there, somewhere. There were russet leaves to crunch under a first pair of shoes and a mother who held so tightly to her she thought she might break from love. There was a new flat near the park and central heating. There were birds to test the first vowels with and a clean squashy couch - the gift of an affluent skip - to hide behind. There was sadness also. Years passed and a dark-haired man danced sprite-like in and out of their lives, leaving emptiness in Rosie's palm where a work-roughened hand should have been. But Rosie was not entirely without friends. She had her mother. She tickled her and read to her from library-stamped books and filled her head with great stories of lost children finding grand homes, of a long-awaited kiss realised at last. There was the dog from down the hall who came to play chasing with her, although it wasn't that much fun because he always won. He had four legs and she only had the two and when she tried to use her hands to make it equal, it slowed her down all the more.

Then, in the school where she found herself one day, she found new companions.

Three (a)

Her hand twitched. It was empty. Something was meant to be there keeping her company, tying her back to the world. Where was it?

'Rosie, stay with it. Stay with my voice.'

But she needed it, him. Did he not understand?

'Tell me more about these friends of yours.'

Friends? Well he was a friend, a special one. Not quite like Peter. Not anything like him. But they had shared much more in a way. She knew Peter would never understand her the way he could. Not even her mother could know the things he knew. Where was he? She needed him, but she could not move. She could not call out for him.

'Rosie,' the voice said. 'Everything is going to be ok.'

If Rosie could have spoken then, she would have told the voice never to make promises it couldn't keep.

Four

It was the morning of Rosie's birthday. In fact, it was April of 1974 and Rosie was three years and four months old. But because she was starting at school she felt she had to mark the occasion somehow. A second birthday celebration seemed best.

It was not going as planned. Rosie knew her soon-to-be teachers at The Park Nursery were awaiting her arrival. She also knew she was late. Her mother was fast asleep and her father was playing hide and seek again, and winning. Rosie had been prodding Sandra in the collarbone for the past three minutes. Sandra woke, sweating. She clutched at the empty space in the bed beside her, her eyes were raw and bee-stung. Then the day, the time, the occasion: they all seemed to come crashing into her memory on top of each other like an unwelcome game of dominos. Without ceremony Rosie was pushed into the bathroom and handed a toothbrush, her hair was scraped roughly into a ponytail. Then she was dressed. All the necessaries were stuffed into a plastic bag acquired on the last milk run. There was no time for proper washing or breakfast.

'Where's Daddy?' Rosie asked as a bruised apple was handed to her and she was steered into the stinking lift. This was no way to celebrate.

'He promised he would come.'

'He'll be there,' Sandra whispered into the lift mirror. She patted on some makeup and fixed her hair across her cheek. Her breath left the shape of a mouth on the glass.

The school was not far, but the journey time was doubled by Sandra stopping every few steps and searching through thin air, sighing, walking on. By the time they arrived the school was buttoned up and still as though it was sleeping.

The call came from the other side: 'Come In!'

Rosie stood outside the door holding on to her mother. If she didn't let go she'd never have to walk through to that other side, she could be anchored there always, kept at shore and safe. Sandra fixed her hair again, followed the command.

'I'm so sorry,' she began as soon as the office door swung open, 'I was working late and then my alarm clock didn't ring. It's been doing that a lot. I have to get it fixed.'

The Lady Behind The Desk watched Sandra as she spoke, her lips which were very full and brown between breath and speech. When she finished she smiled and looked down at her cuticles.

'As long as it's not a habit, Mrs. Cotton. Punctuality is very important to us here at The Park.'

'It's Miss. Miss Cotton.'

The lady made a sound that hovered but did not land. She regarded Rosie from her nail beds, skirting around Sandra as though she had already left the room.

'Is this little Rosie then? Hello Rosie. Are you excited about today?'

Something black and shiny on the desk caught a shard of light and gleamed. A little thing. A toy. Rosie picked it up. It was heavy for something so small.

'Do you like that Rosie?'

Rosie liked it very much. Its solidness comforted her. She could feel it in her palm, feel it, but not feel it at all.

'It's a type of bird,' the lady said. 'A raven. Can you say it?'

'Can you say ray-ven, Rosie? Ray-ven?'

With her sudden animation Sandra's hair shook into her eyes. She folded it behind her ear. The lady behind the desk coughed gently. Rosie looked up at her mother as her mouth stretched and rounded to make room for the bird. A dark shadow hung under her right eye.

'Dad-dy,' said Rosie.

The Lady Behind The Desk stood up and took the toy bird out of Rosie's hands. She put it back in its place. Rosie longed after it, needing it. She wished she could take it with her. It would make an ideal second birthday present. Sandra folded her arms and her narrow chest curved under them like she was folding inside out.

'Shall we go and meet your new teacher? And your new friends?'

The lady left the room. Sandra moved slowly after her.

'Come on honey. Third is the one with the hairy chest.'

As she followed the women out, Rosie looked back at the little bird again. Her first new friend. Before the door closed behind her, she was certain she saw it wink.

Kate The Teacher said hello. Rosie kept her eyes firmly on her shoes; her skin blanched where she held her mother's hand. Sandra tugged at her daughter's grip as quietly as she could.

'This is really quite natural. Don't worry, Mrs. Cotton.'

Sandra cleared her throat and began aligning Rosie's ponytail over and over.

'It's Miss.'

She arranged her hair across her right cheek. Kate The Teacher and The Lady Behind The Desk shared a look they seemed to have recognised in one another before.

'You can take it from here?'

Kate The Teacher nodded.

'Enjoy your first day, Rosie,' the first new lady said. 'Miss Cotton, come and see me once she's off, won't you.'

She turned her back on them and walked down the corridor towards her office.

Kate grinned down at Rosie. Rosie curled into her mother's waist. She could feel Sandra was leaving her already, a tension growing between them like a gradually extending rope. And she hadn't even wished her a happy birthday. As for her father, she had not seen him in days. He had said goodbye, see you later, I'm going to work. He had said he would bring her to her first day of school. A big day for my girl, he said. He had promised he would come. He had promised. She had been taught that promises were made to be kept. But she was at school and he was not there and a crowd of strangers gathered on the other side of the red door, waiting for her. She couldn't recall the last time her father had tucked her in.

'Where's Daddy?'

Sandra's cheeks flared up as though they'd been slapped.

'Everything OK?' Kate The Teacher asked. Her face was very soft.

'Yes, it's fine,' Sandra said. She laughed abrupt and shrill like a tin whistle. 'He's just late. You know. Men.'

She took a shuddering breath and ran a hand along the outline of her face. She rummaged in the yawning plastic bag that dangled at her side, threatening to split.

'Here. Rosie might need this.'

She handed the teacher a breathing apparatus that resembled a small blimp.

'And these.'

Two inhalers. One brown, one blue. On cue, Rosie gave a small cough.

Sandra smoothed her hair down and tucked the hair she had just arranged in front of her face behind her ears. Kate's eyes flicked quickly at her and away. She pushed it forward again.

'Well, I better be off. Be good Rosie won't you. For Mummy.'

Rosie hugged her mother around the knees and wondered if she would ever see her silver-gold hair catch the light like that again, or hear the rumbling sound of her father's voice. She would be like one of those orphans her mother had read to her about she knew it, roving around the city caked in dirt, sleeping under railway arches, eating out of bins. She would learn how to put just enough pity into the question tuppence? and how to fend for herself. She looked up at her mother with big sad eyes as practice. Sandra was overcome at last and shrunk as she walked down the corridor.

'Come and meet your classmates,' said Kate.

29

Rosie compared the clock that was alive against the picture beside it on the wall and worked out that outdoors time would be in ten circles. She had gotten used to this new routine. At first it had been alien to her, this rigid timekeeping, but now she enjoyed carving up her day into different activities. It made it go faster. The large chalk letters on the blackboard reminded her it was Tuesday. Nap time had already been. They were painting now. Until the tenth circle had been drawn all she had to do was keep her elbows in while she was working so she didn't touch against the girl who sat beside her. She kept dragging the back of her hand across her nose, leaving a glassy trail across her skin. It reminded Rosie of the snails who waited for her outside and the game they had left unfinished. Rosie didn't begrudge them their slime but the stuff the girl beside her was producing was unnatural.

'Five minutes until outdoors time boys and girls, so start tidying away your things if you please. Ask if you need help,' Kate called.

Rosie dipped her paintbrush in the water jar, a black cloud uncoiled inside the glass.

'What is *that*?' the girl said.

She pointed to the black shape on Rosie's page. Her dirty finger came closer, too close, and landed in the paint.

'Uh-oh.'

The black had mixed with the blue, and the two had merged. It was all wrong now. The girl giggled. Rosie scowled, something inside her sunk down and out of reach.

'You've ruined it now.'

She picked up her wet painting and stood up, getting in line behind the others queueing for a clean square on the drying out counter.

'It was ugly anyway,' the girl muttered behind her back.

Rosie looked down at the sodden page. She couldn't remember what she had been trying to achieve. It was just blobs. She sat back down again and took her paint brush out of the water, trying to recall what it was meant to have looked like and how she might fix it. But all the paints had already been tidied away. The girl beside her had done a picture of a brown house with a green door. Four thin, pink figures stood in the foreground. A yellow sun shone in the top right corner. The girl saw her looking. She lifted her chin up high.

'That's me and my brother and my mummy and my daddy and that's my house,' she said, naming with her snot-greased hand each of the pale streaks that represented her loved ones.

Rosie looked at the picture for a long time. She looked so long that something else began to emerge, a pattern, something previously hidden in the picture's white relief. Like a green snake emerging from the grass, something was made visible that could not be unseen. Her hand began to move then of its own accord, it lingered over her own painting. The dark blurred figures within sang out to her. The song was sweet. The notes whispered into her ear, they travelled the skin of her arm, they reached into her fingers. She was snared. Her hand spread out as it hovered over her painting. It plunged down into its deepest, wettest part. The cold of it on her naked palm. A small ridge of dark paint rising around it. And as the sunshine next door dimmed then was blocked out entirely, she relished knowing that she had forced that thunderstorm upon the smiling sticks that lived within and that had so shamelessly mocked her.

'Now yours is ruined too,' she said. And she smiled.

The girl beside her started to cry loudly. Instantly. Wound up and let go. It was an awful sound. Kate The Teacher came running over to the scene.

'What's happened?'

'She - she – she,' Snot Face wailed.

'Rosie, did you do this?' Kate asked.

Rosie held up her paint smeared hand with wicked pride. The girl's nose was now pouring freely into her open mouth. Kate comforted the girl at arm's length and sent Rosie straight to outdoors time alone.

The day went from bad to worse then. Before she knew it, Rosie was locked in a battle and trying to find a way out. First it was Snot Face then it was The Wasps. They often tried to pick fights behind the bushes when all Rosie wanted to do was go to the races with the snails or hunt ladybirds. Rosie and The Wasps had never seen eye to eye. They were fundamentally different. Acid and alkaline. Sharp and flat. They were territorial where she liked to roam. It was a free country, so Rosie had heard. But the wasps had made it clear that they felt she belonged on the tarmac with the other humans.

'I don't like it there,' she said. 'They pull my hair and call me Paddy. And that's not even my name.'

'That is not our concern,' they said.

'But I lost something under your bush and I had to get it back.'

'We do not care,' they buzzed.

Their crystal wings went into action. Their speared ends glinted.

'I'm sorry!' she cried, as she stuffed something small and hard deep inside her dungaree pockets. But the buzz of their wings was too loud for them to hear her. Or perhaps they had chosen not to listen.

'Get away!' she screamed, beating at the air around her as it started to hum. As one the colony took flight, pointing straight for her. She ran towards the school doors. She pushed the door open and had almost made it to safety when one wasp slipped through the gap and sank his revenge into her neck. Rosie felt his cruel sharp sting and for the second time that day the anger swelled within her, it took her over, she could not stop it. Rosie caught him and crushed him into pulp.

The door slammed shut behind her, draining her sudden rage. With her eyes still shut tight the reality of what she had done trickled through. One eyelid lifted, then the other. She looked at the mangled body of the insect. One transparent wing was still twitching. Rosie had always thought herself peaceful but now - there was no other word for it - she was a killer. And so young!

Then Rosie heard her name being called. She felt a soft hand on her shoulder. She looked up and saw a kind face, the face of The Lady Behind The Desk, the woman with round brown lips, whose name she had never learned. Rosie blushed with shame for two reasons. One was buried inside her palm, the other inside the pocket of her dungarees.

'There you are. Come with me please.'

As she turned around, Rosie saw that millions of tiny silver fish swam in her dark hair. Rosie walked with the lady, their shoes echoed down the corridors. The long lines of the passages stretched out and it was as though they would never end. The body of the wasp was still hot in her fist. The sun was bright in the sky outside the windows, but the passages remained in shadow. It never could find its way in there, the light, the trees outside were too tall. Rosie found herself before the same green door she had stood in front of that first day, many clock circles ago. It opened and the two entered the room. The lady and Rosie sat down. The lady smiled.

'How are you getting along here, Rosie?' she asked.

Rosie heard a bump against the window. She looked up. It was an angry wasp, beating his body in grief against the glass. Her clenched fist throbbed with guilt.

'Don't open the window,' Rosie said. The lady smiled still.

'Do you like it here?' she asked.

Rosie wondered which of her snail friends had passed the marker first. She had put a bet on the tortoiseshell, but she'd have to wait to find out now. The lady sat before her, barring her way to the playground. Each time she shifted in her chair shoals of whitebait changed direction on her head. Her hand was still heavy with the knowledge of what she had done. Had the lady seen? What was her punishment to be? She couldn't go back out there now. The Wasps were baying for blood. She looked up at the window. More of the colony had joined the scout. They were hovering on the other side, searching for ways in. Whatever her punishment was to be it had to be better that what awaited her out there, even if it meant that outdoors time was over.

'You've been here over a month now. There must be something you've found you like?'

If this was punishment it really wasn't too bad. Although the lady did ask a lot of questions. And stare a lot. Rosie looked around the room, trying to dodge the bright beam of her gaze. Books everywhere. Paper. Shelves. Paintings and drawings, not too different from the ones that she and her class had done. The desk was wide and wooden and brown, scattered with pens piles of paper. The little bird was no longer there. Beneath where it had sat that day was a deep dark ring, like a burn. She chanced a look at the lady. Still smiling, still staring. The moments passed. Rosie realised that something was expected of her.

The lady sensed the change: 'Anything you like in particular? Your lessons perhaps? Your teacher, Kate?'

The buzzing outside the window was getting louder. Rosie would not look. She needed to get rid of the evidence then maybe she would be safe. And these questions were being put to her and surely if she didn't answer one of them now she would be discovered? Things she liked. What did she like? She had to find an answer.

'I like the custard we get at lunchtimes. The chocolate one,' she added to buy herself some time.

'Good,' the lady replied, showing her teeth as her smile opened. 'And what of your classmates? Do you like them?'

Rosie frowned. What ridiculous questions she asked. What had they to do with wasps?

'I don't want to eat my classmates,' she said sternly. She could not be both a murderer and a cannibal in one day.

The lady smiled again, and this time it stretched to her eyes. At the corners, they crinkled.

'Of course you don't. I heard you had some trouble earlier in class though? With Linda I believe?'

Rosie kicked her heels against the chair legs. So that was what all of this was about. Snot Face and her stupid painting and her stupid pink family.

'You know not everyone finds making new friends easy, Rosie. Especially when you come in halfway through a term.'

But she had made friends, Rosie wanted to protest, they just weren't Snot Face and the rest of the stupid boys and girls in her class who always had something to say about the colour of her hair, or the way she said certain words, or her battered, dirty shoes. Her gaze strayed to the floor. It looked far away. Rosie let her fist fall open and felt the relief as the wasp fell down, down.

'Can you tell me a little bit about what happened during painting time?'

Rosie looked up. She wiped her wet hand on her thigh. The buzzing outside the window stopped. For now, she was safe.

She talked and now it felt familiar even though then it was the first time. The lady asked more questions and Rosie answered them. They drew pictures together. The pictures took the shape of familiar things, familiar people. The lady asked questions about these too. After a while, Rosie was allowed back to class. Outdoors time was over. The lady walked her up the corridor to the red door. She knocked. Kate answered. She looked down at Rosie, raised her eyebrows.

'I'll come and talk to you at lunchtime,' the lady said high above Rosie's red hair.

Kate nodded. The lady nodded. Kate steered Rosie to her seat. Linda stared determinedly away from her when she sat down, her pert clean-at-last nose pointing up in the air like a pin.

'Ok, boys and girls. Let's start that again,' said Kate, coming to a rest back in front of the blackboard, where she spent most of her time.

'A for Ap-ple, B for B - B - Bear. Yes. C for ...'

Rosie felt bad for her friends out in the dirt, still waiting for her to come back and call an end to the race, but she thought it was probably best that she give the hive and The Wasps a wide berth for some time. Anyway, she had her little friend hidden in her pocket and that was the most important thing.

'Wait for me, over there. I'd like to have a word with your mother.'

It was the end of the bad day. Children and parents were being drawn back together. Kate sent Rosie to the pine bench under the coat rack to wait. Rosie kept her head down and counted as high as she could go. When she couldn't get any further, she started again. In the tumble of arriving parents and inside-out jacket sleeves and forgotten lunch boxes Rosie disappeared. Children dragged adults out the door towards home with the urgency of those fleeing a pandemic or war. There was no sign of Sandra, but Snot Face's parents arrived, her brother with them. He was older, taller and had brown freckles across his nose. They stood there, and the girl's painting came to life. Kate spent some time talking up close to them while the girl held on to her father's hand and looked as glum and fat-cheeked as she could manage.

Rosie held her hand up before her so that they looked small and her hand big. She swept her hand across them. She did it hard with her arm stiff and straight and her hand shaking. But no storm came. Her powers no longer worked. They were still there: four pink strips unblemished standing in the path of the sun. Every now and again the mother and father looked over towards the coat racks, but Rosie would not catch their eye. She kept on counting. When she got bored with numbers she started on the alphabet.

'A is for Ant, B is for Bumblebee, C is for Caterpillar, D is for Dragonfly...'

'Home James and don't spare the horses.'

The storm had heard her and sent the thunder. Was it thunder or a voice? She looked up. Her father towered above her. She couldn't remember what E was for.

'Aren't you going to say hello?'

Rosie would have spoken had she been able to, but her own voice had left her. It floated above her head somewhere. Rosie could feel her brain jumping up there trying to catch it while her head remained beneath the coat hooks. It was a strange sensation. As dark as he was with his hair and his jacket and his voice, there was this brilliance also that hurt to look at. She looked past him instead. The girl and her pink family had left. So it had worked after all. He had scared them all away for her. Then Kate The Teacher came marching over to spoil things.

'Excuse me, who are you here for?'

He threw his hair back away from his face as he softened his shoulder toward her. It fell well past his shoulders now. Rosie wondered if people thought he was a girl from behind sometimes.

'Me? I'm here for this little lady aren't I.'

He shrugged in Rosie's general direction. Kate did a strange thing then, she seemed to swallow a giggle whilst trying to push a fly off her nose with her nose. But when she spoke her voice was steady.

'I'm afraid only parents - or guardians with a written note - can collect children from The Park.'

'That's just as well then.'

He took her hand. Goosebumps crept along Rosie's forearm.

'I'm very sorry I haven't managed to introduce myself before,' he said. His second hand closed upon their handshake and Kate's hand was trapped in the middle.

'Rosie's father. Her mother is usually in charge of the school side of things.'

All the coats were gone apart from the pink scarf that was always left behind even at the weekends. It was just Rosie, her father, and Kate.

'Oh, I'm sorry, I didn't know you were ... No, that's fine. I'm Kate.'

'Hello Miss Kate.'

'Just Kate.'

'We give our teachers a title where I'm from.'

Kate blinked many times in quick succession.

'Actually, I was expecting Sandra today. She usually comes ...' she trailed into a quiet apology. He grinned it away with his left dimple.

'You see there are a few things that Harriet - the owner, have you met her? She started out working with children for the council.'

Rosie's father shook his head.

'Well, there were a few things Harriet and I wanted to discuss with Sandra about Rosie.'

'Can't you discuss them with me?'

Kate looked at him for a while, very still. Frozen almost.

'Well I suppose I could. It's very important, Harriet has written up a report ...'

'A report? Is my little lady in trouble?'

'No not at all, Mr. Cotton.'

She giggled again.

'It's ___.'

Rosie's ears pricked up and tried to catch the sound of the name, but missed. It was offered to Kate in private as a whisper. Below, Rosie burned with jealously.

'Sorry, it's a habit,' said Kate.

'And I'm no Cotton, that's for sure. Think the old woman would have me deported if I was.'

Kate's giggle developed into an open laugh.

'What did you say your name was again? Catherine?'

'It's Kate,' she said, and her smile stayed still.

'Well Kate, why don't we ... Rosie, be a little dear and wait outside for me a minute.'

The red door closed, Rosie on the wrong side of it. She sat on one of the small chairs lined up along the wall outside. The clock hands moved on. Circling and circling. Each circle Rosie counted. She got to six counts when she climbed into the big chair, the one for mums and dads and other teachers. Her feet dangled high above the ground. Falling would hurt. The fast hand travelled around the clock face. She travelled with it until it made her feel faint. The more she looked at it, the more it took on the appearance of a many-eyed face with three barbed tongues. A ticking monster. The red door remained closed. The longest hand had moved from 2 to in between 6 and 7.

Someone shook her shoulder. Her father. She had not heard him come out. She had her hands over her ears but she wasn't sure how they got there. He walked straight past her. He didn't look at her. The red door stayed ajar, but Kate did not come out to say goodbye. Rosie felt she ought to have said something to her but she didn't know what. She was wary of approaching the room now that all the other children had gone. Something about it said Do Not Enter. It was the territory of pencil sharpeners and crayons and plasticine only. Neutral. It no longer belonged to her. She knew she must be in awful trouble.

'Come on!'

Her father was already at the foot of the corridor. Rosie stamped after him.

Four (a)

'And now I am somewhere else. Somewhere far away. It is cold and dark and bright at the same time and I am up high –'

    'Where are you?' asked the voice.

    'The stars,' said Rosie.

Five

All was still.

Rosie felt strange, as though she had been flattened. She opened her eyes. She was back in her room.

The same shoes, toys and unwashed clothes were jumbled in a heap on the floor, no longer in shadow. The window was back in its frame. A flutter beneath her brought her back to her bed. The Raven was still there, watching. His head was cocked and his watery blue eye observed her.

'We are home,' he said.

His voice was like syrup made into sound. Smooth and rich and refined.

'Did you enjoy yourself?'

Rosie did not have the words to say it, but her eyes shone. The Raven's face grew grave.

'We could not stay up there,' he said.

'Why?' Rosie asked. Discomfort grew inside her like stomach ache.

'The sky was in danger.'

He fixed his bright eyes upon hers.

'How?' she asked.

'Because of you,' he said. 'Because of your tears.'

The bed shuddered angrily beneath her. She wanted to climb down and run to her mother, but the fall to the floor was far.

'Soon there will be no stars because of people like you,' he said. The bed vibrated beneath her again and her knees grew hot.

'Why?' Rosie asked. Her voice was small.

'Your tears are so loud I can't hear myself think. The stars do not cry. They are strong, but when you are sad, they die. Because of people like you and your stupid mother who are sad and weak, the stars will be lost.'

Guilt settled in her, deep among the blankets.

'Don't speak about my mother like that,' she whispered.

'What did you say?' The Raven said.

Rosie's thighs began to burn. She did not want to fight.

'Nothing,' she said.

'Good girl.'

The mattress cooled. The sky grew rosy outside the window, the glowing street lamps fought the waking day.

'I must leave you now,' The Raven said.

There was silence. Rosie said nothing. She didn't want to sleep, or wake. She didn't want him to leave. His deep eyes were upon her like pools.

'We will meet again,' he said.

Do you promise? Rosie wanted to ask, but was afraid of the answer.

His wings shrunk back in on themselves.

'You will need me before the end.'

The bed shook. The bird's neck twisted around, his gem bright eye dilated, his beak shut and sucked itself in and then, he was gone. Rosie sat atop a bed and not a bird and in her hand was a little toy that sat heavy in her palm.

Once she was sure he would not grow large again, Rosie closed her hand around him. She relaxed her body and curled into a croissant shape under the duvet. After some time she fell asleep, just as the sun began to rise.

In a few hours Sandra would wake her for breakfast and all would be as it once was.

Five (a)

'Before the end?' The voice asked, further away now. 'What might that mean?'

'I don't know,' said Rosie.

But she was certain it wasn't anything good.

Six

The sun rose higher in the sky as Rosie slept and soon it had coaxed Sandra awake. She lay in bed still and wide-eyed as the sun pushed against the window. She remained like that for some time.

The flat was still, his absence all the more palpable because of it. Her own breath the only music to reach her. Such a singular sound, how the chorus of their exhalations used to warm her to the morning. She threw the duvet back and rose, pulling a jumper from the chair by the window to throw over her night things. There, revealed: an old shirt of his hidden beneath the steadily mounting pile of cast-off clothes. One he had missed. She lifted it to her nose and breathed in the days old smell of damp sweat and heat and the fading scent of aftershave. How that smell used to wrap itself around her and she could disappear into it, how she had drunk it in with such a thirst. It had been her drug. She would not wash it. It would be the one thing. Just that. She folded it and placed it under her pillow, went out into the narrow corridor that connected the five small rooms of their sparse box flat. The warped wooden floorboards massaged her aching feet after yesterday's double shift. And all that went with it. Him. The worst she'd seen him, banging down the restaurant window. Calling. Screaming. Customers running out the door when he grabbed the manager by the throat ... it was a miracle they had not told her to leave, but how long their sympathy would last was another thing.

As she reached her daughter's room she pushed the thoughts away. She edged through the door and stood in the doorway to watch the little chest rise and fall, the little arms wide and thrown above her head, open and trusting. Only in sleep. The room was filled with sunlight, she hadn't got around to getting curtains. She made her way up the steps of the bunk to Rosie's sleeping form and gently prodded her.

'Wakey wakey.'

The child moaned. Sandra rubbed and rocked and coaxed; she went deeper into her nest.

'But-ton,' she sang.

Rosie went like a stone, she went hard against her. Sandra felt that resistance, something she knew too well. Rosie had inherited it, but not from her. She felt her patience slipping away from her then and tried to grasp a hold of it, she'd had little sleep and a night she was desperate to forget and all she wanted was to get the morning over with. She tried again. She tried to remain calm. But the child would not yield. She could hold herself back no longer.

'Get up. Now!'

The words tore at her throat and she snatched back the duvet. The child's reproach was the first thing to greet her that morning. She had her father's eyes but for the colour, their lovely impossible depth and their way of singing with sadness when they did not get their way.

'Get. The. Fuck. Up. Now!'

The words purged from her, as though they had been pulled. She marched into the kitchen. She needed to channel her energy into an action. She needed to keep her hands busy. She banged the kettle off the sink as she filled it to drown out the needling echo of her own voice. She cringed when she saw other mothers lose it. She had always believed herself to be made of better stuff than that, born to the role. But the echo of her own voice clung to her like a stain, taunting her. The day had not started well. She had important things to discuss with Rosie and little did she want to for she knew that once she let the words loose out of her mouth she would never be able to shut them up again.

Rosie slunk into the room with sullen eyes. Her red morning lips were in a deep pout, her hair a gorse fire about her face. She loitered at the door and twiddled the handle to announce herself.

'Could you leave that please?' Sandra's voice was again straying into a dangerous territory. She held herself. 'Sit at the table.'

She'd laid the squat table as though for a celebration. Two embroidered white linen napkins for two wooden chairs. A knife, fork and spoon sat side by side upon each napkin in neatly descending order. Rosie did what she was told. She pulled the chair out. It was large and awkward in her four years old arms. It scraped across the floor, the legs grating and wailing against the tiles. Rosie looked up at her mother. Sandra closed her eyes, took a deep breath and walked out of the kitchen.

In her bedroom, Sandra closed the door and lay on her bed face down. She buried herself in her pillow. She screamed. Feather quills pricked her face and poked into her open mouth. Her voice did not escape but was swallowed up, she beat the mattress with her fists. When she was done she lay still for some moments. Then she got up and wiped the wetness from her face with her sleeve and tried to do something with her hair. When she came back to the kitchen Rosie was sitting on the chair with her head bent and her hands in her lap as though in prayer. Steam was rising out of the kettle and the eggs had begun to boil. Sandra put some toast under the grill and took two chipped cups from the cupboard.

'You can have some tea this morning if you like,' she said. Her voice held firm this time and did not waver.

'Yes please,' said Rosie.

Sandra slapped the butter on the toast and sliced off the egg tops. They rolled around un-cradled on the plates beside the toast. They would have to do without egg cups if they were to have white linen napkins. Sandra carried the plates to the table and set them down. She sat opposite her daughter. They ate without speaking. Sandra did not taste the food but felt the mechanical working of her jaw relax her. Rosie drank her tea slowly and with pleasure, it was a rare treat. As they were fingering the last crumbs and pieces of egg and it was time to clean up, Sandra found that the time had come to talk about the thing that needed to be talked about. It forced itself upon her, she had no choice. The words themselves were edging their way out between the gaps in her teeth.

'Rosie –'

'Yes?'

Sandra steeled herself.

'Last night –'

The phrase hung over the teapot. Rosie looked at her and her head tilted slightly to one side. Sandra considered holding her breath until she turned blue.

'Rosie, you won't be seeing your father any longer.'

The sentence ricocheted off the four grubby walls of the small kitchen. Rosie froze, her ear and shoulder moving towards each other like lovers.

'Button?'

Rosie's eyes dropped low and to the right as though a far off sound, some movement or disturbance, had caught her attention. Her eyes flicked alarmed back to her mother's face.

'Did you hear it?' she said.

'Did I hear what?'

Sandra became aware of her own heart pulsing.

Rosie frowned. She kept still. Then her eyes bulged in their sockets, on the cusp of outrage and panic. Then they relaxed. Then she sipped her tea.

'Rosie did you hear what I said?'

Rosie gave a short curt nod, her eyes still on the table.

'I'm sorry. I did try my hardest, but sometimes that's not enough.' She sighed. 'Are you alright?'

Rosie nodded again, her nose pointing to her plate.

Sandra stood up. For an excuse to turn away she filled the kettle again and put it on to boil and started washing up. She was struck then of the first time, the first thought. Before she had divided into two. She had always been like clockwork. And then she was late. When she realised it her stomach swooped out of her and the sickness in it was a sensation she

47

would never even now far on the other side of it ever quite forget. The denial came after. 'It can't be that. Impossible. I'm just a little stressed at the moment. I'm tired. All these late nights! It will come tomorrow.' But the next day the bedsheets were still stubbornly white. It was a marker of how desperate the situation was that she longed to sully her mother's precious sheets. She had never craved the coming of her period. It was a monthly nuisance, something one had to put up with. The inevitability of ruined underwear. But now it became an obsession. She pushed a finger inside but it came out clean. Tampons swelled but did not colour. As the days passed and the blood did not the fear intensified. And then: the worry. Her head buzzed with it. It knew nothing but it. What to say? How to say it? How to tell *him* and then *her*? How to tell her mother. What was worse? The knowledge of his disgust, or her disappointment? She convinced herself that he would be happy. She wrote plays in her mind in which the perfect words were said, words that ought to be written in a flawless Edwardian script -

She would be taken in his arms yes and there would be a kiss oh the most magnificent kiss and it would be in the rain perhaps and then they were a family that smiled in photographs stylishly until the end of time. More children would follow after this, the first, two boys and a girl would be lovely. They would buy a house and have a car and they would only put the photographs from the sunny days in frames on the mantle and on the shelves. It would always be summertime in their house, clouds would pass over the roof and hover down the road over the other homes and the beams would light up her windows like they had been chosen by God even though she never went to church. Neighbours would envy their carefree relentlessly happy lives and lambs would leap in the field behind the poppy strewn garden

But he had shouted and slammed the car door and gone to the pub. He had said: *Be rid of it.* How those four words wore away at her like a cancer. What could she do? She had already lost one and how the pain had wrenched her then and she was young and she couldn't help being fertile and it wasn't just her in it anyway! She wrenched down the window and shouted after him. He hadn't looked back. How she loathed the blame for it, as if women could procreate in solitary confinement, like some marine being. Was she a witch who picked the seed from the innocent sleeping man and swallowed it down cackling, somehow fertilising herself through the digestive tract and snaring the man against his will for all eternity? And oh how it had awoken every anger that had ever been felt by womankind in her bones and how she shook with the injustice of it. And how her determination held that she would do something, say *something,* this time she would. And she had shouted after his back and watched him leave. The nights passed and he did not call. The hollow of it inside her all around her and the gnawing growth nestled between her hips. And when he finally returned to her she had lost it all, all her strength was gone. She said nothing in the end. You take care of it. It's nothing to do with me. It. It. It. Nothing. It made her sick to her stomach. Or perhaps it was just the pregnancy.

She swung between choices, unable to settle. *Take care of it!* Marie barked. *Be rid of it!* he commanded. How she had longed for her dead father then. How she had longed for him to hold her and to tell her that what she wanted was right. Then one morning she vomited up her breakfast. She had always wanted a baby, something warm and fragile to hold and love, something that would love her back perhaps unconditionally, something that would always need her as she would need it. A bond for life. A best friend. Would she ever tell Rosie about those nights? Frozen in dread with the worry of it all with the empty space in the bed beside her and knowing, but powerless to stop it, that he was off with *her* or *her* or *her* and the knowledge of it pinned her to the sheets broiling and seething inside, her mouth stretched across her face with the teeth bared and grinding, the squeak of it so spine draggingly awful like nails down a chalkboard or freshly washed wood. The tumour of pain in her chest. The relentless weight of it. Or perhaps it was just the heartburn.

'Mum can I've a biscuit?'

'You're pushing your luck now Rosie.'

'But I want one.'

'You've already had sugar in the tea and that's enough. Don't give me those eyes! We've none anyway.'

'Oh.'

Rosie had this ability to spear her through the heart with one flicker of the eyelids.

'You're wasting your breath,' Sandra reaffirmed. She was certain she would not give in.

'But why can't I have one?'

'We have none and I'm not going to the shop for you to have the whole packet gone by dinner. I don't know where you got your sweet tooth from.'

But of course she knew. They both did.

'I. Nev-er. Get. *Anything*!' Rosie screamed.

Sandra looked at her daughter's face, written with the passion that had reared up from nowhere. A fluttering had started up inside her. Cath from the flat block, who had three boys under seven and lived upstairs, had told her that distraction was the key to her sanity. She grabbed her keys. She would take her to the park.

Just around the street corner, solid grey concrete was swallowed up by bark and leaf and the colour green. The park had laid out a huge spread in celebration of their arrival; the billowing plastic tents of a fairground: Eye-popping, blinding, its soundscape of plinking melodies and the occasional unanimous scream thrilled them both. The park was usually patchy grass peppered with dog waste, benches with mouldings of sleeping men and the odd climbing tree, so the tents and the fairground were asking to be explored. Within minutes, Rosie had made sure she was decidedly lost.

'Be careful!' she heard her mother call from somewhere, but that didn't matter now.

Mud-kneed she crept under table legs and in and out of tents, among the pegs and ropes. Endless rows of cakes and delicious things lined the boards and in her rodent form she made her bid for them. She believed no one could be looking and even if they were what could they do about it and she a mouse? She was too small to be seen. A chocolate bun disappeared, a small iced cake. But as she snuck towards a large jam roll she was caught.

'A thief, a thief!'

A woman with a puff pastry face: Rosie's wrists were seized. She was dragged out from under the table, into a circle of faces.

'Geoffrey, can you believe it - the cakes - a thief has stolen our cakes! For the charity!'

'No!'

'You can't be serious, surely?'

'I won't believe it!'

Rosie stood in the middle of the tent with her wrist clamped inside a cold dry palm.

'Is that the one, there?'

'Such a little thing to be so naughty.'

'Surely she meant to pay?'

Every pair of eyes turned to her. The circle of faces was ever-widening, each lit upon her like a spotlight. Their hot collective gaze bit at her face and her cheeks burned. She looked down at her feet. Black feathers lay in a pile on the grass. She kicked at them.

'Where is your mother, girl?'

'Oh! And we've been up since dawn baking. For charity!'

'I can scarcely believe her capable.'

'Well I will have words. I will indeed have words. Mark me!'

Then – saved. Her mother appeared. Sandra sighed when she saw her.

'What's going on?' she said. Her voice had weights attached to it.

'Oh, are *you* the mother then?' The woman gave Sandra a hard look. 'I was sure she'd been abandoned! I was ready to call the police!'

'Well I'm here now. I'll take her off your hands.'

'Now - see here - your daughter has been stealing baked goods from a charity sale for repairs to the local church,' said Geoffrey. 'What have you to say about that?'

'Rosie never was particularly religious. Like myself, actually.' Sandra smiled.

The woman smiled back, sucked in her cheeks. Rosie was sure she was suffering from toothache brought on by a life surrounded by cakes. The woman nodded solemnly.

'Yes, of course. It must be difficult for you,' she said, and her smile stretched along her pearlescent wet teeth: 'raising her alone.'

Sandra frowned, looked down at the hair on her daughter's head. A miniature red top. She ran her palm along her crown down to the base of her skull. Under Rosie's feet, the black birds' feathers in the grass caught the dying light of the sun, flaring up like the slick green of spilt oil.

'And so far from home,' she continued.

Sandra cleared her throat: 'If my daughter has upset you I'm sorry. But she is only five years old and knows no better. We have to get on now, get home for the tea ...'

Sandra pulled Rosie away before they could ask her for money. As they left the tent Rosie heard the woman's voice again behind her, speaking low, but with such intent that her words snaked through the crowd and tapped them on the shoulders –

'A terrible shame. These days none of them have fathers. And Irish, of course.'

Sandra squeezed Rosie's hand hard, but Rosie wriggled free of her grip. She was drawn to the bright fairground light, a suicidal moth, her mother's calls consumed by the wind.

Sandra hobbled after her in leather shoes that pinched around the emerging corn on her left foot. Her patience had deserted her again, not least because her perm was now violently askew.

'Get. Back. Here. You don't take just things – Rosie, do you hear me?'

But Rosie's second brush with the criminal life was already forgotten. She was transfixed by something else: the gorgeously spinning Wurlitzers. Sandra waddled up beside her and took a firm hold of her arm and tried to catch her breath.

'I want a go,' Rosie said.

'I don't have any money Rosie. I told you that before we left.'

'But ... but ... that's not fair because, why do you go to work?'

Sandra sighed again.

'There are things that exist in this world, Rosie, called responsibilities. The longer you've no knowledge of them the better.'

They stood and absorbed the neon heat and each passing scream. The sky began to grow dull and collapsed in towards them. In the absence of the sun they shivered.

'I think we should go,' Sandra said, turning. 'Come on. We'll come another day.'

'But it won't be here another day.'

'It will be somewhere.'

But they were both reluctant to turn from the bright lights and music and the voices light and full and move towards a home they now knew with certainty would be cold and empty. Their steps were heavy as they left the park, toes dragged, toecaps frayed. Some heaviness, something like foreboding pushed out their bone marrow and replaced it with lead. A shadow passed overhead, and Rosie looked up in time to catch the flight of a dark winged creature. She moved closer to her mother. Their block came into view. Rosie wanted to run but could not move. She could have been glued to the ground.

'Mum I don't feel well –'

'It's your own fault for stuffing your face.'

As they approached the flats, the bushes shook. Rosie shivered though there was no breeze. Sandra unclasped her bag shakily, desperate to get indoors. For the cup of tea it was. She was gasping for a cup of tea ... her cold hands spidered around in her bag for the keys. Then a voice spoke.

'Hello ladies.'

The keys Sandra had just found clattered to the pavement. The sound echoed off the building like an alarm.

It was her father. Her father was here, but he was her father and not. He looked strange, smiled weirdly, a scent rising from him like steam. Against herself, Rosie began to feel afraid, her spine was tingling. Sandra shot down to the floor, grabbed the keys and unlocked the door. She pushed Rosie through first. She followed but was only half in when she got jammed inside the doorway. Rosie turned back to her. A large rough hand was clamped around her upper arm, pulling her back. Sandra resisted but the hold upon her was strong. Rosie watched from the stairs, wanting to run, but not knowing which direction was best. With her one free hand Sandra grabbed the door by the letterbox and tried to slam it shut, but the arm was caught in the gap. There was a cry.

'You stupid bitch!'

The limb retreated.

Sandra snapped the door shut behind her, the thick wall of frosted glass and wood was between them. But at once they heard the jangling of keys.

'Oh no, I forgot,' she said, as though remembering she had left the radiators on.

She came sprinting up the stairs towards Rosie, took her up into her arms and threw her over her shoulder like in Sack of Potatoes. It was a fun though uncomfortable game they would sometimes have played together: Rosie would bob uncontrollably down her back like a ludicrous ponytail giggling almost to the point of throwing up, when just as it all became too much they would fall into the couch on top of one another red-faced and gasping. But in that moment Rosie knew it had lost something essential.

As they reached the first landing they heard the front door open. They still had to reach the next floor before they would get to safety, and even then, he still had the key. Rosie willed strength and speed into her mother's legs beneath her, calling upon the psychic umbilical cord that still united them. She prayed for time. His steps came ever closer, ever louder.

Up another flight, bypassing the lift and powering through to the shared bathrooms on the third floor as the shadow grew into form behind them ... Sandra threw Rosie in, bolted the door. On the other side, something slammed against it. Sandra closed the lid of the toilet over someone's unflushed remains and sat down, pulling Rosie tightly onto her lap. They tried to ignore the stench of blocked waste, the repeated butts against the door. They sat still and waited. The banging door fell into a soporific rhythm. Rosie slipped into sleep.

She was in a wide open space. Grass rolled out from under her toes. It wound up and down in the shapes of hills and valleys and far beyond. She knew the place but did not know how. She looked out over the sea. She smelt the sweet sea air and heard the cry of birds. Dark shapes passed overhead. Shadows rippled across the green. A ram sharpened his horns against a rock nearby. The ram turned his face to her. His eyes narrowed and grew red. His mouth opened and he spoke.

'Get out here you fucking bitch!' he said.

Rosie jumped, and her eyes opened. She was sitting on her mother's lap in a toilet.

'I had a bad dream,' she said.

'I'm afraid this is real life,' her mother replied.

A voice was muttering nearby. The voice of a man.

The handle lowered, bounced back.

'Open the door,' the voice said.

Sandra said: 'Just go home. Please just go.'

'This is my bloody home,' the voice said. The door rattled in the frame.

'I'll get you for this I swear. You'll rue the day you tried to get rid of me!'

Sandra's face was pale, her fingers cold and stiff. She jiggled Rosie on her knees. The night rolled into the early morning. They held tight to one other, eyes wide and alert, arses numb, hoping the door would hold, or he would give up and leave.

'I'm sorry you had to see your father like this Rosie,' Sandra whispered into her hair.

But all Rosie could see was a trembling door. A sudden urge came upon her then and she rooted in her pockets feverishly.

'What are you doing?' Sandra whispered.

'I've lost something –'

Panic was trickling up Rosie's spine. It was now very important that they get out of this toilet and into the flat. She must know where it was ... but she was stuck. She was at the mercy of her mother, who wrapped her around her hands like a balloon string. The door pulsed. The smell faded. Time passed. It was filled with the sound of shoes moving up and down the hall. Of heavy breathing. Of denim clad legs crossing and uncrossing. Of a face passing through hands. Of leather squeaking. Of paper dancing. Of a lid unscrewing. Of lips, a tongue, a throat. Sobs. Repeated words as rage rendered, gave way to remorse.

The words were: 'I'm sorry'

Rosie felt the grip around her tighten. She felt the jittering legs slacken beneath her.

'I know I've been an asshole. You don't deserve it Sandra.'

A bitter laugh echoed in the toilet.

'I don't know how you put up with me. But I don't want it all to have been for nothing.'

The sound of rustling and of sloshing liquid came through the keyhole.

'There are things I've said. Things I've done that I shouldn't have.'

Then his mirthless laugh to echo Sandra's.

'I mean where would I be without you. You know I'd be nowhere.'

No answer from the toilet. The door continued to speak. Rosie willed it open.

'You were the one who wanted this family. Now you want to ruin it?'

Sandra fidgeted on the seat but did not rise to the door.

'Please Sandy. Please darling. I'm sorry. I don't know how many times I can say it. I'm sorry. I'm sorry. I'm sorry. I'm sorry. I'm sorry. I'm sorry. I'm sorry. I'm sorry ...'

Rosie felt her hairline grow wet. Her mother shook behind her.

'I need you you know? I need you so much. What would I be ... oh what would I be if you were to leave me ...'

His voice was a toneless drone, a foghorn. Sandra giggled a little. Rosie thought that perhaps this was meant to be singing. She thought longingly of her bedroom and what she had left there, an essential thing. She was hungry. She was thirsty. She needed the loo. Her own loo. And then, they came: those words.

'I Love You.'

How quickly forgotten his harsh words, his spitting bile, his steel-hard grip. That little phrase was like a spell, Sandra heard it like an oath and became a doll ready to do his bidding, all forgotten. She lifted Rosie off her knees. Rosie stamped her feet and tried to wake them. Sandra pushed herself slowly upright and stood before the door. With closed eyes she slid the bolt across. She opened it. The sky was breaking up outside the window at the far end of the hall.

There he was leaning against the frame of the door, lit from behind by the emerging dawn. He had brought Hollywood with him to the flats of North London. Even Rosie softened to look at him. Dressed in that faded leather jacket of his, the face pale and anguished, the long dark hair. He reached in and pulled them into him. The scent of him was all there was, the sewage a dwindling memory.

'Let's put her to bed,' he said, the edges of his words blurred as though they had been left out in the rain. 'Then we can sort this all out.'

He used his key to open the door to their flat. He stood a moment in the doorway and seemed to swallow up all the light from the naked bulb overhead. Then he stood aside, and the two women followed him in.

In Rosie's bedroom, Sandra dressed her in her pyjamas and carried her up to the bunk and laid her to rest. She tucked the duvet in around her. She did it slowly, a tender ritual. She kissed her lightly on the forehead. She turned off the light. She left the room with Rosie's father - why could she not recall his name? - closing the door behind her gently, so gently.

'Night night, sleep tight don't let the bedbugs bite.'

But Rosie was wide awake. And the thing, the thing was yet to be found. She rooted around under the sheets. Nothing. She padded her hands out over the mattress. Where was it? She tried to retrace her steps in her mind. She needed to find the lost thing. It had to be in her hand now, only then would the panic in her subside. Then she remembered. She luxuriated in the memory and felt the anxiety ebbing away. She slid her hand under her pillow and the tips of her fingers touched against something cool and hard. Then: a crash exploded from the kitchen. The sound of glass shattering - or maybe the earth - followed by her mother's scream. Rosie thought she would go deaf.

The voices were tumbling over each other in a rush now, the vowels smacking together, two opposing gusts of wind. They were outside her bedroom door. Rosie knew with every bit of herself that she was the only one who could stop it. She slid down the stairs of her bunk taking no time to be careful, for there was work to be done.

She stormed out of her bedroom in her star-patterned pyjamas into the bit of corridor between where she stood and the front door. The scene before her was loud and fast, and she couldn't make sense of it. It had to stop.

This is ridiculous, she wanted to say, echoing a voice that lived somewhere in her ribcage: *Whisht now. Settle down. I'm trying to sleep.*

But if she had spoken, they had not heard her. They crashed against one another. The wooden floor groaned beneath them. They were so much bigger than she was, their voices so much louder than the one that lived in her. The light bulb swung above them all and night and day chased one another across the hallway. Something had to be done. She marched between them, right into the middle of it. Her throat ached. They danced above her and she swayed along to their rhythm. Then she felt herself being lifted high into the air, flying away. It felt strangely familiar, she couldn't remember why. And then she was falling back down to earth again, falling and hitting the ground hard and she was on the wooden floor in that narrow bit of hallway between her bedroom and the front door and the back of her head felt wet and light. An anguished sound ripped through the flat blocks. Rosie blinked her eyes open and saw her mother's face no longer beautiful, but sharp and squinted. All of her soft edges had taken on corners.

'You!' She screamed.

The sound of it drilled through Rosie's skull. She knew she must have done something very bad. Her father, an inverted triangle of splintered legs and a wide towering back, seemed to feel the same way. He lifted his arms above his head and shrunk away from that screeching sound coming out of Sandra, from somewhere deep inside her, her own ribcage. His boots were coming ever closer to where Rosie lay.

'Don't you ... don't you dare ...' Sandra said, and it was all breath, as though she was trying to come first in a race.

Then Rosie was caged in by Sandra's legs, her father's legs caging them both, and Rosie felt herself pinned further against the skirting board with every driving moment. She cursed herself being barely out of the womb with only four years in her. She willed herself to grow. And she decided then: I am big. I am strong. With her new muscles, her new strong long bones, she forced her way out of the cage of legs. She was almost out when a knee came from nowhere and nailed her back against the wall. Her breath was squeezed out of her and she shrunk down to four years old. Above her way up above her father was a hammer and her mother a pretty picture with a shattered glass frame hanging lopsided on the wall. The knee released her then, looking for another target. She was not going to be it. She wriggled free and crawled into her room.

In there, she kicked things. The post of her bed. The clothes on the floor. A limp cotton bear. She had a strong right foot for her age. Her desk chair got a good kick. From outside, a scream. She took a step towards it. Her bare foot landed upon some hard angular thing. She picked it up. The little black toy, too weighty for its size. She must have dropped it on her way down. She didn't want it anymore. She threw it at the wall, it bounced off and fell to the floor where it shuddered angrily. Rosie did not care. Another scream. The wall that held the door shook. She ran to it and kicked it. It stared back unmoved. She kicked it again, but it was still just a wall. Again she kicked and again harder and harder. She cared not about the crushing pain in her toes or the dark bruise slowly spreading up her foot.

Then she gave it her shoulder. She gave her shoulder to the wall once more, with more of her strength. Again and again, the wall still oblivious to her marbling skin. She knew the harder she pushed the quieter the shouting would go, until it was a whisper, until it was a breath. She pushed and pushed then turned her body and pushed her hands against the wall with her whole weight behind her legs and the weight of everything, and saw a spark appear before her.

She knew all she had to do was keep her strength and focus trained on that one spark until more and more sparks came and more still, until all those sparks fused together to create a huge blazing fire, enough to make them stop. The sweat rolled down her face and her arms and legs shook and her wrists ached and her neck burned and all of her was sore, but the wall yes the wall was aflame.

Six (a)

'And after that?' he asked

After that - a life without her eyes open in the dark waiting for a sound from the front door, from anywhere, without urging the clock to keep still at the end of school days, as if by controlling the movement of the clock's arms she could by magic make him appear.

'After that I saw a life with no hope.'

'No hope?'

The space between the two end points of the metronome became a vacuum and Rosie had the sensation, if only for a brief moment, of being nowhere at all and being no-one.

'That must have been very difficult,' the man's voice said, breaking the illusion. But only just.

'It wasn't. It was wonderful. I –'

Seven

A few weeks afterwards Rosie was kidnapped.

On the morning of the abduction she was playing in her usual spot - the dirt patch in front of the bushes outside her block of flats - when her mother remembered the toast on the grill and hobbled back in before the smoke alarm woke the neighbours. Rosie did not notice her mother's retreating footsteps, she did not hear the sound of approaching ones. She wheeled her truck forwards and backwards through the mud. Then a shadow swallowed it and her and she was gone.

Rosie felt little fear when the shadow reached down for her and hoisted her up and away. She did not struggle. She did not thrash. She did not call for her mother. She yielded to its embrace and let her plastic truck fall to the dirt. The entrance to her flat bobbed up and down and grew smaller with each step the shadow took. Soon it was out of sight.

Sandra returned. She saw the abandoned truck. She sank to her knees. She called aloud. She tore her hair. She walked up and down streets and in and out of gardens. She searched under bushes. Neighbours opened their doors and came running down the stairs. Cars stopped in the middle of the road.

'What happened Sandra?'

'What's wrong?'

'Is that bastard back again?'

'Rosie - my little Button - gone –'

'Gone?' they cried, their eyes blank with horror.

'How?'

'Gone - just gone –'

And the question they all asked one another late into the night, it was put to friends and lovers, spouses and sisters and aunts:

'But who could have done such a thing?'

Images of men – old, hairy faced with sweaty eyes and heavy breath, dressed in overcoats and dirty shoes - loomed before each of them. They locked their doors and slid the keychain across and pulled their offspring close.

But they were all of them mistaken, for the shadow was no stranger. Rosie's own father had come to steal her away. The flat block neighbours shook their heads in disbelief. Why would a man who didn't show any interest in his daughter want her to himself all of a sudden?

'You don't know him like I do,' Sandra said.

A bleary phone call later that night confirmed her fears.

She confided in her neighbours. She had no-one else. She would not tell her mother. She needed to talk, and talking gave the neighbours a license.

'He's just doing it for the attention love,' The Widow Across The Hall said.

'He only wants what he can't have,' Sinitta From Next Door said.

'He wants you chasing after him all the time,' Cath From Upstairs said.

Or perhaps it was because the police had visited Sandra at the hospital and finally convinced her to appeal for the restraining order. Whatever his reasons, Rosie did not stop to dwell on them. In fact, she was probably the one person involved in the affair who did not notice her own absence. Her mother noticed it. It kept her up at night, pacing gingerly through the hallways when she ought to be resting, hair awry, eyes all manner of shades: red, purple, brown and swollen, a naked cup of tea and the telephone in front of her at the kitchen table. The police noticed it. They walked the roads and knocked on doors asking questions, they searched the canals and the parks and the cars as they passed.

Rosie's father also noticed Rosie's absence from where she ought to be, but he was undergoing a struggle between staying hidden and making sure everyone knew - everyone being Sandra - exactly what he was up to. And through Sandra his former neighbours at the flat block and the Metropolitan police got in on the secret as well. So though the police weren't exactly sure of where it was he had squirreled the child away it was only a matter of time before they found out.

On the first night of her abduction, Rosie let the door to her new bedroom - a blanket-covered sofa in the bare-bottomed living room - fall ajar as she heard him pick up the receiver and start to dial. She knew where those numbers would lead. A moment or two passed and then:

'Sandy.'

The kitchen was a great cloud of silence. Her father exhaled and it blew the cloud away.

'Sandy are you listening to me.'

Answer him.

'Sandra?'

Answer him for God's sake.

'Are you still there?'

Can't you hear him talking to you? Can't you just - ?

Then her father's voice got louder all at once and the one inside her faded out.

'Bollocks! She's my daughter. You can't just –'

He leaned further into the phone as though doing so would bring Sandra's absent face right in front of his own. A long high note sang out of the phone in his hand. A mosquito must have been trapped inside it. The noise inside the receiver grew. His voice rose to match it.

'I will take her if I want, when I want. It's my right.'

You're damn right.

'The amount I've put up with for the sake of the two of you and did I ask for any of it? If she's mine or you've made her mine anyway, then I can have her when I want.'

I am yours, Rosie thought. *I'll be yours.*

Then his voice got louder still. It got too loud.

'Oh yeah? You do that Sandy, call all the fucking pigs you like, call them over to the house with a fucking loudspeaker to tell them what a cunt I am and fuck them all on our bed while you're at it you fucking slut.'

There was a noise like jaw snapping shut and the phone went dead. There was a single wonderful moment of silence. Then he stood up. He kicked the chair. He banged his fist on the table. He pulled at his long hair. He growled and the growl opened out into a strangled roar. He opened the cupboard doors. He slammed them shut again.

'Bitch!'

Open.

'Bitch!'

Shut.

'Fucking bitch!'

Open open shut shut.

'BITCH!'

With each loud noise the pressure around Rosie grew. She was on the bottom of the ocean, the weight of miles and miles of sea was upon her, pushing her down. The door that was her shield creaked ajar and her mouth opened with the cupboard doors and a noise like a bubble popping came out. Her father's head turned sharp towards the sound like a bird's. His face was an arrow coming at her and Rosie shrunk back into the dark corner of the couch. Then it smoothed out, went round and face-like again.

'Come here,' he said. His voice was not loud now, but quiet, hollowed out. The pressure receded but Rosie did not move.

'Come on I won't bite. I'm your dad.'

And he laughed, just once, an open-mouthed thing. His mouth was full of white straight teeth.

'Come here, Rosie.'

Rosie walked into the kitchen. One light bulb hung above the table. She looked away from it afraid of what it might tell her. That was gone now whatever it had been. It may have never even happened.

'Up,' he said, tapping his thighs as though she was a dog. She put a hand on his thigh, tried to pull her way on to that warm place. He laughed again.

'Oh, I forgot you're only a little thing. I do forget.'

'I'm not.'

She was big and strong, she had made herself so. She could make walls scared, though she wasn't sure why. The reason might take her too close to other reasons, reasons she should feel certain things about the man whose lap she was sitting on now. And she wanted to enjoy the warmth of his large rough hands around her and his hot breath on her shoulder.

'My little Rosie. You really are mine aren't you? I'll never get over this mane of yours.' He squeezed her hard around the hips: 'What do you want to do tomorrow? Let's do something fun.'

Rosie shrugged: 'Ok.'

'What would you like to do?'

Activities spun through her mind: riding a Ferris Wheel or going to the zoo or the beach or cycling along the towpath, like she'd heard other families did, other fathers and daughters; pink ones, like Snot Face's. But she didn't own a bike and had no idea what direction the beach was in. She had only a vague recollection of ever being at one and it was all water and no sand.

'Well?'

She was desperate to offer a suggestion, she just had to be sure that it was the right one. She looked around the kitchen for inspiration. A piece of paper with a jagged edge that didn't belong where it was lay beside the telephone on the kitchen table, a pencil beside it. Words like tornados littered the top right corner. Rosie could not read them, but maybe she could sound them out. W for wasp, H for horsefly, O for ... Rosie couldn't think of an insect beginning with O. R for ...

'Stop it,' her father said, closing one hand over Rosie's pointing finger, the other over Rosie's open mouth.

Rosie picked up the pencil instead and below her father's scribblings she began to draw. It helped her think.

'What's that?' her father said, looking over her shoulder and releasing her mouth. He let his hand drift to the table and rest lightly against her free hand.

'A little birdy?'

Rosie nodded. She had managed to distract him. Maybe she should play it safe tomorrow, start with something small. The park, perhaps. She didn't want to go too big on the first try. She might scare him away. She kept her free hand still and quiet beside his and hoped it would not shake, would be indistinguishable from the table.

'That's not bad,' he said, looking down at her picture. 'For your age. How old are you again? Three? Four?'

'Four and three months.'

'Huh.'

He went quiet for a moment, frowning. Then he brightened: 'I used to draw a bit you know.'

He took the pencil out of her hand and his other hand moved from Rosie's to hold the page. Rosie's hand wanted to follow, but she stopped it. Above the bird he began to sketch a large round eye. Thoughts of how tomorrow would be filled up got smaller.

'Don't really have the time anymore though with one thing and another.'

Then the light bulb above his head seemed to come from inside his head and he was lit up. He stood up abruptly, became a straight line. Rosie slid down on top of his feet.

'Will I draw you?' Then without waiting for an answer: 'Ok. Sit over there.'

He picked Rosie up and deposited her on the nearest chair. He turned the page with the tornado words and the bird and the eye over. It was blank apart from a line of typing, two words in block capitals at the bottom that spelt: THE END

He ran his fingers through his hair suddenly filled with a manic energy, a line of explosive powder just lit.

'Ok sit there. Like this - no! - like this.'

Rosie went still and squidgy, became dough. She let him mould her as he wished.

'I will sit here for you Dad Da - Daddy.'

He frowned at her; frowned down at the page.

'My name's Joe.'

A-ha. There it was.

'Don't call me Daddy. I don't like it. Ok.'

It wasn't a question. Thoughts chased themselves around her brain but couldn't find their way to her mouth.

'Quiet now I can't hear myself think!'

Was her mind so loud? Well she would stop thinking. She held her breath and her mind became a white empty room. One wrong move, one wrong word, one more too-loud thought and the brief moment of peace they had found together would be gone. Rosie took what had been offered and put it in her pocket. She was glad to finally have that hidden thing about the man before her and now that she did she always would. It could not be taken away. He may not want to be Daddy but he would always be Joe. She could do a swap for that. She stayed quiet. She sat still. She was a good girl. A good daughter, even though she couldn't say so.

He studied her for a while as though she were just a chair and not a girl that sat in it. He looked at her, around her, through her, down at the page. When he sketched his eyes were tense and focused. She liked being studied by him like this, liked how near he was in the room, definitely there before her. Definitely real. They were really there together in that room, Joe and Rosie (father and daughter) and nobody could tell her otherwise. And if they did she wouldn't believe them.

'Ok. I'm done,' he said after a time that felt too long and not long enough. He handed the page to her. 'I'm a bit shaky, it's been a while.'

She took it from him.

'Do you like it?' he asked, and his voice came out young and small and Rosie wanted to hold him.

Was that what Rosie looked like? She couldn't quite find the word for it. She saw people in the drawing and she wasn't sure if they were her. They were her mother and someone else and someone else though she couldn't think who. But she must be in there somewhere too because above it he had written the name ROSIE. And she knew how to read her name. She found the word for the drawing then and it was: Beautiful.

'Don't you like it?' he asked.

Rosie was on the point of saying, yes, yes, I love it, can we go to the park tomorrow, when he snatched the drawing back out of her hand.

'I told you I hadn't drawn in a long time.'

She reached out for it. *I want to keep it,* she tried to say. But he crumpled it up and held it in his closed fist. Then he opened his fist and it drifted down on to the table and settled upon it, a landing snowflake.

'I'm going to bed.'

He abandoned the kitchen and shut his bedroom door. Rosie could hear him stomping around behind it. Then all went quiet. Rosie reached onto the table and pulled the crumpled drawing close to her. She smoothed it out but the creases still ran through her face. This is what I'll look like when I'm an old woman, she thought. She focused on the pencil lines only. She traced them with her finger in one long continuous movement. Every time she got stuck or side-tracked by a crease and had to jump from one part of her face to the next she started again. She tried over and over until she could trace the whole piece without lifting her finger once from the page. When she was done she kissed her fingertip. Now his drawing was in her always, like his name. She scrunched it back up and put it back where Joe had thrown it. Joe but not her father. Her father yes but still just Joe. She was learning new things every day.

The next morning before they went to the park Joe stood with his back flat against the wall and the edge of the closed curtain in his fingers staring sideways out the window. Rosie sat on the same chair as she had when she was being drawn, dressed in the same mud-kneed dungarees from yesterday, the same striped t-shirt. She was very aware of her underwear. It was hot and sticky and clung in all the wrong places. She swallowed back the feeling in her throat and kicked her heels against the chair legs and waited.

'Ok, we're good to go,' he said at last.

Then the telephone began to ring and he went still. Rosie went still too and held her breath. Beside the phone on the table was an empty space where the drawing had been. When the phone finally stopped he relaxed; Rosie copied him. He looked out the window sideways.

'Ok,' he said. 'We're off.'

On the way to the park they stopped in a shop. Rosie looked up at the shelves behind the counter while Joe got his things. Rows of glass jars filled with boiled sweets stood side by side. She played the game she often played in shops like this where she grew to the height of a giraffe and took a sweet from each jar and tasted them one by one, trying to imagine what that might feel like. Then someone coughed and when she opened her eyes and looked up she realised her eyes had been closed and Joe had been watching her. His mouth was wide and his straight white teeth were out for all to see.

'Pick some,' he said.

'Pick what?'

He pointed up at the jars. 'Just tell the man which ones you fancy and he'll get them for you.'

This had never happened before. Sandra had a mortal fear of Rosie losing her teeth, so no matter how hard she cried, she rarely got treats. She had thrown some epic tantrums in her four years and three months on the earth for very little return. But now sweets were being offered to her freely with no effort on her part. She pointed at one jar, then a second, checking in with Joe each time. With each permissive nod her boldness grew. She pointed and pointed until the bag was round and heavy and the man and Joe her father began to chuckle. Joe paid and stashed his own brown paper bag inside the leather jacket and handed Rosie hers.

'Don't eat them all at once now.'

Rosie took the bag tenderly, terrified it might split.

'Thank you Joe,' she said.

Her father's eyes flicked toward the man behind the counter briefly. Then he frowned down at her.

'Joe?'

Rosie froze. She was certain it was Joe. But what if it had been Jack? Or James? Or something else entirely?

'Where did you get it into your head calling me that?'

The bag of sweets started to weigh heavily in her hands.

'But you said –'

'Don't call me that. Ok.'

Rosie's mouth opened but no sound came out. He looked back at the man behind the counter, snorted, blinked.

'Her own father can you imagine?'

'Kids these days eh?' the man said, moving his gaze onto the customer behind them.

'I don't think she wants these,' Joe said reaching down for the brown bag. Rosie held onto them.

'Do you, Rosie?'

'Yes.'

'Yes what?'

The man behind the counter looked down at his hands. He was going to be no help.

'Yes ...'

Rosie knew she had to say something and it had to be right.

'Yes ... dad?'

'I can't hear you.'

'Yes dad.'

Outside he took her by the forearm and brought his face close to hers.

'Don't embarrass me like that again do you hear me?'

His face was his but not his, as though he was wearing a mask made in his own likeness.

'Do you?'

Rosie nodded. She hoped it would be enough.

'Ok,' he said. He straightened up and looked left and right and up and down the street. Then in a loud bright voice that was all new, he sang: 'Onwards to the park!'

His long strides led them and Rosie ran to keep up. She was on one end of a see saw, not sure when the man who might be Joe or her father or her dad or none or all would suddenly jump off. And yet she felt as though she was on a sort of holiday. And as her most recent experience with him in the square patch of hallway between her bedroom and the front door faded from memory to be replaced by newer nicer things, she found herself desperate to enjoy it.

The next morning, Joe cooked breakfast for her. He fried sausages, which were her favourite. He also made her sweet tea. Cups and cups of the stuff. After the third in an hour she had to refuse.

'I'm not allowed to drink too much,' she said.

'Go on just a sip. I made it especially for you.'

'But mum said my teeth will go black and fall out if I do.'

The thought of it was terrifying. She didn't want to turn out like The Widow Across The Hall who had a cup in her hand at all hours of the day.

'After all the trouble I went to?' he said quietly, his face darkening to the colour of thunder. 'You're an ungrateful little thing, just like your mother.'

She didn't want to be ungrateful. She knew what happened to those who were. She fake-sipped to be polite then poured it in the spider plant when he wasn't looking. It flourished during her visit.

That night he tucked her into the couch. The blanket was a little scratchy and irritated her chin and the sour smell of it tickled her nose, but she kept still. A wrong move could break

73

the fragile moment they shared, the precious minutes of peace. She collected them up, swaddled them, kept them safe. He didn't read her any stories from library books but it was ok. Rosie knew some of them by heart. She recited out loud to herself until she fell asleep.

'Cut that out!' Joe her father her Dad but not her Daddy shouted from the other room: 'I can't hear myself think!'

She learned to whisper and soon after that made no noise at all.

Over the next few days they walked in the park together and he held her hand. Rosie cherished that touch as tenderly as if it were a newborn baby bird nestled in her palm. They never made it to the beach or the towpath but he took the time to pick up leaves and explain to Rosie what they meant. He talked about trees and different sorts of animals, all the things that Rosie loved to hear about. He loved to hear himself talking about those things too, so it worked out well for the both of them. Even if she already knew that this tree was an oak, that bird a thrush, she let him talk. She listened. She made her mind quiet so he could hear his own. She wanted to share something, anything, that would unite them.

'Where's my mum?' she got bold enough to ask on their fifth day together as they fed the ducks in Victoria park. He plucked at the hard leftovers of a granary loaf but did not respond. He was just a pulsing jaw line towering above her, a bulk of jutting shoulders and glassy unblinking eyes.

Rosie had been on holiday with her father Joe for more than a week when they were finally discovered. They were walking back from the shops with freshly filled brown paper bags when the doors of a parked car opened up ahead and three police dressed as people jumped out.

'Stop! Police!' they called, their legs moving fast.

Joe ran. He dropped Rosie's hand and was gone. Thinking it was a game, Rosie started to run too, but her legs were small and wouldn't go as fast. The police people went after Joe and she was left behind. She tried to catch up but as she ran the bag in her hand split. Jewel bright sweets tumbled across the path.

'Oh,' she said, stopping to watch them spread across the tarmac, a bursting firework.

Up ahead a crowd was gathering. Joe had been outrun. He was mainly height and bones and didn't have much speed in him. The police had tipped him over and bound him. People stood by and watched, saying nothing. With a quick halting step they led him into the backseat of their car, which was plain and green and didn't say Police on it like the other ones did. He looked out through the back window at Rosie through a wire cage and his mouth opened and closed. Rosie looked back down at the sweets. The sun had come out from behind the clouds and they sparkled around her. They were too bright. She stood on an apple drop closest to her and the light went out.

'Come on now, Rosie. We're taking you home to your mother.'

Rosie looked up. A policeman was looking down at her. His hand was on her shoulder. She vaguely recognised him.

'I dropped them,' she said, flicking her wrist at what looked like a pool of marbles surrounding her.

'Oh. Your sweets?' he said, looking down. 'Don't worry we'll get you some more.'

With his hand on her shoulder he steered her away.

'I'm sorry you had to see that.'

She looked back once at the car. Joe's face was twisted and wet and his mouth was wide. She was sure he was being too loud.

'I don't want any more,' she said.

The policeman looked down at her. His eyebrows gathered in the middle.

'Are you sure?'

Rosie's shoe caught on something round. She looked down, lifted her toe. Red and yellow. A rhubarb custard. She let all her weight fall into the shoe and felt the little bead give beneath her. Another light went out.

'I'm sure,' she said.

Seven (a)

' - was free.'

    'Free? From what were you free?'

    'I ... was ...'

    'Rosie?'

    'I ...'

Eight

Sea breeze blew through the city. It ran down alleys and skirted apartment blocks. It whittled through gaps in the cobblestones, caressed the faces of greying sculptures and cathedral gargoyles. It whipped up ladies' skirts and stole the hats of men. It circled the flat that Rosie and Sandra shared and slipped through windows left ajar. It whipped their hair about their faces and went up their nostrils and a curious longing neither could explain in words went through them. The coastline was calling. The time to cross the sea had arrived once more.

They left quietly at dawn. They did not tell the neighbours. They did not tell the school. Since the kidnapping Sandra had clung to her daughter as though to the last threads of life and Rosie had never gone back. Her empty seat by the window yawned like an open wound in the classroom but within weeks target and demand had it filled. The replacement student filled up the vacuum, but they couldn't soften Kate's discomfort.

'It wasn't your business,' Harriet told her, behind the green door. The burn mark on her desk was covered over with piles of papers, she had long forgotten what once had sat beneath them.

'How do you know what's happened? They might just have moved borough.' And then the refrain she fell back on when yet another child slipped through their fingers: 'Kate, you can't help them all.'

Kate chewed her lip. She buried her own secret guilt and the unread report at the bottom of a drawer and allowed life to take over. Soon the memory of Rosie was no more than a coppery glint in the sun.

So it was back to the homeland for the Cottons, back across the sea.

'Rosie! We're going to miss the train!'

Sandra wailed from the doorway of the box flat on their last morning as the cab driver's meter ticked on the street. Rosie wound in and out of the rooms, searching. She had forgotten something, something important. What was it?

'Come on!' Sandra cried from the door. 'If we miss this one we'll have to wait for hours at the port!'

'But I can't find my –'

'It's packed, believe me, it's all packed,' she said, pointing at their two meagre suitcases.

Could almost five years of life fit into such small packages?

'There's nothing left of ours here. Let's go.'

Into the taxi and to the train station: a vast room filled with people, the squeak of luggage wheels, the colliding of too many bodies.

'Right, here we are. Platform 14. To Chester. Then we change ...'

And then they were aboard. The train had been oversold and was heaving. Rather than risk a confrontation over seats Sandra dragged her unwilling child out the carriage doors into the chilly space beside the toilets, a familiar fragrance hinting at other familiar things keeping them company all the way to the coast. Tangled bracken lined the tracks. Endless fields of grass and rapeseed sped by. Rivers, willow and the barges beneath, they all got left behind.

'Can trains go on the water?'

They crossed over a bridge straddling the reaches of a lake. Sandra scoffed and shifted impatiently on the hard train floor and felt her voice sink into an ancient tongue.

'Trains on the water? I've heard it all now.'

'But how –'

'We have to take the ferry.'

The station signs stretched longer and longer into a language as foreign to Rosie as mathematics. The train slowed and finally, stopped. Rosie was queasy and light-headed and craved the fresh sea air.

79

They were closer to home now than they'd been in five years and it couldn't reach them fast enough. Sandra brought Rosie out on deck. In the sharp sting of the cold they stayed, drinking in the sea air that seemed to clean them from the inside out. Sandra kept one hand firmly on her daughter's collar as she tried to launch herself through the railings and into the surf. She was muttering something about dolphins.

Sandra had frugality drilled into her marrow and had saved almost all of her tips from the restaurant, dipping into them only at birthdays and Christmas when Joe liked to play his favourite game. It was enough for a modest rent and food for a year in Dublin. In Ireland her Sterling stretched. But it was almost too much freedom for her to handle. She wore each house she moved into like a new outfit, casting it off again, as though it pulled in the wrong places. She would settle on somewhere, sign the lease and unpack their two small bags, but within weeks Rosie would find her staring at the bare walls, white eyed.

    'No. Not here. We have to find somewhere else.'

    'Mummy we just got here.'

    'No. It won't do.'

    It was as though they were trying to outrun something, or find something they had lost, something precious, something treasured. Deposit after deposit was wasted, swallowed up by a string of frazzled landlords. The once lush pool of money began to dry up. Each new house they moved to got smaller and darker. The cold of those first few months in the squat in London returned, no longer a memory. Rough stone floors gripped underfoot where carpets had warmed only months before. Cold walls rose up around them stripped of their creamy wallpaper. They got friendly with the scent of damp. Mother and daughter curled up together in near-empty rooms trying to keep warm as the bitter Irish wind stole in through the windows.

'Remember London, Rosie? The park, your school? Do you miss it?'

They were tucked underneath the blanket together, their faces red beneath the wool. Their shivering kept them awake long into the night.

'I don't know.'

'Don't you ever wonder though...'

'What?'

'Oh, you know. Just things.'

Why would she choose to live like this? Sandra warred with herself constantly, one foot on her next move as a single woman, one edging its way back to the ferry port. She had returned home to a place where she could find help and shelter, where family or friends could receive her, where she and her daughter could live in comfort. But she had returned after almost five years with nothing but threadbare clothes and bitten nails to show for it. She couldn't face those who had warned her, she could not stand to be told she was wrong, that she had been mistaken, that he really was no more than he had seemed. But they were running out of money with alarming speed and Sandra couldn't find a job. When she got down to her last few coins she swallowed her pride and made the phone call that saved them.

And with a clicking step and a brisk knock on the door, she appeared. Glamorous, scrubbed and stern, whose misgiving lips the five years apart had wasted into nothing: Marie.

'No Sandra,' she said, as the door announced her and the slippery walls came into view.

'Why didn't you call before? This place. Six flights up! And the types around here are beyond it.'

Sandra pulled her sleeves down over her fists and bit at her lips.

'We were in better places weren't we Rosie?'

Rosie nodded, thinking wistfully of carpeted floors and heat.

'But the landlords were right wankers, Mum, you've no idea.'

'Watch your goddamn language Sandra.' She peered at her and seemed to see her for the first time. 'You've lost weight. And you sound different. English.' She turned her mouth down and looked at Rosie. 'And Jesus, the child. The size of her.'

Marie's eyes didn't leave her daughter's face then but Sandra would look anywhere but back at her. Rosie clung to her mother's thigh, their suitcases spilling out around them half-emptied, watched by the grease-stained walls.

'Come here you daft thing.'

And Marie held her daughter. Sandra's arms stretched out between them and plucked at the loose strands of wool at her waist. Then something left her, she wrapped her arms around her mother's narrow back and her shoulders heaved and Marie's hand caressed Rosie's cheek as Sandra's leg trembled in Rosie's grip.

'Right,' Marie said at last, pushing herself free: 'We're not staying here.'

Her angular face scanned the room for lost items, her eyes glistening but focused. She kicked things into the case with the leather of her shoe but wouldn't bend to touch anything.

'Zip those up Sandra. Let's get in the car.'

With their two bags in hand they shut the door on the squalid flat and followed Marie down the stairwell to the car. Globes of spit peppered their journey.

Rosie had never been in a car before. It was very grand. No sharing with strange people who stared or coughed, no standing with her face pressed into a rucksack or her mother's waist as the bus or tube swayed, sending strange body parts and their owners crushing into her. The car was exciting and new, even if it was a dull red like the houses that got sucked into the car's slipstream as they passed. Inside it was very clean. The seats were grey and firm. Her seatbelt was sleek and tight and cut into her and told her to sit still. It would not let her look out the window and she had to be content with the canopy of trees that zoomed past the small bit her eyes could reach. The trees melted into a blur. Rosie closed her eyes and felt her excitement move into her throat and leave her.

'Oh Christ!' Marie groaned from the front seat. 'And I've just had the carpets done!'

'Oh Button – what's happened?'

Rosie groaned.

'I can't tell why she's like this. She must have eaten something off?'

In truth Rosie and Sandra had barely eaten in days, but Rosie decided it was not the time to make that known. Sandra appeared in the gap between the two front seats, her eyes pulled tight between them.

'Why didn't you call me sooner Sandra? You knew I would have helped. For God's sake the child is ill.'

'She was fine earlier. She is fine.'

'She is not - would you go away out of that with your *fine*.'

'I'll take her up to Dr. Callaghan tomorrow. Is he still up in the village?'

'He is of course,' she said, her face darkening under the colour of some memory: 'This family is fated to pay that man's way through life.'

Sandra pursed her lips but said nothing.

'I'm sorry I messed up your car Granny,' Rosie said at last, breaking a long silence.

Eyes found Rosie in the rear view mirror, ice-blue, unwavering and cold.

'No, child. No.' Marie said, wheezing: 'Never call me Granny. Not Granny, not Nan, Nanny, Gran or anything like that. You may call me Marie and if you forget it you'll be cleaning out this mess till Christmas.'

'You'd do well to remember that Rosie,' Sandra said from the front.

Nine

Marie's house was much bigger than anything Rosie had ever seen before. It sat nestled among twelve identical others, so when standing at one end of the street she felt she was between two reflecting mirrors stretching into always. It was a peaceful place. It was very quiet. Cars rarely passed until the evening when the few that had been absent parked up silent and still, their power and speed slow-ticking into memory.

Inside it was very clean. The floors and wood surfaces gleamed like water. Rosie thought she might plunge into the table when she laid her hand upon it, so liquid and soft did it look. Crossing the kitchen floor for the back garden was like crossing the sea for the third time. She had to make like a saint and walk the water without sinking. After many successful attempts she began to believe she was blessed with divine powers.

'Out with you! Get those mucky soles off of my floors!' Marie screamed when she found her and booted her out the back door.

'I think your grandmother would prefer you not to wear your shoes inside darling,' Sandra advised a weeping Rosie later in the upstairs bathroom. Her rump was raw from her grandmother's powerful hand. The hoover droned up at them from the living room beneath.

'Why?' Rosie asked, sniffling.

'Because she likes to keep things clean.'

'But why?'

'Because she does.'

'But why Mum?'

'Some people are just like that, I don't know. Now you know what to do to keep her from you with that wooden spoon of hers.'

'It hurts.'

'I know Button. I know it does.'

Rosie took to boating across the floors instead, barefooted, like the ferryman Chaeron. Her mother had read to her about the ancient Greeks in one of those library books that managed to find them wherever they went, and she had always been fascinated by this man forever stuck between the worlds of life and death, sailing between banks, never coming to land. The dining table in the good room was diminished as its wooden chairs went skirting across floorboards as though moved by a spirit, leaving their milky stains on the polished floorboards. Perched inside her makeshift boat, she lugged herself across the kitchen calling for obols and wheezing through her phlegmatic lungs.

Then the house began to tremble as the stairs came thundering down. The all-seeing eyes and all-hearing ears and all-knowing nose of Marie stampeded into the kitchen on the back of some monstrous beast.

'Those chairs were your Granddaddy's favourites!' she wailed, her face large against the ceiling. The windows shook in their frames across the house.

'They're antiques! Far too delicate for a lump the like of you! Get. Out. Of. It!'

'But – I have to sail across the sea,' Rosie cried, one arm twisted up into her ear: 'I left something …'

'Go. Away. Out. Of. That. I've only had the floors done. Out!'

That evening in the bathroom Rosie cried her eyes out on her mother's lap once more.

'I … had my … shoes off …'

'I know darling, I know.'

'I hate her.'

'No you don't. She's family.' Sandra said it with a finality that Rosie knew to leave untouched.

Rosie found herself relegated to the outdoors more often after that, but it suited her. It was where she felt as ease, where trees could be climbed and bushes scoured for willing insects to befriend. And if ever there was cause for complaint with her in the house - often found when sticky hands left their mark on vintage upholstery, mahogany coffee tables, and winking figurines - it was an ideal spot for her to disappear to. She had mastered the art of finding a good hiding place, which was one thing she had inherited from her father at least.

Mealtimes were the only occasions she could be found inside, her shoes removed and her feet on a towel at Marie's insistence. But as Rosie went for the bread with her fingers:

'Wash those hands! Sandra - she's been at those snails again. Can't you do something about it?'

'She's just being a child, Mum. What should she be doing? Sitting in her room and polishing her shoes all day?'

'That would be preferable,'Marie said, but only to herself.

After lunch Rosie was back among the leaves recruiting players for the afternoon games. Scouting snails wasn't entirely pleasant as they smelt like a mixture of damp earth and snot, but she kept her air passages clear with a sniff of her grandmother's prized rosebush, though she had to be careful not to be caught too close to it. Marie was very particular about her roses. If a rogue snail was found among the buds there would be trouble. But the roses were too beautiful not to share. And those dull brown shells needed cheering. Rosie checked the faces in the kitchen window before sneaking over to the scented flowers, daring her fingers to go as fast as lightning and as light as air. Then it was back to the tarmac below the windowsill - the official divide between house and greenery - where she removed her fresh finds from her pockets and lined them up side by side in preparation for the afternoon's events.

'We're going to be great friends,' she announced with a strange pang, one ear on the hidden voices above her head.

Sandra and Marie stood at the kitchen sink by the window. Lunch was done. The crumbs swept. The table was clear. Marie was washing, Sandra drying. The squeak of glasses, the rub of a towel. The room expanded with the calm of those kept warm and fed.

'It's great for her to have her own garden,' Sandra said, gazing out over it, the piece of land almost claimed.

Marie sniffed.

'What?'

'Oh nothing.'

'I know that sniff of yours. Come on out with it then.'

Marie plunged a plate in the suds. It had been scraped so well it looked as though it had been licked clean. A sigh floated through the open window and fell to where Rosie crouched next to the snails.

'She ought to meet with other children,' Marie said at last, shaking wildly from the hips as she circled the sponge around the plate: 'People her own age. It's unnatural for young ones to spend so much time alone.'

Rosie mimicked her unseen.

'You've been here three months nearly. I've never seen her once out on the road.'

'She's always been shy.'

'Had she no friends from school before?'

'She wasn't there that long.'

'She was there long enough.'

Sandra moved away from the window and stacked the glasses in a row on the shelf. Marie watched her.

A small box hidden behind the water pipe caught Rosie's eye.

'There are plenty of children around here she can play with,' Marie went on. 'Get her out from under our feet. Get you out of the house.'

'I've been looking for a job.' Sandra's voice took a back-step and raised its arms high.

'Give you less of an excuse to be in it all the time anyway.'

'It's tough. Jobs are thin on the ground. Everyone's finding it tough.'

'Who's everyone?' Marie asked so sharply the water stopped to listen.

'You know what I mean.'

The water began murmuring again and dishes gave the odd shriek.

'It's not just a job you're after. You need to get out and about more yourself. Pining won't do you any good.'

'I'm not pining.'

Marie grunted. Sandra squeaked a sodden rag in and out of cups. Below the window, Rosie picked the box up. She shook it softly; it rattled. She pocketed it. Then she blew an imaginary whistle and the snails were off.

'What about the little boy from across the road?' Sandra asked suddenly.

Rosie stuck her tongue out.

'Do you mean the Kennedy's boy? Across at number 10? Oh no Sandra. No. We can't have her falling in with them.'

'Why not?'

'That family is full of rot. Mr. Kennedy isn't even the boy's father.'

'What? You can't mean –'

'I do. It was that bloody Winter. Sure you know all about it.'

Sandra took a plate from the washed pile and set to work on it and did not respond.

'It was that South American who stayed down in Mulligan's for ages. Remember him? The artist. Out most days before the Snow with the easel and stand staring at sheep. Stayed on to *learn his English*. English my arse! Go to bloody England if that's the case. Marquez or something I think it was.' She laid a plate to dry on the rack. 'No-one knows how long it went on. Gone now, of course, as they all do. Back to Argentina or wherever it was he came from.'

'I can't believe it of her.'

'Well believe it. The colour of the child! Like rust. And the rest of them like milk.'

Sandra stacked up the plates, Marie poured bleach into the sink.

'No, the Kennedys are no good. And as high and mighty as she was when Rosie came along? Hah. And come to think of it she was probably a month or so gone herself at the time.'

'We can't blame the child for it.'

'You would say that.'

Sandra put the cups away and wiped down the board.

'Right, I'm done,' she said. The words came out weak and heavy. 'I think I'll head to the library.'

'Going out for some fresh air, are you?'

Sandra opened and closed cupboards and her silence was as loud as the snapping doors.

'Well if you are going down there don't forget to ask about the school.'

'Right.'

'Oh Christ! Sandra - tell your child to stay away from my roses!'

Snails in soft pink capes glided past the open back door.

Rosie and Sandra were in Marie's territory now. For free comfortable living and good food, they had to abide by her rules. Marie had tried to impose discipline with punishment, but her grandchild would never fully understand the significance of the wooden spoon, though she had learned to fear it. She flinched now whenever she saw it, even when it lay innocuous beside the pot of soup or stew.

The last beating was a particularly brutal one in response to the mutilation of Marie's beloved winter roses. Rosie whimpered in Sandra's lap on the kitchen chair. Her hair was stuck to her cheeks in long slim strands, her nose wet and streaming.

'You didn't have to spank her, Mum.'

'It's the way to teach them.' Marie washed the wooden spoon vigorously before placing it back in the drawer. 'You won't do it again now, will you child?'

Rosie never quite learned to practice reverence in the garden even then, but she did manage to keep a safe distance

89

from the rosebushes most of the time. Her grandmother seemed to love them almost as her own flesh. It was often wondered if she loved them more than any other living thing since Ned had passed.

'The rose, Rosie, is what you were named after. Did you know that?'

One dry afternoon a few weeks later grandmother and granddaughter were outdoors and back on neutral ground. Spring was getting into its stride and things had started to bloom.

'Your mother was too unwell after you were born to come up with one so I named you. I don't like flowers you know –'

Rosie watched her prune and weed from under the bushes.

'- nature's whores.'

That word. Rosie knew it. But where from and what did it mean? Could she read it written down? She was getting better at reading these days. Sandra's trips to the library were plentiful and she always came back with something new. Rosie loved learning new words.

'What's a whore?'

Marie paused and squinted down at her then went back to pruning, continuing as though there had been no interruption.

'Anyone's and anybody's, most flowers are. But the rose Rosie - your namesake - the rose has self-restraint. Try and grab one too hasty and you'll get a good prick.'

A throaty chuckle escaped her lips.

'Roses can teach us women a thing or two about self-respect.'

Inside Rosie's mind pieces of a puzzle started to fit together. Marie turned around and looked at her.

'Well you definitely have the beauty of them, but it remains to be seen if you've the rest of their qualities. I pray to God that you do. They only yield to a careful touch. Remember that Rosie. Imbibe it. You'll need to with a face like yours. I should have called your mother after them.'

She squeezed the shears smartly and a rosebud fell into the grass: 'Ah bollocks. Whatever you do Rosie -' she jabbed the shears sharply in Rosie's direction '- don't turn out like your mother, you hear me?'

'Why?'

'Oh, you're too young to understand.'

She picked up the bud and threw it into the shrub border.

'If Mum's not a rose does that make her a whore?'

Marie peered down at her granddaughter.

'How old are you again?'

'Five and four months.'

Marie tutted and went back to the bush. 'I swear all that book-reading has gone to your head.'

Rosie picked up a stick and began tracing letters in the dirt. W –

'Your grandfather had a way with them.'

'With what, whores?'

There was something about that word that made Rosie want to hold it in her mouth. The sound it made was like the wind. And it made Marie's face wither as if she were sucking on a sour apple.

'Would you whisht! Roses, I meant. Roses. He knew how to handle them. Your grandfather Ned. The only man I ever met who did.' She sighed, but a warm quiet smile stayed on her lips. 'He was too soft on Sandra for her own good.'

Then the smile fell off and her face was its usual suckered self. Rosie dragged the stick through the dirt. Lines and circles came together to form something that was more than the sum of its parts. Marie began to hum softly, low and tuneless. Rosie watched her.

'Can I help?' she asked after a time.

'No. You'll be cut.'

And all Rosie could do was watch as her grandmother's hands preened and primped, twisting rapidly around the cagey stalks with the shears. The brutal instrument chewed away at leaf and twig and little pools of leaves collected at her feet. She wore no gloves.

'Ah! You bastard!'

Her hand retreated. She'd been caught.

'Were you too hasty?' Rosie asked.

For once Marie laughed: a big open mouth directed at the sky, as though she were sharing the joke with whoever lived up there out of sight behind the clouds.

'You know more than you let on.' She caught Rosie with a shrewd look. 'I forgot that about young ones. It's been so long.'

She laughed again until all of it was gone.

'I only get the odd jab every now and again. It's just the rose reminding me to be gentle. Remember - a careful touch only. What are you writing over there?'

'Nothing.' Rosie wiped out the letters she'd written in the earth quickly with her hand.

Marie frowned. 'You do know how to get yourself in a state. Shoes off before you set a foot in my kitchen. You know what will happen if you forget.'

She returned to the roses, humming. Her voice blended with the music of the garden. The soft flight of the flies and bees, the wind and its leaf shake, the chiming birdsong, her quiet singing. Rosie relaxed fully with her in that moment, the fear of the wooden spoon forgotten. It was the only time Rosie had known Marie not to find fault. She snipped and sliced away, leaving Rosie undisturbed in the dirt. And it was in that moment also that Rosie remembered she loved her. She found at last her mother in the contours of Marie's face and in the way she held her shoulders slightly rounded, a buffeter against loss and harsh times and the cruel winds so common to that place. She moved closer to her then, drawn in by her brief and unusual warmth. She could almost touch it, she longed to be absorbed into it. But once she'd built up courage to go so close she yellowed and reached out a hand to feel the ears of the bud instead. Then a sharp slap caught her wrist. And that was it. No reprimand, no acknowledgement. The work went on. And as Rosie watched the red sting flare up on her skin in the shape of her grandmother's knuckles, the book shut, and once again she forgot.

Nine (a)

'He stands over me and the moon disappears. I can no longer see ... him, anything. And then he ...'

She stopped and tried to catch her breath, but she was suffocating. The air was gone. The taste in her mouth burnt and bitter. Her lips opened and closed but the air stung -

Ten

If it wasn't for Sandra's sixth sense, they would never have made it out alive.

She had never expected the house to catch fire, least of all in the middle of the night when things were unplugged, lights were out and the gas switched off.

'Get up! Get up now!'

She looked soft and unfinished standing in Marie's bedroom doorway, illuminated from behind by the landing light. For a moment, Marie thought it was an angel.

'What is it?'

'It's a fire, Mum. Our house is on fire!'

She fell into hysterical giggles. Smoke snaked quietly past her left shoulder.

'Pull yourself together girl!' Marie was up and conscious and had mustered the strength to slap her daughter around the face. 'Quick! The child!'

'Oh, God –'

Sandra disappeared into the smoke-filled room where her daughter lay. Each second that passed was an age of the earth.

'Get out of there!' Marie cried.

'She won't move!' Sandra choked.

'Just drag her down by the hair if you have to!'

Out they came, alive. Rosie barely knew her own name as they bolted down the stairs, Marie in a nightcap and tutting, as though an unexpected caller had knocked on the door during Coronation Street. The smoke grew tendrils and followed. Sandra used Jane From Next Door's phone to call the fire brigade. She danced on the spot as the dial swung sluggishly, half-asleep itself.

'When are you going to get proper phones over here for crying out loud!' she shouted.

Jane frowned at her from under her hairnet in the kitchen doorway. Then they stood outside and watched the smoke build up like fungus in the upstairs window and waited.

The truck arrived, shining like waxed fruit. Lights blinked blue and white. The sirens woke the whole street. Neighbours emerged with stung eyes, clutching at their chests and covering their mouths in shock.

'What's going on?' they called out to one another through the haze of sleep.

'What's happening, Marie?' asked Mrs. Kennedy.

'Fire,' Marie said, hardly glancing in her direction. 'In the child's room. Lucky to have made it out at all.'

They all looked at the girl who stood blank and wide eyed and heavy. The flames danced in her eyes. She moved towards the fire and stretched her arms out to it.

'Sandra - the child!' Marie called. Sandra jumped and ran, pulling her back.

'Is she entirely right in the head?' asked Mrs. No.4.

'She's not with us now anyway,' Marie muttered.

Rosie broke free from her mother's hold and began twirling on the spot with her hands over her eyes. The neighbours exchanged glances.

'Have you ever seen the like?' Mrs. No.5 whispered to listening ears.

Then the firemen jumped out cutting all conversation dead. They were huge hulking forms of men. Rosie again moved forward, but she was pulled back.

'He's calling ...' she said.

'Who's calling?' said Sandra. 'What are you on about Rosie?'

'He is calling for me.'

'What...?'

'The man ... the black man with the feathers ...'

Sandra looked up and down the street. Rosie raised a finger slowly to the bedroom window. Sandra looked up at it. It looked back, black as a void, flames licking its edges.

'Have you got her Sandra?'

Marie had appeared at her right ear.

'Yes.' Sandra wanted to say more, but Marie silenced her with pursed lips.

'Now hold onto her for God's sake and keep her still.'

The women of the street were furious to be caught in their night things and curlers. Mrs. No.6 pinched her cheeks and bit her lips just short of drawing blood as the uniformed men approached.

'Get back ladies!' they cried.

The women shivered in the balmy heat. The men worked hard. Arms locked, jaw tensed, neck sinew in sharp relief. They unravelled the hose like some preposterous serpent, while the women gasped and stroked their necks, gills aflame, thrilled. The firemen shuddered under the power of the pipe. It had been a night.

It was another one of those shared experiences that drew the community together, as the Winter had. In the days that followed, it was all that was on anyone's lips. Neighbours, spearheaded by the Mrs.' No.4, 5 and 6, called into No. 11 at all hours of the day with cakes and home-baked bread. They were all well aware the kitchen was fine, the quick work of the brigade had stopped the fire from spreading. Mrs. No.6 asked with a glint if she could have a look at the room. The three of them crowded in to feast on Marie's misfortune, gloating that it was not their own.

'No men in the house,' Mrs. No.5 muttered to whoever would listen in the corner of the living room, as Rosie eavesdropped from behind the settee: 'A young mother with a child but no husband, even now after five years in London - and we all know that was the reason she went running over there.'

'And you've no idea how brazen she is for all of that,' spat Jane From Next Door: 'You should have heard the way she spoke to me that night in my own house - and after all I did to help her and her deranged child!'

'Shh,' Mrs. Kennedy said, as her eyes met Rosie's over Jane's shoulder.

But the neighbours hovered still. 'How odd, wasn't it,' they said, 'for a fire to start in the room the child slept.'

'Sure you probably just though the child's hair had gone awry!' Laughed Mrs. No. 5.

It was indecently vivid, so striking, such a *colour*. And so much of it!

'Would you not try to tame it, cut it back, hide it under a hat?' said Mrs. No.4.

'It must attract so much attention. But maybe you enjoy that, do you?' asked Mrs. No.6.

Sandra smiled a tight teethed smile, but said nothing.

'How can anyone be so private,' Mrs. No.5 asked 4 and 6 during a moment under the shadow of the grandfather clock in the hallway. 'Do they think themselves better than everyone else?'

'It's something to do with that child,' Mrs. No.4 said knowingly.

'You know I think you might be right,' agreed Mrs. No.5.

'I still remember her when she was a baby. She used to give me the shivers,' said Mrs. No.6.

Rosie listened from behind the coat-stand undetected. She had heard enough. She slipped into the empty garden. It waited for her always, and never said a thing. Unfamiliar faces peered out the kitchen window at her and she shrunk behind the azaleas.

'Can't we just tell them to leave?' Sandra cried in desperation one evening after a fortnight of visitors. 'Refuse to answer the door? There are things we need to sort out –' she said, stopping the flow of her talk in the heat of Rosie's curious stare.

'They'll get tired of us,' Marie said, not taking her eyes off the television.

Two days later Mrs. Kennedy's youngest had an accident. The neighbours bustled out of Marie's house with the remains of their bakery and clambered over one another to be the first to knock on the door across the road. The boy's birth was only too well remembered. Skin like dirt and hair like oil and the two Kennedys as pale as the moon and the only one likely to have caused it had packed his bags and gone in the night. The other women who had succumbed to him had been lucky or left. The Kennedys were either shameless or brave or both. And she - Mrs. Kennedy - had been so good, helpful, generous, always ready for a chat. She was more difficult to forgive because of it. If you couldn't rely on the good ones what hope was there for the rest? Nearly seven years had passed since that Winter. Mr. Kennedy was believed a saint. He treated the boy like one of his own, no different to the others, all grown up now and far away. They'd never had another. And now this awful thing had happened. The boy's blank bright stare and his unnerving quiet. His dark head stuck at an odd angle and the constant trail of spittle at the corner of his mouth, the strange sound of the wheels as they dragged on the carpet. The bereft silence of Mr. Kennedy, who had been looking the other way when he drove down the road, not knowing the boy was playing out. Suspicion trickled through the street. All eyes pointed towards the door at No. 10 and away from Sandra, Rosie and Marie. The three women breathed a guilty sigh of relief.

But the tragedy lost its appeal, and soon it would be replaced with another. Life on the street returned to routine. What had passed was quickly forgotten. But whenever the chat became scarce, The Fire at No. 11 would be seized upon:

'Remember that night? The terror! The firemen! That strange, strange child ...'

Eleven

Rosie's old room was out of bounds until the man came in to fix it. The Fire had settled in her chest and she woke up regularly in the night gasping for the inhaler. There was another spare room, but her mother insisted she stay in with her, until she healed. Her old, blackened bedroom door was kept shut but it seemed to yawn open as she passed on her way to the loo, drawing her eyes to it as if something ugly and forbidden, something dead, lay beyond calling to her. Since The Fire, she hadn't felt right; it was as though her body and mind had come apart. Something was moving towards her, circling ever lower above the rooftop. Soon it would land. It would make its quiet path down the chimney and into their sitting room. It would creep about the house at night and breathe on them while they slept. She kept out of the house as much as she could, going to the toilet in the bushes during the day instead of inside. Yet she couldn't help but be drawn to her old room. The prospects of entering were terrifying, and she had been forbidden; she knew she would be punished. But her curiosity was stronger.

She listened at the top of the stairs for the enemy, then pushed inside. The starkness of it hit her, desolation lay behind the blackened door. She narrowed her eyes into slits to look at it like she did when something scary came on the television. Through that distorted film everything was kept at a safe distance. All her clothes had been ruined. Her best teddy and companion since birth who had had survived all their journeys was now a pile of ash. All her toys had melted together into an indiscernible lump. All of them? Could that be right?

She edged along the skirting toward the splintered window, trying to keep out of view in case someone saw her from the road. On her hands and knees, she crawled to the windowsill. She raised herself to the ledge, rising slowly over it in case the enemy was weeding out the front. But the garden was empty. It was another one of those grey days, the blank unfeeling kind that gave her the sense she was underwater. It was how she felt most of the time now.

Her bedroom window looked across to the front lawn of Mrs. Kennedy's at No. 10. It was the most beautifully kept lawn on the street, though she'd never admit it to Marie. It had a wildness that hers lacked. Rosie never had shared her grandmother's passion for pruning pruning pruning. Why had she come up here again? Was it the thrill of being found out that lured her or the thrill of such brazen ruin? Or maybe ... She jumped, stinging her palms on the crushed glass littering the windowsill. There was Mrs. Kennedy's son at the foot of the Wisteria bush that spilled across their doorway. Gazing up at her. She hadn't seen him since the accident, but she had heard all about it from beneath the kitchen window. His head was cocked too far to the left, his wet nose pouring into his open mouth. He did not blink. Rosie's stomach turned over.

How fast things changed and changed without reverse. Only the week before she had passed his house on the way to the shops to get away from the searchlight eyes of the three bird-faced women. He had been out there, also alone, playing keep up with a football in the road.

'Dyuwannaplay?' he had asked her.

Rosie hadn't known what to say to him. The girls at her new school down in the village did not jeer or tease, they simply pretended that she did not exist. Some had made an effort in the beginning, but stopped trying when she preferred to sit in the corner with the crayon box, pretending to be deaf. As they skipped and giggled and clutched at one another, Rosie was in a bush rooting out snails. This boy was different. When he spoke at first Rosie had not understood. His interest was like a foreign language. She had blushed and turned away. All the way down to the shop she had practised what to say to him on the way back. (I'd like to play please thank you.) But when she turned onto the road he was gone. She hurried back into her own house with the lumpy brown paper bag filled with twice the sweets - there had been a recent softening in Sandra's sugar policy that she hadn't questioned - clasped against her chest. She moped all night, only managing to empty a quarter of the bag. Why had she turned away? Why couldn't she just be normal and speak?

She hid behind a bush in her front garden the next day, the bag of sweets beside her shoe. She would ring the doorbell and hold the bag over the threshold as a peacemaker and they would be friends. She watched Mr. Kennedy leave in the morning and kiss Mrs. Kennedy hard at the door. She watched the front door so intently she didn't notice her mother skirt off down the path behind her and get into an unfamiliar car at the bend in the road. She watched the door so intently she didn't notice the Mrs.' No. 4, 5 and 6 frowning at her backside in the air as they left No. 11 after another fruitless session with Marie. She watched the door so intently her knees went rigid from crouching. Finally, at around 4pm, the boy emerged. She watched him as he played in the street as he always did, alone with the ball. But she couldn't do it. She had spent so long behind the bush watching the door that the light had faded. She had missed breakfast and lunch and the unfamiliar car that she hadn't noticed had dropped Sandra back off at the bend in the road and she was already back indoors helping Marie with the dinner. He looked up and down the road once and picked up his ball and the front door of No.10 closed him back inside. She'd not had the chance since The Fire, Sandra had been using her in the house like a shield. Now they would not know each other as they might once have.

Perhaps he could have given her something there in the road that separated the two rows of houses, something that might have filled the yawning feeling in her chest that was stretching wider by the day. Maybe there was something she could have given him. She left the forbidden room and the window. She did not want to look at him anymore. The Kennedy boy did not move until sometime later when his mother came and wheeled him back inside.

That evening, Rosie made an announcement.

'I am going to bed,' she said.

'About time. I can put on Pride and Prejudice.' Marie was already on her knees before the video cupboard, honouring the acquisition of the new VCR.

'I'm coming too!'

Sandra followed her to the door.

'But it's only half past eight!' Rosie cried, outraged.

'You'll miss Mr. Darcy,' said Marie. 'Are you sure it's altogether necessary?' She shook the VHS in front of her. 'Rintoul couldn't tempt you?'

Sandra steeled herself against the cover of the VHS.

'No I won't be able to enjoy it. I'll only be worrying.'

'Yes you're right,' Marie sighed. 'Some of us still can't be trusted.'

Marie held Sandra's frowning gaze for a moment before turning back to the television. Rosie looked between the two women, trying to find a way to jump into the pathway of secret understanding they shared above her.

'Goodnight Gr – Marie,' said Rosie.

'Goodnight child,' said Marie. She was giving nothing away.

The room Rosie now shared with her mother had been cleared of clutter. Sandra and Marie had packed most things away in empty suitcases and put the rest away in the drawers. Rosie had caught them at it, and watched through the crack in the door. A bed, two chests, a wardrobe that was almost always shut and one side table with one lamp upon it was the only remaining furniture. Sandra loaded up the drawers and turned a key in each latch. The keys went on the ring and into her pocket. She jangled everywhere she went now. Every night since The Fire, Rosie and Sandra went to bed together. Sandra locked them in from the inside and slept with the key in her hand under the pillow. In the morning she unlocked the door again.

103

But she tossed in the night, and Rosie woke frequently in the darkness. Shadows of things moved and disappeared just beyond the edge of her vision before she could catch them, leaving her with outstretched palms and a desperate need for the bathroom. But she couldn't get out with the key hidden and her mother refusing to wake. Sometimes she was so desperate she went in the corner like a dog.

After weeks of carpet scrubbing, and Marie's fury, a pot was put under the window, and Rosie was tucked up and locked in alone. Most nights Rosie was checked in on, but not for long, when the picture was on pause it jumped and gave Marie a headache. But on other nights the unfamiliar car came and waited at the bend in the road for Sandra and she slipped out as Rosie slipped into another world in the room at the top of the stairs.

Time passed. Things went on. The sun replaced the moon, the moon took over the sun. The routine became lax. Her mother came to bed later and later. Rosie no longer stirred when Sandra's body made its impression on the mattress beside her. Marie took over the watch. She popped her head around the door with a sigh to announce herself, letting a slice of landing light cut across Rosie's ear and nose. Rosie held her breath and kept her eyes shut tight and listened for her mother's step.

Some mornings later Rosie woke to find herself alone. She tried the door, but it was locked. There was no key under the pillow or the mattress or on the windowsill or in any of the drawers. She tried the door again. She hammered on it. She pulled. She shouted through the keyhole. She shouted through the gap between the door and carpet. She shouted at the ceiling. She tried to shout out the window, but it too was locked.

'Help. Help! I need to go! I NEED to GO!'

She heard an oath from the direction of the kitchen, and a raspy breath approached. But it wasn't who she had wanted.

'Where's my mum? Why isn't she in here?'

'Come and have breakfast,' Marie said, turning away.

'I don't like being locked in by myself.'

'It's for your own good child. Now come and have your porridge.'

They sat at the table, the clock filling the silence. Any noise that moved out of the rhythm of the clock hands caught Rosie by the ears. She waited for the sound of her mother's footsteps. They did not come.

'Why is Mum not having breakfast?' Rosie asked.

Her grandmother was hidden behind the newspaper as she answered: 'She's had her porridge.'

'But where is she?'

The papers rustled angrily, snapped in two.

'Christ! I can't concentrate with you and your twenty questions! Your mother, you'll be happy to know, has a job at last. Will that do you?'

'Since when?'

'Since today.'

'Why wasn't I told about this?'

Marie squinted at her, unfolded the paper and disappeared behind it again.

'She told you I'm sure, you just didn't listen.'

Her porridge was congealing beneath her nose, but Rosie had lost her appetite.

'Where?'

'Where what?'

'Where does she work?'

Marie sighed loudly, as though trying to push Rosie away bodily with the strength of it.

'In a bank, child. Will that do you now for the love of God?'

'But where?'

The paper shuddered. Rosie found herself in the garden finishing her porridge on the back step. The door remained closed all morning. At lunchtime a plate of sandwiches and a glass of milk appeared. At five in the evening Rosie was allowed back inside for dinner. Her mouth was bursting with questions, but Marie's face was a shut door. The news played over the radio and they ate in silence.

As they were cleaning away the dishes, the front door went. Rosie ran to it and Sandra nearly tripped over her when she walked inside.

'Jesus Rosie you scared the life out of me!'

She shut the door quickly behind her.

'Where have you been?' Rosie demanded.

Sandra blinked.

'Out.'

'But where?'

'Just out, Jesus.'

'Were you at work?'

'I - yes. I was at work.'

'Why didn't you tell me you got a job?'

'I did tell you.'

'I don't remember.'

'Maybe you weren't listening.'

'That's what Granny said.'

'Well as we all know Granny is usually right.'

'Where were you this morning? You were gone when I woke up.'

'I told you, I was at work.'

'Where do you work?'

'Nearby.'

'Where though?'

'I haven't even had a cup of tea,' she groaned, taking off her coat as she entered the kitchen. Rosie followed. Marie raised her eyebrows at her from the kitchen counter. Sandra threw her coat across a kitchen chair.

'Has she been like this all day?'

Marie nodded.

'Have I been like what all day?'

'Rosie I swear to you, if you ask me one more thing ...'

That evening Sandra tucked her into bed as usual, but Rosie did not sleep. She listened to her pottering about the bathroom. The bathroom light clicked off and Sandra's footsteps came toward the bedroom door. Here they paused, then reversed. They creaked down the stairs. The living room door gaped open. Words were exchanged, she couldn't hear them. The front door opened and closed. Rosie lay awake all night, but the door did not open again.

She so ached with tiredness the next day she couldn't throw questions at Marie. She flopped around the garden and scowled at her grandmother, who she watched from the bushes. That evening her mother again returned late, after the dinner had been eaten and the dishes had been dried and stacked. Rosie shrunk away from her when she came to give her a kiss.

'What's up with you?' Sandra asked.

'Nothing.'

The two women locked eyes above her.

Marie hadn't drawn any attention to Sandra's absences. To Rosie, this was a confirmation. Nothing was said, nothing was explained. Every time Rosie asked questions the women would change the subject with a precise and practised skill. Then one day a few weeks later, something happened that made everything slot into place. Rosie met The New Man.

Eleven (a)

'Then everything started to get worse. Much worse.'
    'You began to lose control.'
    'No. It wasn't that.'
    'No?'
    'I couldn't tell the difference anymore.'
    'The difference between what?'
    But already that feeling was taking over again, and she was sliding away from herself while rooted to the spot, as if the remaining shell of her body was a hologram and she was no more than smoke -

Twelve

It happened spontaneously without warning or preparation and was destined for disaster from the start.

It began at breakfast.

'Look at that sky out there. Blue as anything,' said Marie.

'Isn't it a beautiful day, Rosie?' said Sandra.

'It's alright.'

Rosie was in one of her sour moods.

'Would you ever whisht. A sky like it hasn't been seen in months. Out with you now you're finished your breakfast and not a foot back in here until I say so.'

'And try not to get completely filthy darling. I've a surprise for you later.'

'What is it?' asked Rosie. She discussed with herself if she'd consider brightening up for it. It would depend on the nature of the surprise, she decided.

'Out!' cried Marie.

Then the back door closed, Rosie on the wrong side of it. She slunk back inside herself. An odd feeling of déjà vu took her over, but she couldn't catch the pulse of it. She had an urge to tear up the rosebush, but an image of a wooden spoon stopped her - she ripped the leaves off the spindle shrub instead. Out of fresh ideas on how to pass the time, she ended up in her usual spot racing snails underneath the kitchen window. The sun was too bright and hurt her eyes. She sat against the wall as the race went on and threw loose pebbles into the grass. The hoover sang indoors. Rosie's stomach rumbled. Thirst crept up on her. The sun rose into the centre of the sky.

Her mother popped her head out the door, with a glass of juice and a biscuit. Her hair was curled tightly around pink rollers and she wore only a dressing gown.

'Need anything else Button?' she asked.

Rosie frowned at her, unease creeping up her neck. 'Are you going out again?'

'No. I'm all yours today.'

She smiled brightly. Beads of sweat collected at her hairline.

'What's this surprise you said about?'

'Patience,' she said, tapping her nose. She disappeared behind the door again. Rosie heard it lock.

She moved into the shade under the eaves at the back door. A family of swallows had nested up there and were swooping in and out above her. Everything around her seemed to be moving much slower than usual, as though the goings on of the world were taking place under a body of water she could not see or touch. The snails moved languidly along the ground, or had stopped still. But the race was finally coming to an end: two of her best long-distance sliders were neck and neck at the finishing line. As Rosie was about to take the minutes on her watch for the winner, the door opened and pushed her sideways off the step. There was a crunch behind her. She looked around. The snails were gone. Rosie saw her wide mouth reflected back to her in the shining surface of an unfamiliar shoe.

'And you must be little Rosie!'

And a strange man, the shoe owner, was talking to her. He was all nose and teeth with a bushy yellow moustache that quivered on his top lip like a bleached slug.

Rosie was alone in the garden with a man she had never seen before. How had things changed so quickly? Marie and Sandra were nowhere in sight. He had crept in. He was an intruder. A robber! How did he know her name? Questions tumbled upon one another. Her brain jammed. Escape was the only option. She bolted into the foliage.

'I'm afraid that didn't go very well at all,' she heard him say from her hiding place. And then Marie's voice joined him, and it came out easy and familiar.

'She's just playing strange.'

Why would Marie be so polite to a robber? Was she going to invite him to stay for dinner, like the three awful women with the faces like birds?

Rosie peered through the leaves. Marie was kicking the snail shells off the ground into the grass. She threw a glance toward Rosie's hiding place then turned back to the strange intruder.

'Would you mind helping me with the umbrella?' she said. 'I need a strong man for it and since Ned passed away it's been gathering dust.'

'Course Mrs. Cotton,' he replied promptly. His voice sounded like he was shuffling along on his knees beneath her. Perhaps he was the man who would fix her room. He would repaint the walls and fit a new window so she could start sleeping on her own again. That would be ok.

'Sandra could you come out here please?' Marie called into the kitchen.

High heels echoed across the kitchen floor and clicked onto the tarmac. The intruder moved off to the shed, rolling up his sleeves. Marie spoke into Sandra's ear and Sandra's gaze turned to Rosie's hiding place. Marie went off to the shed and the strange man, and Sandra started across the lawn.

'I know you're out here,' she called softly.

Rosie stayed hidden in the dense border and did not say a word. She watched through the gap in the leaves as her mother, dressed all new in white and shining, tip-toed across the grass and transformed from full human size to a pair of shins in fresh cream-coloured shoes. The shins stopped, and the shoes pointed in the direction of her nose.

Sandra glanced back at the house and bent lower into the shrubbery. Her mouth opened and closed through another leaf-less space that usually only showed sky.

'I know you're in here somewhere. I want you to come and say hello to Mr. -.'

'Mr. -?' Rosie asked.

'Yes, Button. Mr. -.'

'Who is he?'

'He's my friend.'

'Is he a robber?'

Sandra laughed, and her mouth opened wide. Rosie couldn't recall seeing all of her teeth in one go like that before. Their brightness unnerved her.

'No. He's our guest. Would you ever come out? I feel mad talking to bushes.'

Rosie watched the new shoes shifting on the grass in front of her. One kicked out into the air behind her and hovered there, parallel to the earth. From the shins down her mother could have been a marble Flamingo.

'I don't like him,' Rosie decided.

Sandra sighed.

'You haven't said two words to him yet.'

'He crushed Popeye and Olive!'

'He couldn't have known.'

'Well I still don't like him.'

'Please Rosie, just come and have lunch. You're making me look bad. Christ my heels are sinking in.'

Rosie's stomach rumbled. She would have to give in soon, she knew. Then a second pair of shoes - beige loafers - came into view, marching at top speed across the grass. Rosie shrunk further back under the leaves. Then Marie's voice jabbed down at her, sharp and impatient as a stinging nettle.

'Get out here now you little You. Know. What. Or you'll have the wooden spoon for dessert and nothing else!'

'Mum! He'll hear you –'

'He won't. I sent him in to wash his hands before lunch.'

'What?'

'What what? That umbrella was filthy. In you go now you're ruining those lovely new shoes. Rosie out you get or I'll reef you out by the ears!'

'Come on Rosie you must be bloody starving by now.'

'You and your fucking language Sandra ever since you came back. I'd watch that today if I were you.'

112

Sandra sighed again.

'Come on now, Rosie. How about you have some apple tart for dessert rather than the wooden spoon?'

Rosie's mouth was dry. Then it started to water.

'Fine,' she said at last. 'But turn around. I don't want you to see my hiding place.'

The weather held all day. Marie laid a spread on the garden table and they all sat around it on the worn wooden chairs. Rosie's feet nearly touched the ground now.

'I meant to paint them but it's been bucketing all bloody week until today,' Marie said.

Sandra clucked her tongue. Marie raised her eyebrows at her.

'Don't be silly Mrs. Cotton, I'm spoiled rotten.' The stranger threw a hand out that took in everything said and unsaid and smoothed it all out. 'Isn't it great that we got such a lovely day?'

'It is indeed. Isn't it Sandra?'

'It's perfect.'

Rosie ate in silence. The New Man was an unknown quantity and he warranted watching. Sandra was resplendent beside him. Rosie couldn't help but feel proud to have her as her mother. The new dress she wore was made of a beautiful white lace that held her tightly around the waist. With her silvery hair and skin, she was doing a very good impression of Grace Kelly, whose picture she had seen in one of her mother's books. Beside her The New Man looked like a character from a horror film. With his drab clothes and sharp edges, he looked out of place in the daylight. The skin under his eyes was deep and bluish, bruised-looking. His hair was wispy, a soupy yellow. It was a ghost of a colour, the sort of thing you'd see on a creature that lived its life under a rock. Perhaps he was a vampire. Or maybe he lived in a graveyard and buried people for a living.

'A bank manager you know,' Marie explained, answering Rosie's guarded curiosity.

The New Man laughed and covered his mouth. Behind his hand Rosie saw uneven yellow teeth. He lowered his hand and smiled a closed-lipped smile at Sandra. She smiled back. There was a familiarity to the easy way the smiles fell from their lips and it made Rosie go cold. She watched as his hand disappeared from above the table to rest itself on her mother's thigh just above the knee. It massaged her gently there in little circles. It travelled up the leg slowly until another hand, smaller and warmer, stopped it and dragged it back. The faces above remained impassive as Marie chatted on about the food, about the roses, about her plans for her summer garden.

'Are you a keen gardener yourself Mr - ?' Marie asked.

'I've never been particularly green fingered Mrs. Cotton, but I've always wanted to learn.'

'Well intention's the main thing.'

Sandra cleared her throat: 'Have you seen my mother's famous roses?'

'Oh yes. They're something else.'

Rosie was sure she'd missed something. Sandra and Marie were bowing to this stranger and smiling and cutting him the biggest slices of apple tart but when he laughed a second time he bared stained and crooked teeth. When he stood he towered over Rosie. He eyed down his hooked nose at her. His voice was high and thin, and his face was hairy. He smiled often and said everything was lovely, but when Marie and Sandra turned away to point at things his face became sharp and cunning and he watched Rosie with the biting eyes of an eagle. She withered in his gaze. She disappeared into her bedroom after lunch and hid under the bed.

Twelve (a)

'That night, the eagles came and stole my mother.'
    'And the Raven?'
    'I called for him.'
    'But, he didn't come?'
    Her throat stung, even now.
    'No. He didn't.'

Thirteen

And then Christmas Eve was upon them. There was a trapped bird where Rosie's heart ought to be, tickling its wings against her insides trying to escape. She knew nothing but her own ever-mounting elation, but there were things to be noticed. Sandra was cleaning, polishing and re-polishing the dining table in the good room. She was checking the plates for spots and cracks. Marie sat with her feet up in front of the television and watched the specials with a wide brown glass in her hand, Sandra cleaned and polished around her and she did not budge. Had Rosie paid attention to this odd reversal she would have known to be on guard. But Rosie could think of one thing only and that was: Santa.

'Do you think we'll see the reindeers Mum?'

Rosie bobbed up and down in front of the Coronation Street special. She couldn't contain herself. Marie was nestled in the armchair with her feet up on the pouf. Sandra had grown rubber gloves as a second skin.

'Quit your jiving girl,' Marie said, and her words came out slow, wrapped in wool. 'You've my head wrecked.'

'It's rein-DEER Rosie,' Sandra said into the mirror as she dusted the mantelpiece.

'The girl's near gone on eight years Sandra, would you not just –'

Sandra silenced Marie with a reflected glare.

'She needs to be told.'

Marie fixed her gaze on her daughter's closed face in the mirror's surface. She swayed slightly, even though she was almost lying down. Sandra turned back into the room. Cleared her throat, sniffed.

'Rosie, guess what.'

'What?'

Sandra looked at her, opened her mouth. Closed it. Marie clicked her tongue, began to hum.

'Dum, dum de dum, dum, dum de dum ...'

Sandra glanced at Marie. Her face had a sudden violence in it. Rosie looked between them.

'Guess what, Mum?'

Sandra took a deep breath, opened her mouth, smiled.

'I know that –' she paused. Marie's lips parted slightly. Sandra glanced at her and her next words chased each other out of her mouth '- little girls who go to bed early get on Santa's good list! And you know what happens to girls on the good list?'

A fire was lit under Rosie. She jumped to her feet. Marie grunted.

'Oh, I know all right, I know exactly what happens to good little girls,' she said, waving her glass around. Droplets of the brown liquid fell onto the carpet. Sandra winced.

'Your mother was a good girl once, Rosie. Shall I tell you what happened to her?'

She paused and took another swig from her glass and let out a laugh like a bark. A word formed in Rosie's mouth but she knew strongly not to let it loose, though she desperately wanted to.

'You'll leave me again girls won't you? I know you'll leave.'

Sandra turned to her but said nothing.

'The longer you leave it Sandra, the worse it'll be.'

Marie and Sandra held one another's gaze. Rosie was used to these wordless exchanges but still they bored her, especially at Christmas when there were presents to be wrapped and unwrapped and treats on every surface. Rosie tugged at Sandra's jumper. Sandra looked down at Rosie and seemed to remember she was there. She switched back into Mother.

'Why don't we go and get a little present for Rudolph?'

'Ok!'

Marie groaned. 'I suppose you'll be butchering a few of my mince pies now as well as the carrots.'

Sandra pulled off her rubber gloves and marched Rosie out by the shoulders.

'I spent all afternoon peeling those bloody carrots,' came the disembodied shout from the living room. 'You can have the one only!'

And then it was time for bed, to lie awake and wait for the morning.

'But what if he never got my letter? There are millions of children all over the world, how will he read them all?' Rosie asked as she and her mother came to the foot of the staircase.

'He knows child, oh don't you worry, he knows. We all know,' Marie bellowed from behind the living room door. 'Sandra now's the time. Don't leave it until tomorrow.'

'Enough talk now!' Sandra sent her voice into a high sailing arc as she pushed Rosie up the stairs: 'Up and into bed you go. Santa doesn't come to children unless they go to sleep.'

She was kissed goodnight and the bedroom door was shut but not locked as a Christmas treat. The old room had been put back together, but it was still out of bounds. Rosie had argued weakly at first but was secretly glad of it. The nights were long and cold and since The Fire shadows had threatened her from the darkest corners. The women's muffled voices crept up through the floorboards from the living room, rising and falling like the surf.

When she woke the house was still, the television mute and her mother beside her in the bed. She rose and put an eye to the gap in the curtains. The window bit at her. She could scarcely believe the view, it was blinding. The ground outside was covered in pure white snow. The trees puckered underneath it, the ground lay flat and smooth. She had been born in a blizzard and had heard all about it but until that moment it was just words. She didn't know anything could be so perfect.

In the living room where the tree stood and the presents beneath, the room was a picture. Her bike was there in pride of place. She loved it instantly.

'Thank you,' she mouthed in the direction of the chimney. All that was left of their offerings at the fireplace were a few crumbs of mince pie. He had definitely come.

But the garden of snow remained untouched. She couldn't resist wanting to make her mark on it, to sink into its perfection, to have some of it for herself. The satisfaction of plunging her shoes in, the print of her hand, her body. There was nothing like it. She was overwhelmed in it, it was moist and giving as dough.

This is my garden! She proclaimed silently to the world, arms spread wide above her head like this: Y

Then the kitchen window opened. The music of cups and plates greeting one another spilled out, breaking upon her private world. The house had awoken.

'Bloody snow again!' Marie's voice flew out of the window. 'Thank Christ I'm stocked up this time.'

Then: 'What are you doing out there, child? Get indoors!'

'Go up and put on your nice new dress before breakfast Rosie,' Sandra called.

'Never mind that, get in out of the cold! You'll catch your death. Today of all days it's the last thing we need.'

Inside the kettle whistled and the cutlery drawer smashed open and closed. The radio had been switched on for the service and the carols. Rosie added liberal spoonfuls of sugar to her tea behind the women's backs as they demanded utensils and ingredients from one another and the breakfast got cooked.

'Up you go and get changed now Rosie,' Sandra demanded, as though she were a box of eggs or a frying pan.

'You should wait until after the breakfast and tell her first,' Marie muttered.

'Tell me what?' asked Rosie.

'Don't earwig child. You'll end up hearing things you'll wish you didn't. Anyway, who said I was talking about you?'

Sandra could not stand still. Her legs jiggled as she opened and closed everything and walked from one end of the room to the other.

'Where's the - thing?'

'The what?'

'The ... thing. The thing that goes –'

Sandra made a circular motion with her wrist, as though in homage to the royal speech that would come on the television in a few hours.

'What are you saying to me woman?'

'The - thing - that you use to make the eggs go together. You know what I mean.'

Marie peered at her daughter: 'Is it the whisk? It's right beside you Sandra. You'd want to get yourself together before – '

'Up you go now Rosie –' Sandra sang out over the radio, the kettle, the pan, ushering Rosie out of the kitchen. Marie sighed deeply as she turned the sausages.

'- get that lovely dress on and we'll be eating by the time you're back down!'

'And don't forget to brush that mane!' Marie called.

Rosie's Christmas outfit had been bought the week before, it was still folded in the paper hidden at the back of the wardrobe. It was a deep navy blue, the night sky cut and stitched. A ruff of white lace accented the neck and wrists. Marie had turned it over in her hands for almost half an hour when it arrived home, she had another wordless exchange with Sandra that went on for so long Rosie thought they had both swallowed their tongues. She unwrapped the dress that meant so much. It was live water in her hands. She put it on carefully and hurried back down the stairs to her breakfast.

They ate in the good room. Plates of glistening sausages, crisped bacon, yellow eggs, sweet tomatoes, wet mushrooms, and soda. Once her plate was clean Rosie started on some of the chocolate from her stocking. She wasn't told no, and that was enough for her. Then Sandra began to speak.

'Rosie –' she said.

Already it was loaded with warning. Marie's head cocked up.

'I've something to tell you.'

'Ok.'

The chocolate was delicious, even if it was going all over her mouth and chin. Marie winced.

'Mr. - is coming to tea today, and we all know how well you two get on, so that's fine and good –'

'Oh sure we all know indeed,' Marie said in an undertone. 'Child can you not put that stuff inside your mouth rather than anywhere but. And listen to your mother when she's talking to you.'

'Are you listening to me Rosie?' asked Sandra.

Rosie nodded to show listening.

'Get on with it we haven't got all day,' Marie said, pointing to the clock. Lunchtime was approaching.

'Well Rosie - and I wanted to tell you first - I didn't want it to be a shock. The thing is –'

'Just say it woman for the love of God.'

'I would if you wouldn't interrupt me all the bloody time!'

'Language!'

The two of them were pulsing electric wires. Unease managed to find its way through the thick layers of chocolate to Rosie's brain. She turned her eyes to her mother. Sandra closed her own and spoke.

'We're getting married you see.'

And out came a long hissing breath. She looked exhausted.

'Married?'

'Yes my love.'

Rosie's face was a used piece of paper: scrunched up, written upon.

'Who's getting married?'

Marie rolled her eyes. Sandra put a hand up to stop her inevitable quip.

'I am, Button. Mr. - asked me to marry him, and I ... well I've said yes.'

'You're getting married?'

'I think we've established that,' Marie muttered.

'Yes, honey, I am.'

The chocolate Santa Claus was rolling down to her wrist.

'But -?'

'But what?'

'But ... what about - Joe?'

Sandra's face froze. Marie let out a long groan, pregnant with impatience.

'Joe! Ha. Don't make me laugh.'

But she wasn't laughing, and her lips grew thin and sharp.

'Three years since you left London, more than that. The postman hasn't been knocking down my door. The phone hasn't been going off the hook.'

'Maybe he lost the address.'

'Your father Joe knows well where you are and he hasn't bothered once, not once, in all that time to contact you.'

Sandra's mouth was pale. 'Please don't -'

'It's the truth. Accept it before I'm stiff and six feet under and I'll die a happy woman.'

'That's not true, Granny. I know it's not.'

'It's true. True as the snow out there, true as the day you were born. And don't call me Granny.'

'You're lying,' said Rosie.

'I never told a lie in my life.'

'Stop lying.'

'Please the two of you, stop this.'

'Not one phone call,' Marie battered on, ignoring Sandra. 'Not one letter. How long does it take to pick up the phone I ask you?'

'Mum, please -'

'Am I to be shot down for speaking the truth now? In my own house?'

'Shut up,' said Rosie.

'She'll tell me to shut up, will she?' Marie allowed herself a swift incredulous laugh. 'Madam I've had you looked after here. Well looked after. I took you in. I know many a woman who wouldn't. Many of them on this road thought I was mad to. But I did.'

'Just leave it now Mum, alright? Just leave it for the love of God.'

'Neither of you can show your faces outside the front door. I had to go to the first service by myself this morning before I started cooking for you - of all days, Christmas morning on my own - and all the other families sitting in the pews and the looks and the snide comments I put up with every year for the two of you. I will not be told to shut up for that.'

'Shut up shut up shut up! I. Hate. You. I. Hate. This. House. I. Hate –'

'Oh, hate me now do you? Hate this house, do you? I wouldn't speak so soon child, you don't know the half of it.'

'Ok enough now the two of you!'

But Marie would not be silenced: 'Do you know something Rosie? You're nothing but a spoilt brat out to get your way. You have your soft mother wrapped around your finger and I'll be glad to see the back of the both of you!'

Rosie looked at her grandmother but saw nothing. The room had gone dark. Someone was whispering in her ear. Her hands moved over the breakfast plate in front of her. She lifted it and let it drop silently at her feet. It shattered. Sandra jumped at the impact, but Marie stayed still and her eyes never left her granddaughter's face.

'Time for a tantrum is it? Well you didn't lick that off the stones that's for sure.'

'Mum for God's sake let it rest for once! Just let it rest.'

'I told you, you should have told her weeks ago. Yesterday even. Not on Christmas day an hour before the doorbell goes!'

'This wouldn't be happening if you hadn't kept on at her.

You're relentless sometimes, you know that? Relentless.'

Rosie went for the tureen of mushrooms and closed her hand around a lump of them. She lifted her fist and flung them at her grandmother, who ducked.

'You always have to push it.' Sandra's hands framed her head like blinkers and she hid between them.

Rosie moved blindly towards the cooked meat –

'You've never learned to just let people be. We're not all made of granite like you are.'

'That's right Sandra, take her side as I knew you would.'

Marie's face seemed to shake loose, her hand went to her mouth. But when she spoke her voice was hard and cold.

'She knows exactly how to play you Sandra. And she's stone mad. Good luck to him dealing with her. And are you just going to stand by and let her –'

Rosie had stood up. The blue tureen with the fancy handles was in her hands. She raised it over her head.

'Put down the bacon child.'

'Your grandmother's good china –'

'That dress will be destroyed.'

'– and you're already filthy!'

Sandra caught Rosie, sat her back down. Her body vibrated withheld violence. Sandra moved the tureen away. She dipped a napkin in her water glass and tried to get some of the stains out of the silk. Rosie was rigid, unreachable.

'Ok we're all calm now, good girl,' Sandra said in the forced singsong of mothers everywhere. 'Fuck, I don't think this is going to come out!'

And that was when Marie saw her moment to finish it. Her voice was smoother than eel skin as it flew toward her target.

'That's it –' it was as though she was dressing a wound '– it's all been arranged now and there's nothing that can be done. Mr. - will be your new Daddy.'

'What?' whispered Rosie.

'And that's final.'

124

And then Rosie felt herself stretching open, everything disappearing out of her. Her mouth opened wide, but no sound came out. Her body shook. Then the chocolate came mudsliding down her chin and onto the precious lace collar –

'What possessed you to say that, Mum?' Sandra cried. 'There's no hope for this now - and after all he spent on it!'

'It's the truth. And it's high time she had one.'

Marie's voice was hard, but Rosie trembled violently, her wide mouth, slick and brown, open in a silent howl. Marie looked up at the photo of Ned on the wall, drew her hands together.

'Will you shut that one up!' she breathed. 'He'll be here any moment. Some sight to come into!'

There was no time for ceremony, for apology or reconciliation. Rosie was bundled upstairs, assuaged with squeezing and kisses and hugs, the panic of trying to calm her down. Roughly cleaned up and scrubbed, shoved into another clean dress - far less fancy - but clean at least thank God. The good dress was left to soak in the sink. The water clouded up murkily like cold tea. Then the doorbell went, full and resonant as an oriental gong. It echoed around the hallway and travelled up the staircase, into the bathroom where Rosie and her mother stood. It brought Sandra to life. She went straight to the mirror. She fluffed her hair and traced the outline of her lips with her forefinger. She moved without thought or motivation, each lifting of hand to face and pat of fingertip on skin a remembered role, an act committed dutifully to memory and recited without consciousness or feeling.

'I don't like this dress,' said Rosie. Everything that had happened in the last hour had happened so quickly that she could hardly take it in.

'You look lovely,' Sandra replied at once, eyes still and focused on her reflection.

'I want the other one.'

'Well it's ruined now, isn't it? You can't wear it. You ruined it.'

'Sandra!' Marie called up the stairs.

The voice kicked her into a new course of action. Seamlessly she appeared on her knees before her daughter, placating and gentle, now a mother. There were beads of sweat on the top of her lip just above the line of her lipstick.

'Please be nice to him. For me?' Sandra was begging. 'It's Christmas. And ignore your grandmother. It's hard for her without Ned. My daddy. You never even met him.'

She stood up again and smiled into the mirror. 'It might be difficult for you to understand, but ... I sometimes forget you're only eight years old.'

'Nine nearly.'

'Nearly nine, that's right.'

She ran her fingers through her hair.

'Please Rosie, just ... do you remember what it was they used to say in England, about keeping things in?'

'Sandra would you get down here!'

'Stiff upper lip?' asked Rosie, her own shaped into a sullen pout.

'Stiff upper lip. That's the one.'

Sandra was on the verge of tears with the stress of it all. Rosie promised to be good.

Christmas was the one day of the year when it was acceptable to eat dinner before dinnertime. At no other time would Marie have allowed knives and forks to be held until after the hour of six. The meal was to be eaten in those odd hours between three and five, when the light went. Mr.- was unfailingly punctual. He had arrived at the appointed hour just as the old grandfather clock in the hallway began to toll. His promptness made Marie cluck with pleasure, but left Rosie dead inside. That clock like all old things only foretold doom.

'Crisp out,' Marie said as the door revealed him.

'A white one for once,' came the response.

'The first in nine years,' Marie said. 'And by God I hope it's the last.'

Mr.- wasn't a handsome man, but he had dressed himself smartly for the occasion. He stepped over the threshold as though arriving home after a day of work, expanding into it, claiming it as his own. He placed his umbrella neatly in the stand and his hat he laid on the hook. The leather shoes Rosie knew too well had been shined and his thin hair was neatly parted and gleaming. His suit moulded to his long angular frame. But he still looked like a bank manager. The marriage between the two of them seemed a more absurd concept than ever before as he stood in the house. It seemed impossible that it could go ahead.

He took a seat in the living room. The tree winked and the fire roared, but Rosie's drink stung her nostrils. A glass was put in the man's hand and he swirled the amber liquid in neat little circles. He was brown all over, his glass, his suit, his shoes, the yellow brown slug of hair on his lip. He smiled and sipped and observed the shining bike beneath the tree as though it was a mute performer. Mr. - looked at Rosie and turned his smile inside out.

'You were well looked after.'

He nodded at the bike.

Rosie looked down at her glass.

He laughed softly. 'Gone deaf, have you?'

'Answer the man Rosie,' Marie barked.

'But I was told not to speak.'

'Child would you ever whisht with your nonsense.'

'But Mum said –'

'And she's right. Children should be seen and not heard. Isn't that what's said Mrs. Cotton?'

'It is of course.'

'I only reminded her to be polite is all,' said Sandra.

'And you'd be right. You'd be right to.'

'But Mum, you said that –'

'Whisht now child and drink up or you won't get another one,' Marie said, and the tone was enough to silence her.

127

Sandra sat perched on the edge of the hardest chair, her attention lit upon the man like a spotlight. Her eyes darted between him and Rosie so often she could have had a twitch. Marie watched Sandra and the corners of her mouth turned down as though there was something off in her glass.

Dinner was announced. The party were to reassemble in the dining room. Mr. - rose first and extended a hand to Sandra. She smiled and followed him quickly across the hall.

Rosie was left alone in the room with her empty glass in her hand. She wished she could shrink herself to flea size and hide in a pine cone. She crawled around the back of the sofa and hugged her knees into her chest. Behind the sofa there was no dinner, no wedding and no New Man. She hoped they would all forget her.

Then Sandra's feathery voice called into the room: 'Button?'

Rosie held her breath. Her chest was going to burst. Sandra's face appeared over the back of the couch.

'Are you hiding?' she asked quietly. She closed her eyes and took a deep breath. When she opened them again she had been infused with a new energy, a resolve that could not be contested.

'Come on. It's on the table. Everyone's waiting. I'm afraid we're just going to have to go through with it.'

The table was resplendent. The meat gleamed, the potatoes were crisped and coppery like rusted metal and the vegetables glistening and wet. Marie hadn't let them boil over this year. She'd had her head stuck in Delia for weeks. She had outdone herself and Rosie almost forgave her. When the novelty of the first mouthfuls had passed, Mr. - swallowed and cleared his throat. He was going to speak.

'Do you like your present Rosie?' he said.

'I haven't gone on it yet.'

Her grandmother's foot moved under the table, caught her in the shin. Rosie jumped.

'But do you like it?' he spoke into the dish of buttered peas as he piled a second helping on his plate.

'Well I have to go on it first.'

'It was a very expensive model, Rosie,' Sandra said.

The words fell out of her mouth and it was too late to put them back in.

'How do you know?' Rosie asked. 'Santa –'

'I mean, it looks so expensive,' Sandra said quickly.

All three pairs of eyes were on her. Her mother looked strained, her grandmother angry - though that was nothing new - and he was like a withered balloon. Rosie didn't know what she had done to warrant such sudden and intense attention. Never mind - she was full. She stood.

'I'll have a go on it now,' she said.

Immediately the atmosphere brightened. His face opened and the women began to do things. Sandra started clearing up the plates and Marie reminded Rosie not to stay out too long, she would miss dessert. There was a pudding *and* a trifle.

As she wheeled the bright blue bike into the hallway, chatter from the dining room escaped like birdsong. She heaved the front door open, carefully placed each shoe on the slick stone steps. The bike hopped down beside her and onto the thick path. She threw her leg over and mounted it at last.

But she didn't know what she was doing. It was her first bike, she had never ridden before. She was straddled on the frame with her feet planted on the ground, as stilled and frozen as the world around her. It couldn't be that difficult, she had seen loads of people do it, and most were younger than her! She couldn't walk back in and say she hadn't done it, not after the way they had looked at her before. She steadied herself, and puffed her chest out like a robin. She moved down the driveway and out onto the road, where the snow was thinnest. It was blindingly cold. She had forgotten her gloves.

Her feet moved and the bike followed, but they could only go as fast as the snow would let them. In her lungs the air took on sharp corners, but she kept moving, paddled her feet

129

faster still, she would have to lift them. She scrambled for the pedals, the bike veered wildly to the left then crashed down upon her.

She would go again. And again. And yet again. By the fifth try she no longer felt the pain of falling. She began to stabilise. She stayed on for four counts. Then eight quick ones. With each ride the counts increased. By the time she was ready to finish up she could stay upright for almost twenty. She could no longer feel her hands or ears, but she was triumphant. She heaved the bike back up the front steps. Her grandmother went white when she opened the door.

'Jesus! You're fecking soaked through child,' she cried. 'Again! In you get - no leave that yoke outside! I don't want you bringing your muck in here. Upstairs and get changed with you.' She coughed and her chest shook. 'I'm catching my death here. Up now, then straight down for the pudding. Everyone's waiting!'

Rosie was all out of dresses, jeans and a jumper would have to do. Sandra's face sharpened when she reappeared in the dining room. Rosie sat down and attacked the untouched puddings so prettily displayed in the centre of the table. The adults watched her. A slight frown had appeared between his eyebrows.

'Will you miss the house?' he asked at last.

It took a moment for her to understand, everything had been cleaned from her mind by victory. Then she knew. She had almost completely forgotten. A harsh silence settled over the table. It had become a feature of the day. Her mother traced the outline of her face with her fingertips, as was her habit during times of stress. A barely seen nod of the head was all that was needed to inform him that he'd spoken too soon. The tightening of his jaw when he acknowledged it. A dangerous look passed over his face, a barely perceptible glimpse of something more, but shaped immediately as if by a quick wind into a smooth and pleasant mask once again.

It was all explained to her then with great care. The adults softened their voices to a whisper as they talked.

'When men and women get married,' Sandra said, 'it's normal for them to start a new life together alone, away from their parents.'

'Unless you're one of them Indians,' Marie added.

'But why can't we stay?' Rosie asked.

Marie sighed loudly, folded her arms.

'It just wouldn't be right,' Sandra said, raising her voice.

'So after the wedding, your mother and I will be moving somewhere new,' Mr. - said.

'And you'll be coming with us darling.'

'Yes, and you.'

He folded his knife and fork across one another on his plate. He took a deep drink from his glass. There was nothing more to say.

Rosie could have started to cry. She could have vomited. She could have run into the garden, breaking a few of her grandmother's porcelain figurines on the way. Instead she just sat and said nothing and worked through her dessert until her plate was clean.

'Thank you that was delicious,' she said.

Every face was on her, each as expectant as the next.

'I'll clear up now.'

She picked up her plate and spoon and gathered some other things on top. She left the room. She put the dishes in the kitchen sink. She knew not to wash them herself. It was the good china, breaking it - which was likely - would have severe consequences. She walked into the living room and turned on the television. She flicked for cartoons, or a film, if she could find a good one. There was movement and talk in the dining room. The door opened and he came out, followed by the women. He hesitated at the living room.

'Goodbye,' he said.

'Goodbye,' she replied.

He did not come into the room to kiss her, as her mother usually insisted. There were some more words at the front door, but they were quick. The door closed decisively, and he was gone.

Rosie heard Sandra's footsteps linger outside in the hall. She kept her eyes fixed ahead on the screen and the footsteps walked towards the kitchen. The door was pulled shut. Rosie turned the volume down and their voices, though low, carried through to where she sat.

'You should have told her sooner like I told you to,' Marie was saying. 'Let her get used to the idea. It's a lot to take in at once, especially for a child like her.'

'But it came so quickly I've barely had time to get used to the idea myself.'

Rosie knew, even without being in the room to see, that her mother's hand tugged at the neck of her dress and her eyebrows puckered at the centre as she spoke.

'Well there's nothing to be done about it now. You've given your word and it can't be gone back on.'

'I know.'

'For Christ's sake Sandra, you should be grateful a man such as that thought to look at you, let alone propose, and you lugging that bastard around.'

Rosie pocketed another word she would have to learn how to spell.

Rosie heard her mother shout: 'Jesus Christ!'

The dishes sunk to the bottom of the sink with a clang.

'Quiet now or she'll hear you for feck's sake!'

'Me, be quiet?' Sandra let out a laugh like a bark.

Rosie made her breath go shallow and silent.

'I meant no harm at all and you know it –'

'How can you –'

'It's the truth! You know it, I know it, sure everyone on this bloody street knows it. It's a wonder a man will look at you at all now. In my day –'

'This isn't about you and dad. This is a different world. It's 1980 in a few days for God's sake!'

'It's not as different as you'd care to believe. Not here anyway.'

'And it's almost nine years since all of that, can't you just let it lie?'

'It will never be let lie, as you've got a child sitting in the living room to remind us all of it every day –'

Rosie shifted on the seat. She had been sitting so still her right leg had gone dead.

'- and there's the other matter to deal with, that he knows nothing of. Though as difficult as she already is, I can't imagine he'll even notice. Let's pray he doesn't anyway. Whatever you do, don't say a word.'

Sandra groaned and when her voice came out it was muffled, as though it was trapped beneath something.

'I don't know how I'm going to do this.'

'You'll make it work. You have to.'

'Maybe –'

'No Sandra. There's no maybe about it,' Marie said, and it was clear from her voice that the conversation was over. 'You'll be marrying him within the month and that's that.'

The kitchen door opened and shut. Footsteps tramped up the stairs. The cool silence of the house returned, broken only by the scraping of tableware against the sink and low sounds from the television. And that was Christmas done with for another year.

Fourteen

The marriage was far less spectacular than Rosie had imagined it would be, they dressed in their best and made their way into town by train. Rosie wore her Christmas dress. After a few soaks it had been restored to itself, but it was still cold and when the wind rushed on the platform it blew up and showed the tops of Rosie's tights even when she held it down.

'That boy over there's looking at your knickers,' Marie whispered.

'He wasn't.'

'He was. I saw him.'

'Mum leave her be would you.'

On the train, Sandra fidgeted and sat with her back like a wall, desperate not to crease her own new silk dress. She couldn't stop sweating in it. She held her arms out at her sides, trying to air herself out.

'Sit still woman or you'll be soaked through by the time we get there,' Marie warned her.

They sat on the train all the way into the city and it felt like any other day. They didn't set foot in a church. Some former relationship of his had made it impossible, though it wasn't talked about. Instead, the wedding took place in a stuffy room that reminded Rosie of her school principal's office. It felt like going to the doctor's, except everyone wore suits.

The guests were few. Rosie and Marie on the bride's side and a brother on the groom's. After the rite was performed they had lunch in a hotel restaurant nearby. The white tablecloths were stiff and grainy under Rosie's fingertips. Crumbs from the complimentary bread basket were scattered the length of it and prickled her elbows.

'No elbows on the table!' Marie's lips were white and invisible, imploring the ceiling for answers. 'Christ the child's manners and in a fancy place like this!'

Rosie couldn't seem to do anything right. Her mother had barely looked at her all day and every glance Marie threw in her direction was loaded with warning. The two men laughed loud and long and patted each other on the back as though they were the only people in the room. The women spoke in low conspiratorial voices. Rosie, as neither a woman nor a man, felt smaller and more insignificant than ever before and sniffed the dark drink that Mr. - had poured for her, searching for poison.

Then - how had it happened? - it was the day of the move. Rosie tried to hold on to the few days and hours she had left in Marie's, she tried to collect them and bottle them up and hide them under her mattress, hoping they would hold still and nothing would ever change.

But the day came regardless. Packing everything up, she didn't understand how things spread far apart could double in size when pulled together, or how things had a way of disappearing just when she needed them. Her grandmother helped. She had a knack for finding a lost thing.

'Who will you shout at Granny when I'm gone?' She asked her.

'Whisht now child.'

Marie turned her back and bent low over an open suitcase, folding things already neatly packed. Rosie was certain that with no one to scold or blame anymore her voice would go hoarse from lack of use.

His car, grand and gleaming like his hair and shoes, could take all their things in one trip. The bike was secured to the roof rack with a tight double knot. Despite reassurances it would hold Rosie had visions of it taking flight behind them once the engine ran and disappearing into the wild.

They were ready. Marie raced in and out of rooms and up and down the stairs collecting wayward objects and filling up forgotten spaces in the cardboard boxes as if she couldn't wait to be rid of them. Her eyes moved between the grandfather clock and her watch with such frequency Rosie asked her if she was going blind.

135

When the clock sang out, Rosie went cold. A familiar feeling of dread returned, sitting on her shoulder like a dark creature. And another feeling - the certainty that she had left something behind, something vital, for which she didn't have a name.

Marie closed her inside her arms; she could feel her ribs crushing into one another, bone squeaking against bone. Her slim pink lips planted single, dry kisses on their cheeks.

'Call me when you get there, won't you?'

Transfixed by Mrs. Kennedy's winter garden gone wild across the road, she couldn't seem to look at anything else. Sandra caught her gaze but couldn't reach it.

They walked to the car. He was already in the front seat. He nodded at Marie. Her lips stretched across her face. She sniffed.

'Alright then. Good luck you two.'

'Talk to you soon Mum,' Sandra said, hugging Marie again, holding her tight.

'Alright. On you go.'

Marie broke free, walking slowly back to the house, without turning. Sandra got in the front, Rosie in the back. Everything was cream and brown and leather, as she had expected. When they looked out the window Marie was nowhere to be seen. They looked back at the house as they reversed out and drove away, as the next door neighbour's driveway swallowed up the old brick, the windows, the net curtains and white wooden window frames, the creeping roses and the closed green front door. They looked until the very last centimetre of house was visible. Not a twitch of a curtain to reward them.

The road sped beneath the wheels quick as a river. The sun was bright and proud above them. Rosie felt it mock her. When sunshine visited that place everything glowed, but Rosie wanted rain and fog to press down upon her, to hold in resonance the ache that would not lift.

He did not speak, kept his eyes on the road. He drove three clicks above the limit, his chest forward thrust, already at the end point. He drove as though slackening would offer something unpleasant to slip inside the open window and sit beside Rosie on the backseat.

'Not long now,' he said.

Fourteen (a)

'When I walked through the door I knew. Something was coming.'

A swollen pause. The metronome tripped through the silence; an empty street, mist-fallen, a lone horse clopping through the dark. There was a sharp breath:

'Do you think a part of you had already started planning then?'

It was a question she could not answer, brazen and ridiculous in equal measure. It made no sense.

'How could I have?'

'With you, Rosie, I am learning that anything is possible.'

Fifteen

The staircase beckoned, and what lurked upstairs. Though there was still no light on the upper landing, Rosie went up alone.

Her feet followed the twisting passage of the stairs. Each footstep left a clear stain in the dust. The upper landing unfolded in still silence. Someone was waiting to greet her. A man. Not a man, a painting. A portrait. Only the glint of the golden frame and the white of his teeth. A smile twisted his lips, his floating face. He looked at Rosie. Straight at her. His smile pressed out, went flat, his eyes hollowed. She passed quickly, afraid to let the eyes into hers, the smile to press upon her own. It slid alongside her, the portrait's eyes following her every move, its stare examining every turn of her heel, every curve of her, every inch. Dread settled on her shoulder, its wings tickling her cheek. All the rooms were hollow black, burnt out and destitute.

'Lunch!'

Sandra's call came from below. The silence that cushioned her words meant the work must have stopped downstairs. Her voice was so far away in the vast new house she could have been calling from another land.

Rosie would not waste time investigating bedrooms. She knew she would never sleep upstairs, not near him. She sprinted back down the steps, taking two at a time when she could manage it. She kept her eyes on her shoelaces.

Sixteen

When Sandra came in to light the fire in Rosie's bedroom, the first argument began. Another failed attempt to get some heat going in the grate sent her voice echoing down the passages.

'Can you come and help me with this?'

Eventually as though it had flown there, a response came.

'Can you not light it yourself?'

His voice arrived before he did. Then he stepped into the room and shook his head.

'This place is the size of a study for God's sake. With all those grand rooms up the stairs.'

'You are very far away down here.'

Sandra lit another match and let it fall into the grate. It flared up briefly and went out.

'You don't want to be too close to us is that it?' he asked.

A burst of fire flared in the grate, making his eyes glow hot. Then it went out. They were yellow pale again.

Rosie lined her new teddies up along the wall side of her bed and shrugged her shoulders. She couldn't say a thing; the words would not form in her mouth. Perhaps the man who lived at the top of stairs had put a curse on her, struck her dumb. Even if she could have spoken she knew she would not be believed.

'I know what it is,' he said. 'You're afraid.'

Rosie picked up one of the teddies, a soft black creature with glassy blue eyes. She held it to her chest. 'I'm not.'

'You are. You're a little scaredy cat.'

Sandra stood between them and cleared her throat: 'Are you going to help me light this damn thing or not.'

He turned slowly to face her. 'Excuse me Sandra?'

Sandra dropped her gaze.

'I've been at it for hours.'

He held his hands up and shook them. 'Women! The

dramatics.' He winked at Rosie. She stationed the black bear beside her pillow. He would have the honour of sleeping beside her on the first night.

'You've been in here all of twenty minutes.'

'I'm not used to it. We had central heating before. And a gas fire in the living room.'

She glanced quickly at Rosie and away.

'Look at you with your fancy central heating and your gas fire.'

He cast an appraising eye over her.

She said quietly, 'It's not such a new thing.'

'Well it'd be a waste here. These beautiful pieces of eighteenth century workmanship for nothing.'

He ran a hand across the cool, smooth surface of the marble fireplace.

'I'm not saying to get rid of them - but you know it's worth thinking about.'

'Is it now?'

Sandra turned the box of matches over in her hands. Rosie watched it twirling between her fingers. The wind danced through the chimney, moving in time to the matchbox.

'We could light them the odd time just. When we have people over,' she suggested.

'Have them just for show now, will she?' he asked the ceiling, as though there wasn't a third person in the room.

'Not just for show, no, I meant we can –'

'Beautiful pieces of work like this. In this beautiful house.'

'No, it's - it's a bloody nightmare trying to light the damn things!'

She slammed the box of matches on the mantelpiece shelf and turned away.

'So she'll have me paying for the coal and the gas! I'm made of money is it?'

He took her arm then and she faced him. Rosie shrank against the wall. Her chest felt light and ticklish. Something about the scene brought on another feeling, illuminated by the naked light bulb above them. One she had felt before.

'I've been standing here for half an hour trying to get this thing to work –'

'And what?'

'I'm worried.'

Sandra looked towards Rosie flat against the wall, her eyes wide and silent in the low light.

'Of course. The little princess.' He released her arm, hitched his trousers up around his waist. 'Get her to throw that blanket around her if that's what this is about.'

'It's not that.'

'What is it so?'

Sandra opened her mouth, closed it.

He grabbed the matches. 'It's an unnecessary expense, is what it is.'

Pockets of light rose up and fell, bright and briefly warm.

'You've had it easy, you two. Your mother may never have had to work a day in her life with that handy widow's pension and all her dead husband's money at her fingertips, but not all of us have such luck. I had to fight my way to where I am today.'

He stepped back from the grate.

'There now. All done.' He set the box of matches back on the mantelpiece. 'What would you have done without me?'

Sandra watched the fire spread, her irises red with it.

'I'm going to get an early night. There's plenty to be done in the morning.'

He gave Rosie a swift smile, his teeth glittering. Sandra turned to follow him, snatching the matches as she went.

Sixteen (a)

His hands closed around her throat, icy cold, the hands of the dead. She struggled beneath his weight, heavy and hard. She tried to breathe. Her legs were pulling away from her body, pulling away and opening and she could not stop it. The hands closed around her throat. Feathers brushed the skin of her face. She could not breathe. His fingernails bit into the skin of her neck, like teeth.

Seventeen

There was one thing Sandra was glad for in life and that was the kettle. The morning in that bare old house would not beat her, even as her slippered feet gathered inches of dust from the floor and cobwebs leered at her from every corner. She could have her cup of tea. Then they would set to work. She had not slept. The weight of him beside her in the bed, his heaving back, his hot breath: these were things that could not be escaped. They had spent the night together before, but only in snatched moments; those rare and novel morsels of freedom had tasted sweet. She would have to get used to sleeping beside a man again. She had grown accustomed to sleeping beside her daughter, whose small form moulded instinctively to her own, moving with hers. But he claimed the bed, and she had to cling to whatever space was left to her. The night before they had not made love. She had been ready for it, anticipating the cool touch of his red-tipped fingers on her waist. But within minutes of his silent undressing, his roaring breath had commanded the room. She lay awake dwelling on the fight, the choice she had made not to speak. He turned over heavily.

She knew then that he would spring his lust on her when she least expected it. She would have to prepare for it, him marking his territory in every corner of the enormous home. Hers now. Theirs. She consoled herself that it would wear out with time. Each night would soon be routine, her naked self indistinguishable from the sock drawer, another piece of the furniture. She did not mourn the inevitable, but longed for it.

As the kettle built steam she took a cup from an open cardboard box and unwrapped it and carried it to the sink to rinse. But she saw a sight that made the thing slip from her hands, and as it splintered around her ankles she was powerless to stop it. Rosie stood on the other side of the window in the garden, holding a small black kitten. The morning mist curled about her, now hiding her from view, now revealing her. She was motionless, knee-deep in the grass. Her night-gown was soaked, the white cotton thin and sheer across her body, which, Sandra realised, had started to burst open in odd places. Her skin was the white of bone, the bow of her lips a gash across her face.

Seventeen (a)

'Bring her back,' the voice said.

This one was new. Another person come to strip her down, to poke around inside her. Did that even matter now?

'But we're so close now.'

This one was known. Inseparable from her own now, almost.

'The deeper you go, the more dangerous it is. You know that better than anyone.'

Silence then. Empty space broken by whispers that moved like the feet of little mice.

'Continue,' it said.

Eighteen

The embers had burned down and extinguished, the room was bitterly cold. The fireplaces were exquisite, stealing attention in each room like a fine woman, but when Rosie awoke shivering, her icy breath the only thing she could see before her, their beauty seemed cruel and unnecessary and all she wanted was a radiator. She didn't like the fire burning beneath her as she slept. She knew it could not be trusted.

Beneath the duvet, the sheet was wet. There was a bathroom just down the hall, all she had to do was pull back the duvet, get out of bed, and open the door. It was only a few steps from there. But it was pitch black in the room, the air chilled her bones and no one had fixed the hallway light bulbs.

Her feet shrunk from the wooden floor. The doorknob was like a frozen thing, she thought her skin would stick to it. She twisted it, pulled the door towards her. Colder air crept in along the narrow gap.

'Hello?' she called.

Her voice was big, stupid. She put her hand to her throat, it felt tender, bruised, like it didn't want to work. The hallway returned a deep silence. She knew she should not leave the room. Something was waiting out there, she could almost hear its breath. She shut the door again, hid under the covers in the damp. But her stomach swelled with pain. She would not be able to hold it until morning.

She unlocked the window and looked down, making sure the distance from ledge to earth hadn't yawned apart noiselessly in the night. The fall to the ground was where she had left it yesterday afternoon. She climbed through the frame and dropped.

Wet fog clung to her nightgown. She softened into it. She could have been on the moon, inside the fibres of a cloud. She would not be seen from the windows. She found a bush in the front garden and crouched behind it.

It was pleasantly cool in the mist, warmer than the bitter cold of indoors. The tiredness had lifted from her. She didn't need to go back to bed.

Her feet cut a brave path through the mist. They tasted gravel, stone, earth, grass; they were her eyes. Objects offered themselves to her randomly, a brick, a stone, the limb of a tree. A hedgerow. She allowed these things to guide her.

And then her hands and feet found their way to growth that was springy, hollow. She felt into it. Beyond drooping curtains of ivy spaces between the leaves revealed an opening, a hidden lane. The length of it waned into the distance, a well. She pushed through.

It closed in around her. She lost sense of who she was. Was she her mother or her father, a stranger, or herself? She was walking – no – she was gliding, floating, flying. She stretched her arms out into empty space. The ground was damp and stinking. She walked for minutes, hours, years; she had to follow until the end. There was something up ahead, she knew it. Something she had been looking for. Something she needed to find. She moved closer to it, it moved out of her reach. The tunnel, the lane, the dark pathway, went on. And then she was in a thicket, she fought her way through, hacking and pulling through branch and twig and blade. And then she was falling.

She was in a crowded clearing, surrounded by high trees. The light was just beginning to come through, a warm reddish sort of light. It lit up the ground where boulders stood between grass and weeds and the tall trees. But they were not boulders. Tombstones sunk into the earth. It was a graveyard, consumed by grass and dandelions, eroded by weather and apathy. Where was this thing she had been searching for?

Then the leaves whispered, the branches creaked. Something was up above, watching.

'Hello?'

She could feel eyes upon her. She knew she was not alone anymore: 'Who's there?'

Then a voice came back to her.

'You found me. After all this time.'

It came from nowhere, everywhere at once.

'I'm up here.'

Up in the branches of a tree, barely seen. A flint of blue, a black feather.

'Who are you?' she asked.

'You don't remember me?'

'No.'

'You will.'

Rosie was certain she knew the voice, but she could not name it.

'Who are you?'

Quiet laughter echoed around the clearing, rich and smooth and warm. It was not her mother's or Marie's or her own. Its sound thrilled her. It was a voice she knew, but knew not at all.

'Show me who you are.'

'Oh, it's too soon. Far too soon for that. But you'll figure it out on your own in time.'

She did not want to press him, she knew that would be unwise. She feared she would anger him. She did not want to think what might happen if she did.

'What is this place?' she asked.

'A home for the dead among us.'

'What do you mean?'

'Take a walk and see.'

She walked among the stones, careful not to wake those who slept beneath. The markers were half-sunken ships, barely staying afloat. The dead pushed from below, desperate at a second chance at life, the ground rose and fell, the stones tilted and cracked. She read the inscriptions:

Beloved Father

and

Beloved Daughter

and

Father and Child, together

THE END

It began to rain, but she wasn't wet. No - she was wet, but the rain did not touch her. It wasn't rain at all. It was paper. Pages. Pages that belonged in books, scribbled upon, defiled. They fell around her, littering the ground like a thick carpet of snow. Exhaustion swept over her.

'I think I should lie down,' said Rosie.

'Yes I think you should,' said the voice.

'But how do I get back?'

'Try over there,' it said.

'But how do I ...'

But she knew that he had gone. A black feather fell from the tree. Rosie walked towards it, picked it up. Above her the canopy of leaves danced openly, hiding nothing.

She was walled in, surrounded. She would have to lift herself out. She reached up. The high wall grew, ranging into the sky. She was cold and her feet were stiff. Her nails dug into the pockets of moss that grew between the bricks. She hoisted herself up. Sweat dripped into her mouth.

She reached the top. The new house rose up before her grey and proud and she felt a strange sense of relief. She would drop into the garden and slip in unnoticed through the back door. As she fell, a heaviness came into her body and a lightness into her head and she was being stretched apart. She hardly felt the impact when she hit the ground. The grass came up past her knees, her feet sunk into the waterlogged earth. Strange noises came to her. Thin, weak cries. The touch of things against her skin, soft and feathery, was pleasing. She looked about herself and saw nothing, though the sensations continued. She needed to get back to bed. And yet - there was the kitchen, there the door. She was shivering, but though she willed herself to move forward she found she could not.

Nineteen

The cup shattered around Sandra's ankles. She prayed to God it would not wake him. She had to get Rosie in before she was caught by pneumonia, or a worse fate. Her tea was forgotten.

Halfway out the back door her daughter turned to face her. But she didn't look at her. Her eyes were open, blank and staring. An old feeling of unease swept over Sandra. The kitten was in Rosie's arms, mewling to be let down. Sandra tried to prise it from her, but she would not let go. The mother cat watched from a safe distance, ready to spring.

'Where did these come from?'

Rosie mutely lifted one arm. Sandra followed it. It led to the wall that encircled the garden behind her. An old grey stone, thick and mossy, standing many feet high. Rosie jabbed her arm toward it, making low moans. Her skin was littered with gooseflesh, dirt stuffed under her fingernails.

'What's happened to you?'

When she took her arm, she had touched a dead thing. She steered her into the kitchen.

'Where have you been? Why aren't you in bed?'

'I was in bed,' Rosie said at last.

Her voice came out small, as if it were travelling a long way to reach her.

'You must have been out for hours.'

Rosie did not answer. Sandra shook her:

'Come back to me!'

Sandra slapped her; Rosie went limp. Sandra pushed her into a chair. Rosie's hands fell into her lap, closing the struggling kitten in. One hand was balled into a white fist, guarding something within it. Sandra tried to ease it open and Rosie's head drooped to the side, exposing her neck. It was bruised, with little red flecks along her tonsils, deep blue marks around her neck like soot.

Then, an interruption.

152

'Morning.'

He strode into the kitchen. There was a brief silence.

Sandra moved toward the kettle, her heart pounding.

He cleared his throat:

'Sandra.'

She turned to him. Behind him, Rosie sat on the chair beside the door, staring out. He hadn't yet seen her.

'I shouldn't have shouted. I'm sorry.'

She placed a smile across her mouth. 'I know,' she said. 'Will I bring some tea up to you?'

'No, you're alright, I'll make my own.'

She bent over the cups, breathing slowly. *Leave. Please.*

'It's not a bad day out,' he said.

She opened her mouth to speak when a strange cry escaped him:

'A cat!'

Sandra looked around. The mother cat had slipped in, crouched at Rosie's feet, transfixed.

He took a step back, he was afraid. His eyes set on Rosie: 'It was you, wasn't it?'

Sandra caught him in his stare, a starved and desperate look, the sort of look that sniffed around corners and hid in shuttered rooms. She moved between them, her tone as light as a spring breeze.

'Do you know I think they must have already been living in the garden when we got here, I kept thinking I heard odd noises yesterday when we were working. Rosie must have opened the door when she got up this morning and they sneaked in.'

She handed him a cup, freshly washed and filled.

He sniffed, narrowed his eyes, but took the offered tea.

'Never been into cats,' he said. 'Nasty things.'

'They're no harm,' Sandra said. 'They're just hungry.'

She moved around the sink pretending busy, urging him to leave. She had to get Rosie back into bed without raising suspicion.

'I don't like it,' he said, and his voice started to rise then. 'I can hardly understand how you're so blasé about the whole thing.'

'I just don't mind them.'

'Well I want them out.'

'You're the boss,' she replied, and she smiled again.

'Right,' he said, and the hungry look fell away at last. 'We can get started on the living room after breakfast.'

Sandra nodded.

He was watching Rosie again, but from the side of himself, as though to look directly would cause great pain.

'Awfully quiet this morning, the two of you.'

'I think,' Sandra said, 'Rosie may be unwell.'

'The dust getting to you is it?' he said to her. 'Or is it the ash?' Then:

'Sandra you'll catch your death if you stand there in that.'

'I'm alright,' she said, arranging the slip she wore. She had not yet unpacked her dressing gown.

He tapped impatiently on the sideboard. He looked out across the overgrown garden, looked back towards them.

'You won't get away with that sort of carry on here Rosie,' he said. 'I know your mother lets you away with murder, but I won't have anything like that again in my house. No strays or insects or whatever it is you do be messing about with.'

'She didn't know it would upset you.'

'Well she knows now.'

He raised his voice and hardened it and addressed the top of Rosie's head.

'I'm going easy on you today as your mother says you're unwell, but I won't be so nice the next time. Do you hear me?'

'I think she might have a temperature. I should put her back to bed.'

'Do you hear me?'

Languidly Rosie rotated her head towards him, her eyes flat and shadowed. Her hands fell open and the kitten was revealed. He stepped back. Sandra took a deep breath.

'Miaow,' Rosie said.

'Miaow, Miaow, Miaow.'

The cats outside took it up and a chorus of yowling filled the morning kitchen.

He cleared his throat, moved back towards the door: 'Will you get a hold of her Sandra for crying out loud.'

Sandra shook Rosie again and she fell silent.

'She's not well,' she said, swallowing over the hard nut in her throat.

'I can see that.'

He hitched his trousers up and paced the kitchen, avoiding Rosie's unblinking stare. At the sink, his shod feet crunched when they hit upon the broken cup. He looked down, but made no comment.

'Aren't you putting her to bed?'

'We were just going as you came in.'

'Well go, then.'

Sandra hoisted Rosie to her feet. She had warmed up but shook still, her arms long and purposeless at her sides, the one fist still tightly rolled. Sandra involuntarily touched her fingers to her forehead, stomach and shoulders.

'We're getting a dog,' he said behind them and the kettle whistled for the third time.

Twenty

Rosie was in bed for a week with the flu. By the time it abated, and she was well enough to leave her room, the house was clean and painted and all the furniture had been arranged as though it had stood there always.

Rosie entered the kitchen, the room smelt untrodden and untouched. The fresh paint on the walls making a stab at brightening things. The table and chairs were arranged neatly in the centre. It was altogether new.

'There she is at last,' Sandra said, her face splitting down the centre with relief.

'Back in the land of the living,' Mr. - said.

Rosie took a seat and a steaming bowl of porridge was placed before her. She and the house had got off to a bad start, but this breakfast would be a peacemaker. She asked for some toast. Mr. - watched her as she ate.

'You're looking well,' he said.

'The life's back in her,' Sandra called from the toaster.

'That must be it.'

'How are you feeling Button?'

'Fine.'

The porridge was too hot, but Rosie swallowed it down. She devoured the buttered toast.

'Is there any more?' she asked.

Sandra cut three more thick slices off the open loaf.

'That appetite of yours is back anyway,' he said, his mouth turning down.

'A healthy appetite,' said Sandra.

'Is that what it is.'

'I'm hungry,' Rosie said through a thick mouth.

'I can see.'

He turned to the window and stroked his moustache. When he looked back, he was smiling again.

'I've a surprise for you later,' he said.

'What is it?'

He tapped his nose.

'Just you wait and see.'

'But what is it?'

Rosie looked to her mother, who caught eyes with her and winked.

'If I told you it wouldn't be a surprise, would it?' he said.

'But –'

'Right,' he said, downing his tea and standing, and arranging his pants. 'I'm off to work.'

He kissed Sandra briefly and was gone. The front door shut. The two women were alone at last. The sudden ease in the room was palpable, its silence crisp and warm. Sandra wiped her hands on a tea towel and came and sat beside her daughter. She was bright and full of lightness.

'What do you want to do today?' she said.

When he returned later that evening they were where he had left them, and it was some moments before they realised that something else had arrived too. When Rosie saw it, she edged away, afraid that if it got too close it would snap at her heels. On tiny splayed legs it sniffed around the new territory. Rosie backed against the radiator.

'It's only a little thing,' he said, laughing. 'You are a scaredy cat.'

'What type is he?' Sandra asked.

'Breed,' he said. 'A German Shepherd. My grandfather kept them when I was young. Used to hunt with them in the woods near the farm. I've always wanted one of my own.'

'A hunting dog?'

'That's right.'

'But what if he hunts the cats?' Rosie asked.

'What of it? They're only cats.'

'But they were here first.'

'Sandra would you ever explain the laws of property and ownership to your child because I think she's missing the essentials.'

With a sudden and unexplained mirth, the dog skidded into the next room. It stopped at the door that led into the garden and scratched at the wood.

'He can already smell them. That's my boy.'

Then it crouched low. A long yellow ribbon pooled beneath it -

'The carpet for fuck's sake,' cried Sandra, 'when there's lino in here!'

'And they told me it was a fella - I'm drowning in women.'

It was then, when she had finished, that she padded back across the kitchen and curled into a gentle yielding ball at Rosie's feet. A wet nose examined her toes and the shallow webbing between, greeting them with one meek lick. And that was it. Love.

Luckily for the cats the dog was a soft-natured thing. Rosie took it upon herself to act as its primary carer and friend and started by giving her a name. Dog. The local school didn't have room for her until the Autumn term and she had months to keep herself occupied, and with Dog came purpose. She rose early at the sound of an alarm clock to feed Dog and let her out whenever she went into a low squat by the door. The hours ticked by unnoticed on dry days when she ran in circles in the garden hunting magpies and Dog chased her and them both. In the evenings as the sun set, Rosie sat on the back step with the animal clamped still between her thighs and brushed through her hair, freeing it of the clots and tangles accumulated from a day spent rolling under the willow tree with the cats and vaulting through overgrown grass. And once a day at least, she brought her for a walk.

Together they explored their new home, a twisting maze of interlocking streets and paths. It was a place of shadows and secrets, where the hidden could stay undisturbed, where things could get lost and forgotten, and always remain. It could surprise without a moment's warning. A road could narrow into a secret path and an alley open to reveal a wide green field or a forest. Losing oneself was natural here. Each house in the area sprung up like an independent ecosystem, an organic life form born of the earth. Rosie's house was the grandest of them all, and the land's central point. But the grassy roads were almost always deserted. It was only rarely that Rosie caught a glimpse of the existence of others, rarer still of other children. She knew then that her and Dog were the sole survivors of some terrible tragedy - until they returned home for dinner.

When life was found, she became a hunter. Together Rosie and Dog reverted back to a time when the land free of tarmac and unpopulated by cars and houses was overgrown with moss and flush with rivers, when the encroaching forest, kept in check by hacksaw and chain, still ruled. Dog's snout lengthened, her teeth grew sharp, her fur deep and lustrous. Rosie's limbs grew long and muscular. She could outstrip deer and keep pace with her companion, her wild hair streaming behind her like a battle flag. They ran the passageways that cut behind houses' backs, stalking their prey.

One person came into their sights more regularly than any other, a dark-haired boy with a peculiar bobbing gait. Rosie knew him only as a back, as long legs and bouncing hair and the odd compartmentalised pieces of face, fragmentary glimpses through the leaves of a concealing bush or tree. When he stopped, Rosie and Dog stopped. If he took a shortcut, Rosie stealthily followed behind and earmarked the path for future use. He had never caught them.

'Keep close Dog,' Rosie whispered, and she obeyed. They were skilled hunters and no boy could ever outwit them.

Twenty-one

They were camped out behind a fuchsia on the look-out. Dog stood to attention. Rosie used her hands as binoculars and scanned the area.

'Nothing to report.'

Dog barked once in response.

'Wait –'

There was movement across the road in the pale green bush. Then he stepped out shoes first and the long length of him after. She tried to commit his face to memory, but he turned his back to them and crouched behind the bush and stared back up the road.

'What's he up to Dog?'

Dog growled. The boy went stiff.

'Shhh!'

But it was too late, their cover had been blown. The boy bolted.

'After him!'

The stranger's pace was determined. Rosie's breath grew heavy as she tried to keep up, she had eaten too much at lunch and a stitch spread across her side. She stopped to catch herself; in that moment, their quarry slipped out of sight. Dog whined and set off again dragging Rosie behind her, following the scent. But he had turned into air. Walls rose up on either side of the street, walls and thickets seemingly impenetrable, and he was gone.

'Bollocks! We've lost him. This is all your fault.'

Rosie folded her arms and fell into a sulk on the curb. She threw pebbles at her toes, resigned to boredom for the rest of the day. Then Dog's bright bark shook her out of her gloom.

'What is it?'

She circled three times, her tongue shivering and pink and dripping from her jaws. She barked again.

'Ok, ok. I'm coming. This better be worth it.'

Rosie followed. They ran along a passageway and down another road and up a lane that connected to: yet another road. Then Dog paused, circled along a stretch of hedgerow, and sat promptly. Rosie looked up and down the road. It was deserted. Something about the stretch of hedgerow, the empty road, the grey covering of cloud, spoke to her of things but half-known, but Dog was up again and scratching at the leaves. Then she vaulted through the hedge. Rosie blinked. She heard something move up ahead. She followed.

'We've got him now,' she whispered.

On tip toe, she advanced, Dog's breath now warming her calves. A shadow grunted, writhing as though in pain, injured in escape. Easy prey now. Hers to claim. But as she got closer to him, she saw it was not a him, but a her, and not just a her, but another him, and it wasn't *him*. They were older too, almost grown. A boy-man and a girl-woman. The boy-man held the girl-woman against the wall, he had her pinned there, but she did not resist. They were very close together - too close - Rosie's skin went taut and hard to see how close they were, their tongues touching and trailing each other's faces, their hands moving up and down their bodies like rats. The sharp curve of their shoulders was exposed to her, their jackets hung off the crooks of their elbows, shielding the grind of their pulsating hips. She knew she shouldn't look but she couldn't stop.

'Fuck off you little perv!' The boy-man gasped, making Rosie jump. She hadn't realised how loud she had been breathing. The strange rhythmic dance they were both a part of did not pause. It was hard to tell who and what belonged to whom. They moved and breathed as one, fused somehow, closeted behind the soft drapes of the boy-man's falling jacket. The girl-woman giggled.

'Horny little bitch,' she breathed. 'Go home – go on!'

Dog dragged her away. Rosie tried to keep her eyes on her shoes. She couldn't resist a quick glance back.

A world had opened. The secret lane Dog had discovered became an obsession. Thoughts of moving shadows framed her every thought. She ventured back alone disguised in the dark and she watched each time, sharing each intake of breath, each undulation, wondering what it would be like to be inside one.

She crept upstairs at night to listen at the bedroom door her mother shared with him. Most of the time she heard nothing, deep breathing only, or an occasional grunt. But there were those times when the grunting was different, when it was quick and rasping, when the little moans crept under the door frame and out into the hall to where she stood. Sometimes she heard words. A soft *no*, a gentle *stop*, a pleading *come on* and then, *yes*. Over and again, the word *yes*. She did not understand the words, they had new meanings she could not grasp. She held her breath and tried not to imagine it but images of hands and tongues intruded, reproducing wet limbs and mouths, and her face grew red. She ran down the stairs, eyes shielded from the watching portrait, and breathed again once she was safely locked inside her own bedroom. She tried pacing to work off the heat in her cheeks. But the heat spread down her neck and over her chest and all the way to her belly and beyond. Against her will thoughts of the young stranger who still eluded her capture obsessed her. He pressed her shoulders against damp rock up the lovers' lane, there was no-one there but she and him, her lips were hard and red and her hands trembled as the heat built and set her ablaze and the new mirror over the mantlepiece reflected a strange auroral spectre back into the fire-lit bedroom from its watery surface.

Twenty-one (a)

'I wish I'd never gone up there.'
    'Why?'
    'I couldn't look at him after. And he saw it.'
    He noticed everything with those eagle eyes of his.

Twenty-two

Dinner was over, and Rosie had been sent to bed earlier than usual with no dessert. Her fire had not yet been lit. She was being starved and frozen to death. The cold air seeped in through the sash windows, but she couldn't bring herself to go back out and ask for help, not after how the clock had eaten up the silence between the three of them like the cracking of a whip. She would do it herself, but she wasn't allowed and she didn't know how.

The other reason she could not move was looking down at her. Up on the ceiling directly over her was a spider. She shivered, paralysed; if she moved the spider would leap into her hair and crawl all over her bare skin. In theory, Rosie liked spiders. Number one reason: they were insects. Number two reason: they pulled silver thread from their stomachs and knitted it into glittering webs. In the rain each thread trembled, the raindrops clung to them in pearly globes and when the drops fell, and this was the number three reason, Rosie heard beautiful music playing. The spider was quietly spinning herself a bed to settle into for the night, but Rosie was uneasy. Though she liked the spider's talent for three reasons, she also knew the capabilities of those many legs that could probe into nostrils and throats like ghostly water reeds. She screamed.

The bedroom door opened. Mr. - entered.

'What's happened?' he said.

Rosie pointed to the small black speck on the ceiling.

'Oh-ho-ho,' he said, the yellow moustache quivering. 'Sure it's only a little thing.'

'I can't sleep,' said Rosie.

He looked back into the hall and shut the door behind him. He came and sat beside Rosie on the bed. Rosie drew her knees into her chest under the duvet.

'You're probably right not to you know,' he said, in a whisper.

Rosie's eyes grew wider.

'Didn't I ever tell you,' he said, tracing circles on the sheet near Rosie's feet, 'about the little girl who went to sleep with a spider?'

'No.'

'Shall I tell you the story?' He stroked his moustache lightly as he looked into her eyes. His fingers strayed towards her feet as they followed the pattern on the duvet cover. Rosie curled back her toes.

'Ok,' she said.

'You have to promise me that you won't be scared,' he said. His voice was so quiet she could barely hear him speak.

'I promise.'

'And that you won't tell your mother.'

Quieter still.

'I promise.'

'Ok,' he said.

He arranged his legs on top of one another. He turned to face her and folded his hands into the dark concave crevice in his lap. Rosie's eyes were drawn to that place, to the spot beneath the interlacing weave of his fingers, the darkness there. She looked up and he was smiling at her, thin and long. It sliced across his face.

'Are you ready?' he asked. His tongue darted out and wet his stretched lips.

Rosie nodded. And he began.

'This is the story of a young girl I knew once. She was a lovely little girl, young and sweet, though she could be strange with you and had an awful temper sometimes. But other than that, she was good. She had lovely skin like fresh cream. Her eyes were bright like the stars in the sky. She loved animals and insects and things that grew, and played outside all day, even when it rained. One evening after she had eaten her dinner and helped her Mammy and Daddy clean the dishes and sweep the floors, she went to her bedroom to get ready for bed. But a spider was waiting for her.'

165

Rosie's chesty breathing; his sibilant words.

'The girl loved insects and thought the spider no harm, he was just sitting on the wall in her room, no different to the way this spider is sitting on the wall in yours.'

He gestured easily to where the spider clung. Rosie's eyes were like beads in her head, watching her. Mr. - continued.

'This girl played with insects all day and had no fear of them. She thought nothing of the little eight-legged fella sitting up there on her ceiling above her bed. She took off her clothes,' he said, 'and got into her nightgown. It was her favourite one. It was white and it had lace all along here.'

He pointed to Rosie's chest. His fingers were inches from touching her.

'She got into bed and fell asleep. But later when she was snoring softly and moaning, with her mouth thrown wide open, the spider opened his eyes. He had lots and lots of them you see - did you know that spiders have hundreds of eyes?'

The question threw her into the spotlight, she had expected only to be a passenger in this story. She nodded, but could not speak. He smiled.

'Do you like my story?' he asked in a voice closer to breath than sound.

'Yes,' said Rosie.

'Are you sure you want me to go on now? Are you sure you're not too scared?'

'I'm not scared,' said Rosie, impatience building. It was essential that she discover how the story would end.

'Where was I,' he said. 'Oh yes. The eyes. So. The spider looked down at the little girl with his hundred million glittering eyes as she lay there snoring, sleeping away peacefully. He looked down at her and he saw - what do you think he saw?'

'I don't know,' said Rosie.

'Go on, guess.'

'I don't know!'

'Fine, I'll tell you. He looked down into her wide open mouth and he saw ... a cave. A place he could call home. He climbed down his string and dropped down beside the sleeping girl on the bed –'

His hand assumed the crouching shape of a spider beside Rosie's hidden thigh.

'- then his eight legs tiptoed across the pillow, leaving the pattern of his eight feet behind him on the linen. He climbed up her hair –'

He walked his fingers along the twisting red strands that lay across Rosie's collarbone.

'- and up her earlobe –'

His fingers tip-toed across her ear.

'- and over her cheek and up onto the tip of her little nose –'

He poked her, once, on the nose.

'- then he crouched his legs down low and took a big leap down the dark hole of her throat.'

And he placed a finger inside her mouth.

'The little girl was so deeply asleep that she never felt a thing.'

As he removed his finger from between Rosie's teeth, the tip of it stroked her inert tongue.

'What happened then?' asked Rosie.

Mr. - wiped his finger on his thigh before continuing. It left a faint stain on his pale cream trousers. He cleared his throat.

'The next day she got up as normal and went about her day, not knowing what lay inside her, waiting. Days and weeks went past. Everything was just as it always had been. Then, one day, the little girl was sitting at the table with her family having lunch, when she gave a little cough. It was just a little cough so nobody noticed, not even herself. But then she gave another cough. A bigger one. Her family looked at her then. Their daughter wasn't one for coughing. She was usually such a strong healthy child. She gave another cough that was even

167

bigger again and this time a tiny little black thing flew out of her mouth and landed in the salad. She gave another cough and then another and another, and with each one little spiders came flying out of her mouth, from her nostrils, from her ear holes - they even came out from the corners of her eyes - until the whole table was crawling with the things. Her family ran out screaming as the little girl I once knew choked to death alone on the kitchen floor.'

'She died?' asked Rosie.

'She died.'

The spider twitched. Throughout the story Rosie's eyes had rarely left her.

'Please don't crawl inside me while I sleep,' she said.

'Oh you can't be too careful,' Mr. – said, speaking to the wall. 'You can't trust a spider to keep its word when they never talk back.'

Rosie's shoulders contracted up to her ears and she pulled herself into a tighter knot under her duvet. Mr. - leaned in close to her and spoke into her ear.

'There is something I could do,' he said, 'that would help you sleep easier.'

Rosie looked at him: the veined yellow eyes, the wide long nose, pockmarked and littered with broken veins like many tiny rivers. Flecks of potato hid in between the bristles of his moustache.

'What?' she asked.

Twenty-two (a)

A creaking tread approached the bedroom door. The shallow breaths were coming closer and with them, something worse. She pushed her little talisman down inside her jeans, opened her window, and jumped.

Twenty-three

As her breath took on the form of a spirit before her, she wished for Dog. She had forgotten to bring her, as well as her coat. She balled her hands up in her jumper and bent low to begin a conversation with a worm.

'Hello worm,' she said. 'How are you?'

'Oh I'm alright,' the worm said.

'You look awful cold down there with no clothes on,' she said. 'You're even worse off than I am.'

The worm hadn't a chance to respond before a rustle in the bushes hauled Rosie's attention away. She stood up erect and still and assumed the attitude of a stone.

'Hello?'

Her voice was absorbed into the watching forest. She dared not speak again. There was such a silence and a stillness, and she knew not to break it. Someone somewhere was watching her. It was after the forest had settled that the sound started up again, a hand probing for the last sweet in a crinkled paper bag. Rosie whipped around to face it as it approached her and she could do nothing as the interlacing branches of a nearby shrub parted to allow the dark head of someone rise up. And then he was before her. A living breathing thing. There was a familiarity in the way he held his shoulders and in the length and stain of his hair and she knew then, though perhaps she had known when the first leaf trembled in the wood, that it was him: the boy. His face was unified at last, unobscured by brick or bush. He was a real thing. His hair was long and it fell past his chin. He was a creature of the wood.

He smiled and as he did a deep vertical groove appeared in his right cheek, with a smaller one shadowing it on the left. The right dimple looked so deep that Rosie wished to bury her nose right in it. The thought of being so close as to do that put her in mind of other close thoughts and she looked down at her feet, hoping he could not read them on her face.

'Hello,' the boy said.

'Hello,' said Rosie.

He seemed tall, from what she could see, he was almost swallowed up by green. He had small plump lips and a long nose that rounded slightly at the end like a flower bulb. His eyes were wide and round and so blue that the sun shining in a clear sky could not match their brilliance. She had seen eyes like them before.

'My name's Peter,' he said.

'Peter,' Rosie repeated.

'What's your name?' Peter asked.

'Rosie,' said Rosie.

'Hi Rosie.'

'Hi.'

The words came out of their own accord as though they had been biding their time all along, waiting for their chance. The involuntary workings of her mouth surprised her, but as the boy continued to speak she forgot that she was meant to be mute and found she had things to say. Rosie almost stretched out to touch him, to make absolutely sure he was not a dream. As she watched him she saw a new thought form behind his eyes. She saw it grow, a balloon blowing up. He looked into the grey distance, through the trunks of trees, questioning whether or not to express it.

'I saw you talking to that worm,' he said, and the next words came out in a rush: 'you do know that worms can't talk and also that they can't even hear.'

This was news to Rosie. She'd been having two-way conversations with worms for as long as she could remember. She wanted to take back some of those close thoughts and replace them with ones that were far less soft. Who did this boy think he was?

'Maybe they don't talk to just anyone.'

She jutted out her chin. Peter chewed his lip.

'What's that you're holding?' he asked.

171

The question shocked her, but then she felt the stubborn weight hidden inside her pocket and relaxed. In her hand was something else entirely. Rosie admired the boy then, he hadn't given up on her already. Perhaps he would redeem himself.

'A nettle-beater.' She held it up for him to see.

'That's a stick,' he corrected, and he looked skyward. 'A branch from this oak tree.'

Close thoughts with the boy were moving further and further away. Redemption also seemed unlikely. Perhaps Rosie was doomed to solitude for eternity.

'It's actually a nettle-beater.'

Peter divided his gaze between Rosie, the tree, an undefined spot in the distance and Rosie again so quickly he might have brought on whiplash. Then he shook his wild hair out of his face like a wet dog and opened his mouth to speak. Rosie had had enough of that.

'Do you want to fight?' she asked.

'A fight?' he said, as though unaware such a thing could exist.

'En guarde!' cried Rosie, not waiting for an answer.

She had seen a man with a sword say this once on the television and had always looked for opportunities to use it. Now that she had spoken to the boy, and even learned his name, this seemed to her a natural progression of events. Her face was twisted with rage as it bounded towards him lit by flames masquerading as hair, the red mouth stretched open, the teeth of a wildcat framing her ululating tongue. Her eyes would burn a man alive. Peter had to come to his own defence or surely perish. He seized the first available weapon he could find, a sodden branch half the size of Rosie's and held it in front of himself just in time. The blows hammered down against him and had she not been such a little thing he would have been destroyed. But he held his ground and when she finally flopped on the earth he went and sat beside her at a safe distance.

'Have you made other friends here?' he asked.

'No,' Rosie said between breaths.

'Because I know you just moved in.'

'How?'

Peter sat serenely as though nothing out of the ordinary had taken place, his breath calm and unlaboured.

'I've watched you.'

Rosie looked at him sideways. So this boy, Peter, could stalk. He could also take her in a fight. Her respect for him was growing. Peter shredded the grass under his knees.

'I don't know that many people around here either,' he said. 'I've lived here always.'

'How long is that?'

'Nine years.'

'I'm nine years and five months old.'

'Well I'm ten in August, so I'm actually older.'

Rosie sniffed.

'Do other people live here then?'

'Of course.'

'But there's never anyone around.'

'Everyone is in school.'

'Why aren't you?'

'It's Saturday.'

'Oh,' said Rosie. 'But if you're not in school because it's a Saturday and other people aren't in school then why is there nobody here?'

'We're here.'

'Apart from us.'

'Well it's cold today, even though it's May and really shouldn't be. But then again in our temperate oceanic climate, the weather can be unpredictable.'

Rosie looked at him and wondered if her face was reflecting the squeezing feeling in her brain. Was this boy a book, or a person? He continued on -

'In the holidays though there are loads of other kids our age. They mainly are in my class.'

'So there are others,' she said to herself.

'Are you in school?' asked Peter.

'Not until September.' She plucked at her trousers. 'I'm not very good at school,' she said, still remotely amazed at her ability to form words out of doors and even volunteer information. 'Well, I don't like it.'

'I'm really good at school,' said Peter. 'Especially science. I can tell you all about these trees and I can tell you why I know worms can't talk. Do you know what tree this is?' he asked, pointing above their heads.

'An oak.'

This was a game she could win.

'Ok, that was an easy one, especially seeing as I just told you what it was before. What about this one?'

'Beech.'

'I thought you said you weren't good at school,' he said, suddenly suspicious.

'My dad taught me the names.'

'Oh yeah I've seen him, the tall man. Is he nice?'

'No - that's not ... that's Mr. -.'

'Mr. - ?'

'Yeah.'

Peter threw his gaze off into the distance again, his face heavy with thought.

'Where is your dad?' he asked.

His face was so open, Rosie could have moulded it into any shape she desired.

'He's across the sea and he can't come back.'

But had he not wings ...? Or was that someone else? Her hand strayed to her pocket then dropped back onto the grass. She couldn't let her thoughts wander there today.

'Why not?' asked Peter.

'The waves won't let him.'

'Is he in Gibraltar?' Peter asked.

'What's Gibraltar?'

'Do you want to come and see my room?' Peter asked. 'I'm doing an experiment.'

174

'An experiment?'

'And I can show you on my Atlas. It's ok if you don't want to.'

'What's an experiment?'

Peter smiled. 'I'll show you if you like.'

Twenty-four

Rosie was only the second female to grace Peter's bedroom after his mother, Sharon. Sharon was always bringing them tea and juice and biscuits with marshmallow on the top. Rosie was very fond of her. Whenever they were deep in an examination of a leaf under the microscope or mixing things they'd stolen from the kitchen cupboards in Peter's chemistry set, a part of Rosie's mind stayed at the door awaiting her gentle knock. Then her magnificent breasts and the laden tray beneath them would announce her around it.

'Hi, you two.' She moved aside papers and notebooks and jars filled with slimy things on Peter's desk, and set down the tray. 'Just a little snack in case you were wanting.'

'Mum!'

Peter scratched at his ear, his psoriasis behind his left temple flared up in times of stress.

'I was at a crucial moment in my examination!'

'Even Einstein had to stop for tea and biccies.'

She liked to watch them while they ate, ask them questions.

'How's my little Ginger today?' she asked.

'It's Ro-sie, Mum. How many times!' Tiny flakes of dead skin went airborne.

'I don't mind,' Rosie said. Sharon could have said anything to her at all, she spoke to her as though she were cradling petals under her tongue. She covered the top of her teacup as Peter's scalp came flying towards her and tried to look anywhere but at his mother's chest.

'Stop at yourself.'

Sharon beat his hand away from his head. Peter's scowl deepened.

'You're looking a bit flush there, Ginger. How's the forehead?' She placed a palm to Rosie's skin.

'Hmm,' she said. 'A little warm, but nothing to be alarmed about.'

Peter folded his arms and pushed his teacup away.

'Alright,' Sharon gave a soft laugh, 'I'll leave you to it.'

She picked up the tray and used her left hip to shimmy around the door. Rosie stared after her.

'Finally,' Peter sighed. 'Come here, Rosie, I want you to look at this. It's really cool.'

He took her hand and led her to his bed. He sat down upon it and tapped the space beside him. The bed was soft and squeaked slightly when she let her weight fall on it. Peter made an involuntary giggle and hid his teeth behind his hand. When he let his hand fall away he was chewing his lips. Rosie watched his pulsing mouth, wondering if he had yet managed to draw blood. Then she looked at his eyes. The right one began to twitch.

And then he was coming closer and Rosie had nowhere to go. And then he was closer still and the earthy smell of him overpowered her. Rosie closed her eyes. And then the smell moved away, he was moving past her. He picked something up off his bedside cabinet and sat back upright, safe inside his own field of space.

'Oh sorry,' he said.

Rosie had a sudden urge to push him off the mattress and watch him tumble onto the floor.

'I was getting this.'

He held up a clear plastic box with something big and black stuck inside.

'Look at it,' he said, handing it to her.

Inside the clear casing was a large black beetle with wide pincer jaws. He was stuck between two thick sheets of hard plastic. Rosie turned the cube over in her hands, mesmerised by the smooth curved shell on one side and the soft underbelly on the other.

'Let's look at it under the microscope.'

He took her hand again, clammy now. He pulled her back over to the examination desk and slid the case under the magnifying glass. He stuck his eye in the microscope. Rosie watched him, this was the time she often did her own examining. On this occasion she discovered that Peter had one brown freckle on his neck just below his earlobe. It was calling out to her fingertip.

'Amazing,' he said.

Rosie's finger stopped dead in the air.

'Astounding. Rosie you have to see this.'

He got out of the seat and pushed Rosie into it. Rosie looked into the eyehole. What had been a plain black beetle was now an explosion of colour: sapphires had been hiding in its wings, tropical seas and late summer skies and midnight. The beetle held the universe on his back, Rosie was walking the skies, hopping from star to star, zooming forward and back through time. And the beetle was no longer a beetle, but another creature that was also made up of the two different coloured faces of the sky. And then he was a man. A man who called out to her silently through a wire cage. And then something warm touched her cheek and guided her eye away from the man and then a mouth was opening and closing before it, but it was a boy's mouth and not a man's. And then the mouth opened out into a nose and cheeks and a chin and eyes the colour of the morning and messy brown hair that knit it all together and then sound came into the mouth and Rosie could hear and feel again and she knew that his hand was gently but firmly holding her cheek, and he was speaking to her.

'What did you say?' Rosie's ears were filled with a strange fizzing sound, everything felt far away.

Peter looked at her and did not blink.

'I said - why do you look so sad?'

She couldn't answer, his eyes were too blue. Then the soft knock went at the door behind them and they both jumped. Peter's hand fell to his side. Sharon stuck her head slowly around the door. Rosie tried to sit still.

'Dad's home Peter, come down and say hello.' Her mouth opened wide around her next sentence as though her teeth were trying to jump out of her gums. 'Will you be staying for dinner again Ginger?'

Rosie stood up. 'I can't.'

Peter took the box out from under the microscope.

'Mum said she would make roast chicken if I stayed at home tonight.'

Sharon nodded and glanced at her son, who turned the Perspex cube over in his hands.

'Peter will walk you home, won't you love?'

Peter nodded. Rosie knew her cheeks were blooming again. She cursed them.

'You're always welcome though, if ever ... well. You know we're always here.'

Sharon closed the door behind her. Rosie and Peter listened as her footsteps echoed into silence.

Twenty-four (a)

I think I must have willed him back to me that day. Because after that came the first phone call.

Twenty-five

The new stereo fit into her room perfectly. It wasn't yet Christmas or her tenth birthday, but it was bought for her all the same. She had been good Sandra had said, before squeezing her so tight she thought her head might burst. Rosie was not going to argue with that.

She was listening to a new tape her mother had bought her. The Bangles. Three girls with hair as big as Rosie's were on the cover of the cassette box. Rosie knew almost all the words now.

The door handle turned. Sandra was taking some time off work at the bank since the nanny had handed in her notice. Mr. - had grudgingly agreed, but despite the rest, her face looked tight and pinched.

She winced at the chaos of the room. Rosie turned to look at her.

'What's that look about?' Sandra's voice was already building a wall.

'Nothing.'

'Well wipe if off you then.'

Rosie clicked her tongue off the roof of her mouth.

'Excuse me?' Sandra's eyebrows were dangerously close to her hairline, her lips dangerously narrow.

'Nothing!' Rosie breathed.

'Good.'

Sandra hesitated then. 'Someone's on the phone for you,' she said at last.

Rosie narrowed her eyes at her mother. Sandra returned her stare, her mouth set shut.

'For me?'

Sandra nodded. Rosie couldn't believe it. It was some sort of trick.

'Who is it?'

Sandra turned and left, and Rosie heard her steps retreat down the hallway. Rosie ran after her and came to a skidding halt at the hall table where the phone was stationed. Sandra gestured to it, started rearranging the bouquet of lilies on the hall table. Rosie reached down to the mouthpiece. She lifted it to her ear. It was surprisingly light. She had hardly held it. The phone didn't often ring in that house. When it did, there was only one sharp voice she expected to hear.

'Hello?'

Sandra lowered her head and walked smartly toward the kitchen and closed the door behind her.

There was no answer from the other end but no breathing either, as if the person skulking behind the adjoining phone was holding their breath, or dead.

'Hello again?'

There was an intake of breath through the nostrils, a kettle whistling in the distance. Then, finally, sound.

'Aren't you grown up.'

The line was rough, scratchy, it was difficult to grasp at familiar words. She did not recognise the speaker.

'Sorry, who is this?'

Another pause. Longer still.

'It's your dad.'

Was it possible that time could rewind? Rosie stood at the hallway table with the phone in her hand, there she was, she was solid, she was there. But colours and objects lost their value and form around her and the room faded and disappeared.

She was no longer there, no longer at the hall table. She was somewhere else. A plain room with one couch and one television and a blue and white painting of shapes melded together to form a figure leaning against the wall not yet hung. And there was a man with black hair that fell past his shoulders like a woman's and eyes that could cut a path through the surf and large rough hands. His scent was smoke, it was sour, warm.

And it was the thing about him that she remembered, though she could not recall his face. She reached her arms up toward him, tiny fists opening and closing like a blinking light. Large hands, strong arms received her, held her close against that scent and a scratchy chin. Dad. A foreign concept. Perhaps she had come to forget that she had one, or that such a concept even existed. But when she heard the voice of this man on the phone, the man who was hers, she felt a strange yearning. It may have always been there. It may have burrowed an empty cavity in her heart and she had filled it in with piles of earth, so that any cry, no matter how loud, would not be heard. But now her heart was on fire. The burn of it. The white-hot cut of it, a warmth that did not soothe. She knew dads only from the television. They brought their daughters for ice-cream, had stern words with them when they were getting on their mother's nerves, took them kite-flying and helped them learn to ride their first bike. They'd feign an interest in puppies and ponies and the colour pink out of love. They'd laugh when they said something silly and artless and ruffle their hair. Rosie didn't know much about them. She had learned to ride her bike alone. She was yet to fly a kite. But could she fly ... with him? Her thoughts flew down the hall and into her bedroom to a heavy little object buried under her pillow: the thing she had been sure she had lost once, and the thing that had found its way back to her.

Back at the hall table, the walls had solidified, the phone was no longer suspended in space. She tried to manage the speed of her heartbeat. Her silence was heavy. The man on the phone spoke into it, and once he'd started it seemed he couldn't stop. He had cleaned himself up, he said. He was sorted, had stopped drinking. He had a good job now, a steady one. He was a different person. He was new. He was better. Though what could he mean by different or new? Rosie did not know the original.

'I miss you,' he said. 'Do you know that?'

Rosie had a sense that she was required to say something, and it had to be right.

'Yes?' said Rosie. Had she done it?

'You've no idea how much I've missed you.'

She must have got it right after all.

'And your mother. But I know she's moved on now and I don't blame her.'

Rosie made a listening noise.

'He sounds like a great man,' he said. 'Is he a nice man?'

Rosie thought without letting her thoughts range too far. What was there to say about him?

'He's going grey,' she said. 'But his moustache is yellow.'

The man on the phone - her father, your dad, not Joe, a name she had suddenly remembered as being significant - laughed. It was a warm and rumbling sound that thrilled like the first warning of thunder. She wanted to curl up in the melody of it and find rest. Involuntarily her mouth spread out wide and her face lifted in a smile.

'Your grandmother doesn't like me I'm afraid,' he said. 'Years I tried to get in touch with you and your mother, and she never let on. Told me to ... told me to take a running jump, that's what she did.'

His words came falling out on top of each other as though this chance, this conversation, was a dripping hourglass, and if he didn't get it right before the last grain fell his last opportunity would be wasted.

'I had nothing else to go on. I thought I'd never talk to you again. And I know I'd taken a bit of the long way around, but ... well when she let slip your man's name and where he worked, I managed to track you down alright. Though he doesn't know, so don't tell him.'

Rosie said nothing. She had nothing to say. He spoke into the silence as though fearful of it.

'You should have heard her when I rang the first time though. I mean I knew she was a hard woman, but the screams and shouts were something else.'

He laughed out loud, and another smile threatened to stretch along Rosie's mouth.

'I'd say the neighbours had something to say about that.'

Rosie smiled for real then, and three women with faces like birds came to mind. Her dad, Joe her father, spoke again, and his voice was entirely different as though he'd been possessed.

'You can F off! Make no mistake about that, young man! She's only just got her and the wee one's life back on track after you and your messing! So you can piss off back to wherever you went in the first place! She's married now, to a good man with a good job and they live in a nice big house down by the coast and –'

Rosie laughed. She had almost forgotten it wasn't Marie she was talking to. That it was someone quite different to Marie. Her laughter opened her up and he slid in craftily.

'Is it a nice house?' he asked.

'It is very big.'

He went quiet. His sudden silence after all his talk and laughter unnerved her and she pushed against it.

'It's very cold and damp though.'

The line went still, and the only sound Rosie was aware of was that of her deeply held breath. The phone cord creaked as she twisted it around her fingers. Pots and pans were clattering showily in the kitchen, but the thing at her ear held only silence. She felt she had lost him again, she could think of nothing to say to hold him. Her mouth was dry, her throat clogged with wool. Then he spoke.

'I still have our drawing,' he said.

It was Rosie's turn to go silent.

'Are you listening to me?' he asked. His voice was becoming more known to her with each sentence. He was a jigsaw puzzle she was slowly fitting together though she had lost most of the pieces.

'What drawing?' she said.

'Don't you remember? I framed it. It's in the living room on the wall.'

'What is it of?'

'What is it of?' he repeated. His voice had shrunk. 'It's of you Rosie.'

'Of me?'

'Yes.'

That word came out like a hammer.

'Did that ... did that really happen?' Rosie asked.

'What do you mean?' he said. His voice was brittle and young.

'Nothing.'

She could not get the thoughts in her mind to line up. The pieces of her jigsaw were scattered everywhere.

'You must have been about four or five then. You came to stay with me, remember? Your mother wasn't well at the time.'

He let this sentence hang for a moment. Rosie did not take it up.

'Well I remember anyway.' His voice had gone brittle again.

Memory, dreams began to merge. Words shaped like storm clouds, or tornados - wrong words, words she could not spell or say - on a piece of paper or a page and being watched closely and cupboard doors closing loudly...

'I think I remember,' she said at last.

'Do you?' His voice soared upwards. Rosie had the sense of being lifted into the sky by it, of being taken away.

'Yeah. I think so.'

He said nothing then, but Rosie could hear his wide smile as loudly as a spoken word.

'I want to see you Rosie.'

The words came and could not be absorbed and yet they sunk in too fast and set into motion a rapid chain of thoughts and feelings that Rosie could not contain. She would see her father again, smell that scent she remembered so well, though she could not remember his face. Would he still smell the same? Rosie tried to hold the giddiness in her chest. She could not run into her mother after the call. She could not predict the reaction. She was not to fall prey to hope. Something told her, some deep memory, that it was dangerous. She must keep a part of herself hidden so she would be safe. But she wanted it, she couldn't help herself. Her throat withered like sand.

'Where will we meet?' she asked.

The date was set for one month from then at a hotel in the city. As the day approached Rosie felt she had slipped through a crack into the space between words, and she was there alone. She bumped into furniture and door posts and was often found staring out windows at sights beyond the naked eye. Rosie was forbidden to tell anyone. Only her mother knew. She swung wildly between a nauseous, inhibiting apprehension and an excitement so powerful she began to lose all sense of balance. She fell over with alarming regularity, and got so many stings and scratches from nettle dens and patches of briar that Sandra ran out of Savlon twice in a fortnight.

'Are you ok?' Peter asked when he caught Rosie staring up into the interlacing branches of a tall tree, her head bent back so far her neck looked unhinged.

'You seem weird.'

'I'm fine,' she answered, unblinking, and her voice rose like a clarion. 'I just thought I saw something ...'

She refused dinner invitations to Peter's house, preferring to be alone in her bedroom with her stereo. Her regular presence around her own house made it inevitable that Mr. - would notice the change in her.

'What's up with you?' he asked whenever he caught her enduring stare.

'Nothing,' Rosie replied quick as a bell, buoyed up with the act of defiance she and her mother were soon to commit.

They were to meet him in the hotel car park. Sandra had invented an excuse for them to get away for the afternoon - they were going into town to do some shopping.

'What will he say when we come home with nothing?' Rosie asked.

'I will worry about that,' Sandra said.

They waited. Sandra jiggled her knees beside her in the car. The keys in the ignition bounced off her right leg, ringing like chimes. They waited.

'What does *my* dad look like?' Rosie asked after a period of silence. She was just getting used to the phrasing and hadn't got the inflection quite right. She was hoping to come off as nonchalant but kept getting stuck at smug.

'Don't ask me that.'

The muscle pulsed in Sandra's jaw.

'How will I know what he looks like?'

'I will know.'

'But I want to know.'

Her mother sighed.

'Ok.'

Then her smile released. She leaned towards Rosie and her hands gathered around her opening mouth:

'He looks just like Mr. Darcy.'

Her eyes lit up and she laughed. Again, she was the mother Rosie knew. It had been a long time since they had been together.

'The way he would smile at you, in that melting way, as if you were the only woman in the whole world ...'

Her face was beatific, then sank. It was a mask of worry once more. Rosie supposed her dad was handsome, he must be. But she would decide for herself, she had that choice now. Expectation rose in her like bile.

Clouds passed. Their faces darkened and brightened in the mirror. Sandra got out of the car and went into the reception to make an announcement. She returned to the car. Still, they waited.

'Do not tell your stepfather anything of this Rosie, you hear me?'

She would not tell him anything. But what did she have to tell? When they had to turn the headlamps on to see outside they accepted it was time to go home.

'That's your bloody father all over!' Sandra's teeth were clamped around her tongue. She started up the ignition and the gears crunched. 'This fucking car! I swear to God, Rosie, if I ever get my hands on that man I will rip him limb from limb! I am a stupid woman. A stupid stupid woman...'

But what did that make Rosie?

'Really, what was I expecting?' she asked the rear-view mirror as she reversed wildly. Then, before she changed gear: 'Rosie stop that! For crying out loud, you're ten years old.'

She grabbed Rosie's thumb out of her mouth. Rosie had not noticed it against her tongue. She let it drop into her lap and it lay there, inert and wet against her pubic bone.

'You're not too disappointed, are you?' Sandra eyes were large in her face.

Rosie looked down at her wet thumb watching it slowly air dry.

'I shouldn't have let it go ahead. I should have listened to myself. I warned you, didn't I?'

Rosie rubbed her thumb against her jeans.

'I told you this would happen. That man will never change.'

The car pulled out of the hotel car park and onto the road. Sandra began to laugh. It was the sound of an empty tin can.

'Whatever you do, Rosie, don't tell your grandmother about this. Oh Jesus, I couldn't take it.'

Sandra muttered under her breath all the way home. Rosie said nothing. She could not speak.

Twenty-five (a)

'Do you want to stop?' Dr. Waters asked. 'It's ok if you feel you can't go on.'

'No.'

She was seized with a reckless impatience, even as the weight pressing against her chest grew heavier still.

'I want to keep going.'

So many questions had been opened up and she had to close them, each and every one.

Twenty-six

Sandra had a friend over. The woman's name was Jennifer. She'd been at school with her, before Marie had hauled her out and locked her inside the house. She was one of the few Sandra had managed to get back in touch with since. All the others had been swallowed up. They'd married, or moved away, or had just forgotten that at one time in their lives they had been friends.

Illicit cigarette smoke swirled above the kitchen table. Sandra and Jennifer reminisced about hiding around school corners and shivering with the fear of being caught. Sandra knew she ought to have impressed the rule about going outside, but it was raining. She'd left the windows open and hoped for the best. She felt a strange thrill as she pulled in on the butt and felt the nicotine hit her bloodstream. She hoped the smell would not cling.

'So how's about you then?' Jennifer asked.

After treating her to the story of her life, it was Sandra's turn.

'Oh you know. The same.'

Jennifer raised an eyebrow, looked around her without subtlety.

'Well apart from all this. I'm working flat out. That desk chair is welded to my backside at this stage.'

'How's the new nanny?'

'Oh you know the way they are. Young, hungry all the time. Always looking to move on.'

Jennifer sat forward in her chair. 'Why's that?'

Sandra shrugged and shook out the lengthening ash from her cigarette tip. Her hand trembled slightly over the tray.

'Is Rosie not soft on any of them?'

'Rosie's always out somewhere.'

She blew out the smoke and fanned it away from her face and clothes, stiff and new.

'He's a bit tight with the money for them. So I chance a few extra quid at the end of the week, from my own wages. But anyway.'

'The wages he pays you,' Jennifer said.

Sandra coughed.

'In the evening when I'm home she usually heads off out or stays in her room. Rosie's always out of doors in the day anyway. Maybe it's the house.'

Sandra cast an eye down the long dark hallway through the open kitchen door.

'I don't know. I took the first girl who turned up, I had to go back to work. Your man was going mad to get me back in the office.'

'Keeping an eye on you, is he?' A keen smile crept around Jennifer's mouth.

Sandra gave a brief shout of a laugh and dragged deeply on her cigarette. Her painted lips left a broken mark around the butt. She leaned as close to the window as was possible, her long hands fanning the air around her. Jennifer watched her but her expression did not change.

'How's your girl anyway. Is she getting on alright?'

'She's ok,' Sandra said. 'She's getting to that difficult age.' She flicked some fallen ash off her thighs.

'Has she made any friends?'

'Yes,' Sandra replied, with a sudden wild happiness that caught Jennifer off guard. 'One. A boy. Peter is his name. He lives down the road.'

'Have you met his parents yet?'

'Not yet. But I will soon I'm sure.'

With a little shaking of her head Jennifer took a sharp intake of breath. 'You really should, you know. You've no idea what they're like. The father could be a paedophile.'

'Could he?'

'Oh, you get all sorts around,' Jennifer went on, as though discussing the weather. 'You can't trust anyone.' She took a slurp of tea. 'So, what's this boy like then?'

'Oh. I don't know.'

It would have been wiser, Sandra thought, to have spent the day alone with her daughter. She hadn't spent time with her, it felt, since they'd sat in a hotel car park. And what a shambles that had turned out to be.

'I've actually never met him,' she said.

Jennifer held her with a spearing look: 'How long have they been friends?'

'The past six months. Therabouts.'

Sandra felt herself slide back out of the room as Jennifer started to talk, a part of herself preserved and untouched. Jennifer's voice travelled some distance before it reached her.

'Months! And you've never even seen him?'

'No.'

The words left her of their own volition. She wanted to say: *I don't know how things are meant to be done*, but stopped herself.

'How old is Rosie now?' Jennifer kept on. The sentence was a steel rod.

Sandra looked at the clock. The hand hadn't moved.

'Ten.' Was that it? 'Ten and a half.'

She was no longer sure. She wasn't fit to be a mother. She had known it all along. Jennifer's expression boldly confirmed it. Yet she still felt compelled to justify.

'She hasn't had that many friends. She's always been, you know.'

'What?' Jennifer asked. When Sandra did not respond, Jennifer raised her eyebrows. 'Are you sure it's not –'

'What?' Sandra had given her a license with the question, she knew it. She braced herself.

'Well, and now I'm not saying this is what's going on with Rosie, and I'm not trying to panic you –' her urging tone was at odds with her words '– but a friend of mine had a son and they were very close and then, she got pregnant.'

Jennifer paused for effect and Sandra felt herself being sucked in.

'Everyone was delighted - no more so than the son himself, he'd always wanted a little brother or sister he said - and they waited for the day, and they were all so excited about the new baby. She went shopping for the baby's clothes with him. He helped pick out the cot and everything - he was more hands on than the father.'

Sandra nodded, waited for it.

'But it was very sad in the end, because at seven months she went into an early labour and that was it. Gone. She'd lost it. And nearly died while she was at it. They couldn't help her until the sepsis set in. Weeks she was away. And the son asking his father every day, where's my little brother? Where's my little sister? Where's my mummy? Then he had to be told. Soon after that the child started up about his new friend Jack. Me and Jack this, me and Jack that. So she asked him to bring Jack over for dinner. And he did. But Jack didn't come.'

'I don't understand,' Sandra said.

'Oh her son introduced him alright. Had a place set for him and everything. But Jack was nowhere to be seen. He wasn't real, is what I'm saying. He was all in her son's head.'

Sandra lit up a second cigarette off the dying embers of the one in her hand. Jennifer watched her, kept up the unrelenting flow of her talk.

'She brought him to a child psychologist and he said it was post-traumatic stress. Something to do with the grief. And this on top of everything else she had to deal with. She was sick for months.'

'That's awful,' Sandra heard the words come out of her mouth without feeling them.

'Anyway, as I said, I'm not saying that's what's happening with Rosie, but. And you're not pregnant are you?' She scanned over Sandra's slight frame, went on without waiting for an answer. 'All this change. The new man. Leaving your mother behind. This house. You haven't heard from Joe yet, have you?'

'No. Not yet.'

'Bastard. I always said –'

'I know.'

'We all knew what he was.'

Sandra sighed. *We did.*

She watched her cigarette burn down between her fingers. When the hot ash fell onto the bare skin of her hand, she didn't flinch.

'How's the new man anyway?' Jennifer said with a new brightness to her voice. 'Still honeymooning?'

'It's all so new.'

'Yes it'll be like that. Still though. A big house like this!'

'It needs a lot of work still.'

'It's lovely. It's coming along definitely.'

'We're nowhere near finished with it.'

'It'll get there.'

They drank their tea, cold now. Sandra did not offer to make a new pot.

'How's your Mark?' she asked, after a time.

'Oh, he's alright you know,' Jennifer said. 'The usual. Did I tell you he got the job in the electricity company?'

'You did.'

The clock ticked, the hands barely moved. Rosie appeared in the doorway.

'Where were you?' Sandra asked loudly, relieved at the diversion, relieved her daughter was beautiful and here and alive.

Rosie noticed the other woman and closed her mouth. She did not like Jennifer.

Then Sandra let out a wail: 'What happened to your face?'

Rosie had an angry welt across her right cheek.

'Some boys in the field,' she said.

Her eyes were on her shoes, she was hanging off the door handle, barely moving her lips.

'What did they do to you?'

'They tried to take my bike.'

'And?'

With each question Sandra's pitch rose. Jennifer shifted uneasily in her chair.

'Then they hit me.'

'Oh my darling! Are you ok?'

She was upon her with her arms about her and Rosie was squirming. Sandra held tighter. She tilted Rosie's head back in both hands.

'You smell like smoke,' Rosie said quietly, their faces close. Sandra released her.

'How did you get away Rosie, if you don't mind me asking?' Jennifer asked.

Rosie looked at her quickly then back to her mother, directing the answer to her as if it were she who had spoken.

'Peter came. He stopped them. He hit them back, and they were bigger too.'

'Peter, was it?' Jennifer asked. 'Who's this Peter?'

Sandra inhaled deeply. Rosie did not answer.

'You can't be leaving your daughter out alone now, Sandra, if there are boys like that around. I'd never leave my Cormac out alone. I'd be mad to.'

'Where is Peter now?' Sandra asked.

Rosie made a graceless gesture towards the front door.

'Why don't you invite him in?'

'He's gone up to his house with the bike. He said his dad will fix it.'

Jennifer began rummaging in her bag behind them. Sandra clenched her teeth.

'What's wrong with it?'

'With what?'

'The bike, the bike.'

'Oh. The boys kicked it in.'

'Well, maybe I could - or your stepfather could have a look at it. He'll be good at things like that. He is the one after all who - well. He's knows about those kinds of things I'm sure.'

196

'No!'

Rosie said it with such force Jennifer's rummaging stopped. Sandra stared at her daughter. Her soft face had hardened into marble.

'Peter's dad will do it.'

Jennifer appeared behind them holding out a tube. 'Here you go. Put this on the sore bit.'

As she was unscrewing the lid, Sandra took it from her.

'We have some in the cupboard. I was just about to get it.'

'You looked like you had your hands full.'

Sandra turned back to Rosie, whose expression had not yet softened. 'Darling can I get you some sweet tea?'

She steered Rosie into her seat at the table.

'Peter's mum invited me up for dinner.'

'Again?'

Jennifer gave a small cough. Rosie got up to leave.

'Wait! Wait.'

Sandra grabbed her keys and pulled on her shoes from under the table,

Jennifer loitered awkwardly by the sink.

'I'm coming up with you.'

Rosie marched up the road and Sandra followed behind at a pace, her shoes pinching slightly around the corn on her left foot. She was half-expecting Jennifer to be right and Rosie to lead her to an abandoned park, or one of those hiding places she was so partial to. She was pleased and relieved when Rosie slowed and turned into the driveway of a modest home. Rosie stood on tiptoe to knock three times on the door. Within seconds it was opened by a smiling woman, lit with warmth and the scent of boiled vegetables.

'Ah I was wondering when I'd get to meet you,' the woman said, standing aside to allow Rosie to power down the hallway. Sandra watched her daughter's hunched shoulders and clenched fists smartly follow a remembered path.

'You must be Rosie's mother.'

'That's right.'

'I'm Sharon. Come on in.'

She took Sandra by the hand and shook her into the house. Still holding on, she led her into the kitchen. There was light everywhere.

'I didn't catch your name?'

'Sandra.'

'Lovely.'

She eased her into a seat at the table, already full. Rosie and the boy, Peter, sat opposite with their heads together, whispering behind their hands. A man who must have been his father sat beside her. His face was set and impossible to read, his eyes golden, warm as softening butter. His and his wife's met stealthily and each time they sang, communicating noiselessly across the kitchen counter. He sat and smoked beside Sandra saying nothing, and offered her the pack. She took one gratefully. Sharon busied about boiling water, checking pots and pans and opening and shutting cupboards. She came over with a mug of tea and a loaf of bread and cheese on a wooden board and placed it in the middle of the table. Rosie dove straight into it as though she'd never been fed and Sandra almost excused her, but when she looked up and saw the indulgent expression on Sharon's face she knew her words would be wasted.

'Your daughter's got a great appetite.'

It was said with approval. The silent man on Sandra's left gave one nod of agreement. Sandra tried to fan the smoke away from the food.

'Ah don't be worrying about that now. They're well used to it. I can't get him to go outside, hard as I try.'

The man shook with noiseless laughter at Sandra's shoulder.

'Have some yourself,' Sharon said.

'No, I couldn't.'

'Are you sure now? It's there if you want it.'

'I'd better wait.'

Sandra's stomach rumbled.

'Suit yourself,' Sharon said with a light shrug.

Peter's father was loading up bread with a thick layer of butter and wedges of the crumbling white cheese. Sandra's mouth watered as the three of them ate around her. The two children chewed their food in unison. They could have been the only two people to exist in the world. Sandra couldn't take her eyes off them.

'Terrible it was today what happened,' Sharon began, disappearing out of sight and delving into another cupboard: 'Never known that sort to come around here.'

'I know. I'm only glad nothing worse happened.'

Sharon took a deep throaty breath of assertion and arrived chest first at the table with a tub of antiseptic.

'Look into the light for me now, Ginger,' she commanded.

Rosie obliged, snapping out of the exclusive world that left Sandra feeling as though the far side of the table was another country.

'You're too pretty for big boys to be hurting you like that,' she clucked, massaging ointment onto the mark on her cheek. Sandra watched her gentle, measured movements with a sort of ache.

Rosie said, 'It happens to my mother all the time and she's the prettiest woman I've ever seen.'

Silence hit, eyebrows contracted all around. Sandra knew she ought to speak, but it had been said as though she weren't even in the room, as though she were no more than the smoke that coiled above her and clung to her hair. She couldn't find her voice.

Peter's father cleared his throat. 'Let's have a look at that bike, shall we?'

The children followed after him, the two women left in the silent kitchen.

'Thanks for all your help. With the bike, and Rosie, and everything –' Sandra began. She wondered if once she'd started talking she'd ever be able to stop.

'Don't you worry yourself about it, it's a pleasure.'

Sharon smiled at her and held her gaze. Sandra looked away.

The metallic sounds from the garden broke the stillness indoors.

'Will you stay and have something?' Sharon asked.

'Oh no, no. Thank you, but I'll eat with my husband.'

'If you're certain.'

Sharon took a pile of plates out and set them on the side. Sandra took it as her cue to go.

'What time shall I collect –' she nearly called Rosie by name, but thought better of it '- my daughter?'

'Don't you worry yourself about that. Peter always walks her home.'

'Oh no, he doesn't have to.'

'He wants to. It's so nice for them to have friends isn't it?' Sharon said, and Sandra wondered if only she could have recognised the pleading note in her voice.

'We should let them enjoy each other.'

Sandra stood and stubbed out what was left of her cigarette and smoothed out her clothes.

'Anyway, I'd better get on and start the dinner.'

'Yes, you'd better,' Sharon said gravely. She came beside her and squeezed her hand. Sandra felt compelled to leave.

'Goodbye!' she called over her shoulder. Peter and his father looked up from their work briefly. Sharon saw her to the door and wrapped her bones in a quick rough embrace before shutting her out into the night. As she stood in the dark outside the closed house, Sandra realised that Rosie had not come to say goodbye.

Twenty-seven

A strange thing had happened. Rosie had died. No one had foreseen it, least of all herself. It was Hell she was going to, that was certain. It was dragging her down, legs first, the dull ache below the waist was proof enough. She must have been very bad in life. She tried to piece together how it had happened but the pieces kept slipping through her fingers. Essential information was missing. She was playing Hangman with herself: searching for the final letter and hiding from it. How had it happened? She had been running in the field, forced by Peter to join in with the local children in a game of chasing. Then she had died. She hadn't enjoyed either experience.

'Rosie are you alright? Are you ok?'

'Peter just give her a moment.'

'Should we call an ambulance?'

But vision was returning. Snatches of sound. Sensations. Tender sacrum on a firm soft surface. Damp sticky hair across her cheekbone. A deep nausea that required immediate attention. Voices, familiar. Other familiar things. Solid-looking and of the earth, things that did not belong in a place of fire and pain. Was this the end? Curtains, carpet, the chandelier now webbed, the smell of Dog? On the couch in the sitting room, in her house. She could feel her mother near, watching. There not there? Living wetness in her hand. Now a dry hard palm. But life, there was life in it. And still that dull ache below the waist. Lost, her soft bed beneath her floating unsupported. Everywhere and nowhere at once. In this room, or somewhere else entirely at another point in time? Her mother was there, watching. And someone else: a quiet presence, there all along. They were witnessing her death and neither of them were doing anything about it. Rosie struggled to keep her eyelids open, to stay with the world. Letting them close would be the final surrender.

There was a part of her that wanted to. A knowledge in this slipped space, like a stitch dropped, that this had always been so even from the very beginning of life. She had never settled but straddled the worlds always. A choice would have to be made soon. The television was on there in Hell: was that flickering light the waltzing flames or the changing pictures on a screen? All she could hear was a high-pitched sound. Unrelenting, headstrong, a constant alarm. And something else far beneath that, a faint doleful click. Someone else was there now, watching. In the corner a dark man stood. Shadowed, barely seen. Only the white of his teeth and the blue of his eyes. Him.

'He is here.'

'Rosie, can you hear me?'

'Tell him, tell him –'

'I can't understand her.'

'Tell him to go. Tell him I don't want him anymore.'

'Maybe I should leave?'

'She's babbling, Peter.'

'He's calling my name.'

'Rosie.'

A voice. Her mother's. It contained a barrier, a closing gate, within it.

'Enough of that talk now.'

A strong force, a dry hard palm against her cheek, knocking at the door to Hell. Was communication possible between the worlds? All these unanswered questions. All these open doors. A choice would have to be made soon. A choice would be made for her. But not yet. The door was still ajar. She had not died at all. She tried to raise her arm to show them, to warn them about Him, the man who stood watching, but the power of the dark place had made her weak. But she would warn them, whoever they were. Her mother. Yes. Her mother and Peter. And ...

'What is she pointing at?'

This was a young voice. One she knew.

'She's delirious.'

This was one she knew better. It lived in her.

Rosie commanded her eyelids open. They responded. She looked into the corner. It was empty. He had gone. Had he ever been there? Ceaseless, insistent, the ringing in Rosie's ears went on.

'Who left the phone off the hook?'

She felt a barren palm press down firmly on her forehead. Its touch opened up a small gate and sense began to trickle slowly through.

'My dad, *my* dad, my *dad* ... He said he would call.'

'Whisht now.'

'I'm cold.'

From Hell to Antarctica. She was shivering. She was buried beneath another blanket, another layer of earth. It was tucked in around her tight and neat. She would never get out. It started to shake vigorously.

'Peter what are you doing?'

'I'm creating kinetic heat.'

New hands, hot and wet. Rosie squirmed beneath them. Something about their touch felt wrong and dangerous, a crossing. Especially now that she had died and come back. If only she knew why. The Angelus came on, softening the flickering light, quenching the flames. The droning bells cut through the ringing in her ears until it had faded entirely. She was safe. She may not be going to Heaven but at least she was not stuck in Hell. She looked around the room, reacquainting herself with the things she knew were real. Walls, solid walls. Carpet. A smiling Dog. A frowning mother, a pacing friend. She was back. She had survived her first death. Peter appeared before her, his face strained and blotchy. He turned and said something in Sandra's ear, then swallowed saltily, and was absorbed in his dancing fingers.

'Go get me a glass of water,' Sandra commanded him. 'And close the door. And take your time!'

'What happened?' Rosie asked.

'You had an accident.'

The door closed behind him. Immediately Sandra undressed Rosie from the waist down. She did not resist, she didn't have the strength. Her jeans came off, long grass stains all over them. Then off came her knickers: light blue all over. There was a black gash across the crotch, like tar.

'What is that? What is it?'

'Don't worry Rosie, everything is going to be fine. Lift your hips.'

It was like pushing against a ton of steel. A towel went underneath her, and another above. The blanket went on top just as the door re-opened. Sandra balled up the dirty clothes and stuffed them under the couch. Peter came in with the glass, which he had filled right to the top. It slopped everywhere and splattered the carpet.

Rosie was too aware of her nakedness underneath the narrow throw. The wetness at her crotch, the dull ache below her waist. Her wet palm. Dog licked at it. She was there beside her, had always been. She whined softly. Rosie would sneak her into her bedroom that night if she could get away with it.

'Are you better?' Peter asked. He resisted the call of the couch arm, paced before her on the carpet instead. He was plainly fighting an urge to run. Rosie's stomach tensed and the nausea that had been hiding reared up.

'Oh fuck. Peter run and get me a bowl and a tea towel would you.'

He was gone and back again and the inside of the bowl and a wet towel to the forehead became her best friends. Thanks to Peter her hair remained clean. She wished he would leave.

'I'll never play chasing again.'

'Sorry,' Peter said.

'Chasing or no chasing when it's your time it's your time and there's nothing that you or I or anyone can do about it.'

Peter frowned at Rosie and Rosie, through her nausea, back at him. Sandra was talking in tongues. Rosie watched the question on her own mind begin to sprout as Peter took a breath, but Sandra was too quick.

'She needs sugar. Peter would you ever go into the fridge for me and get her some juice.' She hesitated, went on. 'And there's some chocolate in the press beside the oven.'

This was new. Sandra had closed a tight grip around what Rosie ate. She was at *that age*, though whatever that meant, Rosie did not know. Biscuits and sweets were limited to Saturdays, apart from when she was up in Peter's where an unlimited supply was at her beck and call. Rosie's face fell back to grey.

Peter returned with the gifts. Strength was returned to her. Peter's feet danced like rain on the carpet. All three of them knew, though not all of them quite why, that this was a place for the two women only.

Your mother will be wanting you home for your dinner Peter,' Sandra said.

'Oh yeah.'

'It's after five.'

'Is it? Well I'd better go.'

'Ok.'

'Ok.'

'Bye.'

'Bye.'

There was no wasted time. The doors of the living room and hallway shut like echoes. Mother and daughter and Dog were alone again. Rosie's body relaxed. She took another sip of the juice, another bite of the chocolate. The taste was like medicine. There was no pleasure in it. She could barely lift her arms.

'Am I going to die?' she asked.

Sandra laughed. Her teeth shone as they caught a gleam of failing evening light. Her wispy blonde hairs tickled Rosie's face as she fell forward. She was released, she was young again, but only for a moment.

'No not quite,' she said.

'Then what is wrong with me?'

Sandra looked at her and seemed to hold her bodily with her gaze, to cup and caress her face, to hold her there with it. The passing lightness had left her and Rosie noticed for the first time the very fine lines that had formed around her mouth and eyes. There was a moment where she seemed to consider whether to speak at all, where Rosie believed her question would always be left there hanging in the space between the couch and the chair before the carpet began. Then her mother's face closed in, and the lines around her mouth deepened. She spoke and her voice was without passion or effort. The words came out bare and naked as the sun:

'You're a woman now.'

Twenty-eight

The Thing That Happened Next was something that no one wanted to discuss. But as much as Rosie tried to drown it out with the volume button on her stereo it still came into that space between the brain and the eyes, blurring her bedroom into nothing. Each playback of the event was more vivid than the last, the colours were brighter, the outlines bolder. Nothing could push it from her thoughts, not even the hours spent hovering between stop and record waiting for good songs to come on the radio.

Her mother had decided to go out that night with Jennifer. Rosie had tried to stop her. She couldn't understand why she would leave her alone in the house, with him. But more still it was a strong feeling that could not be pinned down, a tingling in the invisible umbilical cord that still bound them both. That old sense of impending doom.

'Don't go,' she pleaded.

'I need a break,' Sandra sighed. 'Rosie, I need some time to myself.'

'But why?'

'Don't start.'

'Please don't go, Mum. Please don't leave me here.'

Sandra had hesitated then and Rosie had thought herself safe. Then Mr. - came walking down the corridor, and Sandra became liquid and flux and spun like the wind.

'Don't be ridiculous,' she said, and Rosie still remembered the exact shape of her smile as she said it and the way it had blinded her with its force. 'Whatever can you mean? You'll be fine. You're a big girl now, remember. A woman.'

And she had winked.

'I'll look after you, won't I?' he said.

Rosie held to her mother's sleeve and spoke low and rapidly into her ear. She was losing her. They were losing each other.

'Please, please, please don't –'

'Let go of my coat now.'

There was a quick kiss to the forehead, and she made for the door.

'Remember what time you're to be back?'he said.

Sandra had stopped then, her hand on the handle. Rosie couldn't bear to look at his face, imagining it was enough.

'I remember.'

'I want to hear you say it.'

Sandra's shoulders lifted and rounded, very gradually, and still she faced the door.

'Twelve o'clock, I'll be home.'

'You will.'

And she was gone before either of them could call her back.

Rosie went straight to her room and locked her door. She lay awake all night, her hand closed into a fist under her pillow. Hunger built, but the kitchen could not tempt her. She heard her door handle rattle. Gentle words were said, dangerous and low. She pretended to be asleep. She watched the clock. It slowed. The minutes took hours. The small hand went past twelve. Rosie flitted in and out of consciousness. A dark man stood in the corner, a winged man, an angel. No - it was just a shadow, a sly trick the moon was playing on her. Footsteps hammered down the hallway. At times the noise outside her door was deafening, other times soft as a tearful sigh. At a quarter past two in the morning, Rosie found herself on the floor of her room staring at the clock, afraid to let her gaze stray into the mirror above the cold fireplace for fear of what she might see. Noises came from the hallway: mumbling, the dragging of heavy things. Glass clinking against glass. His words, his voice, his sudden, violent singing roamed through the house where he physically could not reach. It skirted around corners and swelled to a deafening wave.

At five past three and thirty-three seconds, the front door opened. The interrogation began immediately. It echoed down the hallway. It echoed all over the house.

'Where were you? Who were you with?'

'We couldn't get a taxi.'

'You're drunk, you whore.'

That word was destined to follow Rosie around through life.

'I'm not –'

'I saw. I saw you. I heard what you did. I had someone watching you.'

'What the fuck are you talking about?'

Then Rosie's name was being called and she was there under the enamel lamp in the kitchen as though under a spotlight, caught in the middle of a scene that for all its horror remained stubbornly real.

Sandra was stuck on the kitchen floor curled around the table leg, holding on for strength. She could not get up. She was broken.

'Ro.Sie.'

The two syllables were tight with panic.

'I. Can't. Move.'

He was standing over her. So still. A painting. Not real, not living. Impossible that he could be. Rosie had not woken. She had fallen asleep and could not wake. Her mother lay crumpled at his feet. Blood pooled around her head, thick, plastic red. He was tall and stiff, without pity, cold and clear. He had been cast in steel.

'I didn't do it,' he said.

Rosie dragged her out. He did not move, only watched with his ogre eyes. Rosie tried to get her on her feet, tried to help her walk, but Sandra could barely stand. She leaned all her weight upon Rosie. Rosie almost fainted under the strain and the stinging billowing smell of her mother's breath. The effort was huge. Could a dream be this real? He stood and watched, but did not follow. When they reached the sanctuary of her bedroom, Rosie again locked her door. Sandra grunted as Rosie laid her gently down. Her mouth puckered like a baby searching for a teat. Her skin was white as bone.

'Don't. Don't go Rosie. Stay.'

'I'll stay.'

'I'm sorry. Sorry I left you.'

'Whisht now,' Rosie said. 'Sleep.'

Rosie pressed play on the tape recorder. A mix tape she had made that morning sang them to sleep. She climbed in beside her mother on the bed and moulded herself around her, taking care not to press too heavily against her back. The deep cut under her eye leaked red on the pillow. The door rattled.

'It's the wind,' Rosie said.

When her alarm clock rang for school a few hours later Rosie did not stir. She waited until she heard Mr. - leave for work. Marie's number was in the leather address book beside the phone on the hall table. She kept her explanation brief. There was a clatter at the other end, the sound of a door slamming. Marie had wasted no time on goodbye.

He came home that evening in a high, generous spirit. Sandra's absence was not mentioned.

He heaved an enormous tree through the door, breezed about getting things out of the attic, flinging open cupboards. The smell of pine needles was so strong it was almost nauseating.

'Look at this Rosie. You'll like this. This is really something.'

Out of a plastic bag came a cardboard box containing a Santa Claus doll that stood almost as tall as Rosie's knee. Rosie was not impressed.

'I'm too old for that stuff,' she said.

He held her look until her gaze fell away.

'I'm nearly eleven,' she mumbled.

'Don't go ruining it for me now.'

Rosie's heart started to move in an odd, staccato rhythm.

'There was a time when you wouldn't shut up about this fella. Don't you remember?'

He set the doll on the table and fumbled around its back looking for something.

'It's one of them robotic things. There's a switch somewhere. Ah here it is.'

A song squeezed through a pipe. The doll's face stayed frozen as it sang, its eyes lit up red like a devil. He moved away from it and all went silent. After a minute he moved back in front of it and off it went again.

I saw mommy kissing Santa Claus ...

'It's presence sensitive, isn't that something?'

... neath the mistletoe last night!

The sound was fragile, thin, painfully sharp. He jumped back and forth in front of the singing doll, waiting for it to come to life.

'Jesus it's something alright!'

And then Sandra was home, borne in by Marie, whose eyes flew around from object to object landing nowhere, never once connecting with Rosie's, and nearly falling out of her head when he offered her a cup of tea. And had it ever happened? Sandra was stiff, holed up; she couldn't get up or down. She walked with a frame like an ancient and yet nothing was said. Had she, perhaps, always been like that? Rosie played the night over in her mind so many times the fabric of it softened into dream.

Back in real time, Marie was changing the sheets upstairs as Sandra wept and shook in the bathtub and Rosie was awoken out of the memory by a tap at her bedroom window.

She pulled the curtain aside. Behind it there was nothing but empty space, a blank and sullen window. She returned to the book she was reading, only to jolt up again when the tapping resumed, frenzied and deafening. She tore the curtains aside and opened the window. There was nothing there. Nobody. Then something caught her eye. On the windowsill lay a single black feather. Its presence thrilled her. She picked it up. A thud came through the ceiling, from the small box room at the end of the upstairs corridor. The room her mother now slept in.

The door to the room was ajar. Through it, her mother slept.

'What happened?' Rosie asked. Her left ear had already begun to burn. The portrait of the man leered at her waiting back. She never went upstairs if she could help it.

Marie silenced her with a finger, went back to arranging the duvet. She was speaking in tones so gentle and low Rosie was sure she was imagining them. She spent most days at the house now, arriving after he left for work and leaving before he returned. She moved around the room picking up clothes and shoes and piling up the sheets in the corner. Sandra's face was grey and troubled against the fresh linen. Rosie became aware her hands were empty. She walked along the landing looking for the lost thing. She did not look at the man in the frame. The feather had vanished. The light through the window was failing, and the loss of light meant the gain of him. She wanted to kiss her mother goodnight before his return, before he swallowed her up for the night. She turned back around, but her grandmother barred the way, close enough to bring on an arrest. Her lips were thin and pale, and her teeth glistened between them.

'Why didn't you help her? You should have stopped him.'

Rosie had lost her tongue. Marie took her arm in her grip and her nails bit into the flesh of it, like little teeth.

'All you do is think of yourself. Down there in your room all day listening to the fancy stereo your mother bought for you with his money without a care in the world. Do you ever look in on her? Do you ever answer her when she calls?'

'I –'

'No. I do that. And all she's done for you. You've no idea the sacrifices she's made for you. She could have had everything ...' Her words were being pushed through a sieve, struggling, faltering, and then they were being slapped down into a pan of hot oil: 'You're. A. Sel. Fish. Lit. Tle. Thing. Just like that father of yours. You. Make. Me. Sick. Go and follow him across the Irish sea and drown yourself in it while you're at it.'

She started to cry. She turned away and walked down the stairs. A moment later the front door opened, then closed.

Rosie sank onto the floor. Her mother's breathing was laboured and tender through the open door. She drew her knees into her chest and fastened her arms around them so they pressed into her heart. The light bulb flickered above her. Only yesterday Marie had changed it. Through the banisters the window's failing light opened up a square of her garden, and what lay beyond.

Something about the hidden space behind the wall called to her. It was a forgotten errand now insistent and intruding, lit up with some unearthly power, sprawling into her thoughts like the branches from the trees that stretched their limbs from that place onto their land. But what was beyond the wall? She knew it was something and she knew it was important. All these open doors. She couldn't see them but she knew they were there. If only she could answer the question on her lips: *why*. It would mean something soon, but what? A dark feathered bird burst through the canopy and flew off, far and out of sight. Why was its shape so familiar to her?

The smooth sound of canvas sliding against wall approached. Rosie was alone and not alone, her mother no longer present. She jumped up and ran down to the living room taking the stairs two at a time. She did not look left or right.

All she wanted was cartoons. Something light and easy to occupy her until dinner, when the enamel light would illuminate only two heads at the kitchen table and the yawning space between them. She relaxed as she entered the television room, already watching them in her mind, leaving behind the space her body was forced to occupy. Then the familiar tune started up. She had forgotten the Santa doll hidden behind the door. The batteries in it were dying and the singing sounded shrill and strange.

Twenty-nine

The second phone call came at the tail end of a string of unfortunate events.

The three of them were watching television. Four, counting Dog. Sandra flicked through the channels, watching as a talking man turned into another man, a woman, a fish. Then two shows worth watching came on and there was a clash. Rosie wanted to watch David Attenborough talk about animals; her mother favoured a soap opera lined with cobbled streets.

'Cut that out, you two. Just leave it on that,' he said, and a line was drawn.

It was the soap opera. Rosie folded her arms and her mother arranged herself cat-like on the sofa. As she stretched herself out, her back cracked slightly. These days, it barely drew a wince. The cut under her eye had faded to a clear, flesh-toned scar. It could only be noticed up close. Sandra appeared to have forgotten all about it, but Rosie had caught her rubbing cold cream on it when she thought she was alone. To all of this, he remained oblivious.

Then the phone started to ring. He looked around at the two of them, sighed, stood up to answer it. A man and a woman were shouting at each other, in a kitchen. The man slapped the woman across the face and the woman began to cry. The room became tight with unspoken words.

'How did you get this number?'

The mumbling came, not from the television speakers, but from the hallway.

'There's no way, no way, absolutely *no* way ...'

His voice slunk in through the door. His voice was a car speeding toward them.

'- I don't *have* to tell her anything. And mark me, boyo, I won't -'

215

Rosie and Sandra caught eyes, looked away. Rosie watched the rain, Sandra the television. The sound was down at one bar above mute.

'Well I'll sleep here beside the thing day and night to make sure that never happens!'

'Who's on the phone?' Sandra called at last through the gap in the door.

Then he was bashing the receiver against the wall in a sudden brutal rage. Sandra sat up knees-pressed, feet flat, searching in her cardigan pocket for something. She drew out a packet of cigarettes. She was halfway through opening them when she seemed to think better of it and folded them back in. She dug her nails into the arms of the sofa.

His laboured breathing and his absence was all there was. Then:

'Somebody would like to speak to you, Rosie.'

He returned, sat beside Sandra. She tightened into the arm of the couch. He stared at the wall. The nutty squeak of his teeth, the fists trembling in his lap. Sandra turned her head towards the window.

Rosie approached the hall table where the receiver lay, inert and innocent.

'Hello?'

The line crackled. Static, electric. It sounded far away, from another world. Perhaps an underwater one.

'Rosie. Is that you?'

'Yes.'

She knew that voice.

'It's me.'

She knew it well.

It came to her at night at the moment precisely before she passed between the worlds of waking and sleeping, when she could be anything or anyone and go anywhere she chose. When she was unlimited. And that strange sensation again of the world carrying on around her at hyper speed as she remained behind stuck still and frozen in time. Her father talked but she could not answer.

'How are you my love?'

Her throat had shut and she could not draw breath.

'My dearest?'

The rain stopped, and a shaft of light broke through the clouds, illuminating the hallway. She held her hand up to it and cast a shadow on the wall behind the phone. Her hand became the dark mass of a bird.

'Rosie, I'm sorry,' he said.

Rosie tried to silence her breath.

'Something ... something came up that morning and it ran over and then when I got to the airport I was too late. I was mortified, and I couldn't ring. I tried to, but I couldn't –'

Rosie listened to him, her mouth held tight. She felt nothing, she made sure of it.

'I tried my hardest Rosie. I was doing it for you, you know. Don't you know that? I tried my hardest, but sometimes in life that's not enough. You'll learn that the hard way, like the rest of us ... are you still there?'

'I'm here.'

'Good ... oh bollocks.'

There was commotion at the other end, and the bright clash of metal against metal.

'Sorry I'd almost run out. These bloody things! Me on this like a muppet and you there with your own fancy phone.'

Rosie said nothing.

'Aren't you going to ask me how I am?' he asked.

'How are you?' she asked obediently.

'I'm good. Getting better all the time. Onwards and upwards!'

His voice fell back to a gentle entreaty.

'I'll never forgive myself for letting you down you know. It will not happen again, you hear me? It will never happen again.'

His voice was a fist pounding a table, a hammer.

Rosie's throat unstuck, enough for yes and no and I don't know. She could think of no questions to ask of him and even if she could, she knew her tongue would not let her. She was aware that the television had not been turned back up in the next room. To fill the silences her father repeated questions he'd already asked. He wanted to speak to her mother.

'That fucker - sorry, Rosie - doesn't want me to, but you'll get her for me won't you love?'

Love. It was strange to hear him use such a word. Many people called Rosie love, most of them those she did not know or little wanted to. The ladies at the fruit market called her that when they passed the apples down to her. They scrunched their faces up and were all smiles, all teeth, but as soon as her mother's money hit their palms they saw straight through her to the next.

'She's in the sitting room.'

'Well go and get her then.'

Rosie lowered the phone. Distortion crept through the ear piece. She returned it to her ear.

'What did you say?'

'Oh,' he said. His voice had a heaviness to it and for the first time Rosie was aware that he had aged: this man she knew well but knew not at all.

'All I said was it's a long way away over there. Across the sea.'

Rosie pressed her cheek and ear against the sweaty phone. Her cartilage felt bruised. She could hear her own blood pounding.

'Go and get your mother for me now.'

'Ok. Dad –'

'Yes?' he asked. The smile in his voice could not be unheard. Rosie allowed the sound of him, his rolling vowels, the thrill and warning of his bass notes, to settle deep inside her ear. She let it collect in there. She bottled it up.

'What is it?'

She corked the top and sealed it with wax.

'Nothing.'

She laid the receiver back on the hall table and opened the door. It creaked. Both of them stared ahead at the silent screen. She walked in. She just stood there. She had walked out on stage but couldn't remember her lines. Sandra watched the television with such intent a bomb could have exploded at her feet and she would not have flinched. He turned toward her then and looked at her once. Once was enough. Rosie walked past him. She took a seat back on the other chair and curled her body tight. She hoped she was the only one who could hear her heart beat. She swallowed down the spittle that filled her mouth and it went off like a gunshot. The receiver lay off the hook on the hall table. After some time, it started to beep.

Then dinner time was upon them and what had passed was mentioned no more. He insisted on doing the cooking. He'd been down to the nice butcher to get the sirloins and wouldn't let anyone else get their hands on them.

'You're not going near them Sandra,' he said. 'Sure, you always cremate the damn things. You got that from your mother.'

Sandra's laughter was tight and stretched and brief, and she went out the back door to smoke until it was ready. There was asparagus and potatoes along with the steaks. He took the plates out of the oven and arranged them on the sideboard. The worktop was crowded. Plates, pots and pans were everywhere. He separated the food: flopped boiled-to-death, soggy spears onto the three plates, slapped on mounds of lumpy mash and divided up the bleeding meat.

'Rosie come and get your dinner,' he said.

She came toward him, hesitating.

'That one,' he said. He pointed to the plate resting on the hob.

She reached out to take it, closed her fingers around the lip and lifted it up. Immediately it sprung out of her hands, tumbled to the floor and split. The food spilled out everywhere.

Dog trotted over to devour it. Rosie held her hands out from her body and stared at them in shock. They trembled before her. Red welts had formed where the plate had touched her skin. The hob was glowing. She ran to the sink and let the cold water go over them. The skin blistered angrily under the running stream. She could never remember if it was cold or hot water that was meant to go on a burn.

He looked at her fleetingly, a child caught in an act of wrongdoing. When she caught his glance, he looked away.

'You did that on purpose.'

She was doing everything in her power not to cry.

'I didn't do it,' he said. 'You ought to be more careful.'

'You did. The ring was on.'

'Oh, was it?' He turned it off. 'I forgot.'

'Mum my hands hurt.'

Her eyes began to water. She cursed them.

Sandra had been hovering at the bit between the garden and the back door. Then she came slowly to her. Rosie winced at her touch. The damage was obvious, too obvious to be explained away or ignored. Sandra turned and looked him. She did not blink but glared, the stare was absolute. She guided Rosie into the hallway. Broken bits of plate lay scattered on the floor before them. Sandra kicked a rogue piece away. It shattered against the wall near the oven, close to where he stood.

'Where are you going?' he said, turning.

Sandra grabbed coats and keys and pushed Rosie out the front door and shut it behind the two of them without a word.

Rosie eased into the little red car that was Sandra's own, a small and insignificant thing next to the one he drove. Sandra was somewhere else entirely. She had a far-sighted focus that Rosie had never seen in her. With mercenary efficiency she slotted the keys into the ignition and started the engine. She reversed out of the driveway instantly and at full speed. The front door opened and he came towards them, still in oven gloves with a tea towel over one shoulder and a greasy spatula in one hand.

'Where in the God's earth do you think you're going?'

And though he did not raise his voice out of doors, the threat in his words was clear. But Sandra was stopping for nothing and no-one and flew away leaving him in the doorway.

'The dinner's fucking ready!' he called.

Where were they going? Rosie thought better of asking. Her hands throbbed in her lap and felt twice their usual size. Her stomach grumbled. They drove on. The fields were swallowed by more and more houses and the towns moved closer together. After a time, Sandra stopped at a long row of houses and shops that stood opposite the sea. A chipper's bright lights slunk in the car windows. She left the motor running and disappeared inside. She came back to the car soon after bearing two grubby steaming packages. It was too hot to taste and singed the roof of Rosie's mouth.

'The car will stink of vinegar, but so bloody what,' Sandra said, and she thought about smiling.

She spun the car around and parked up at the promenade so they could look at the sea, which was in a rough mood. The waves toppled over one another, pushing and heaving each other out of the way in their desperation to reach the shore. It gave Rosie a strange sense of déjà vu.

When they were full, Rosie took the empty papers and braved the wind and rain to throw them in the nearest bin. She lingered a while out in the crisp air, the sea spray spitting at her from below. She offered her scorched palms out to it, it offered relief in turn. She licked her lips and they tasted of salt.

'Come on now. You'll get wet,' her mother called.

She got back in. Sandra turned the key and they were off.

They were driving fast, nowhere in particular. The rain swelled. It battered down on the roof, on the windows. They drove around for what could have been hours. The rain did not ease. Where would they sleep?

'Are we calling into Granny?' Rosie asked.

'No.'

Rosie knew Sandra would not go to her mother's now. Not again. Especially not since

Rosie didn't want her worrying about them again, anyway. She wasn't as strong these days. She, too, like the skin around Sandra's eyes and mouth and her father's disembodied voice, had aged. The Thing That Happened Next had taken it out of her. And she was getting on. They all were. Rosie was a woman now. Once a month black tar filled her knickers and beneath her jumper two alien mounds were beginning to form.

Eventually, Sandra gave in and turned the car around.

'When we get in, go straight to bed, ok?' she said.

Rosie pretended not to hear.

The house was a closed door when they arrived back. It seemed to suck them towards it. Sandra put the key in the lock and turned it gently. Inside, there was nothing there, no one. He must have cooled off, forgotten about it all, gone asleep. Perhaps he had even realised his mistake. It would all look better in the morning.

The sitting room door opened and a dim light cast them into half shadow.

'Did you have a nice time? '

He had waited up, was smiling broadly. It gave Rosie chills to see his teeth shining through the darkened hallway.

'It's very late isn't it?'

The bright joyful voice was all wrong on him. Rosie started to feel sick.

'Well you must be tired Rosie.'

'I'm not.'

'Nonsense. You should get to bed or you'll have no energy tomorrow for what's his name, Paul –'

'Peter.'

'Exactly.'

She found herself encircled around her mother's waist and was holding tight, the way a small child clings to their parent's leg. But she was already past her shoulder in height.

'Off you go now. Let your mother come and talk to me in here.'

She could not let go. She would stay there all night if she had to. She saw that his patience was wearing out, she could not give up ground. Then Sandra took Rosie's hands and released them.

'Yes you must be tired darling.'

She kissed her on the forehead and gave her a little push to send her on her way. Calm radiated out. She smiled tenderly as she turned to follow him through the door.

'Night night. Sleep Tight. Don't let the bedbugs –'

The door shut behind her and swallowed her up. She was gone. Rosie stood for some time stranded in the hall, a strange hunger coming over her though the fish and chips lay heavy in her stomach. After a time, she went to her room. She lay down on the bed and put her burnt hands over her ears. It was long after the embers died in the hearth that sleep finally came.

Twenty-nine (a)

She did not move. She did not breathe. She was grey. She opened her mouth to say the word, but it would not come out. It was stuck in her throat.

But a third person was in the room - the cave - he ate up the light from above. Matted straw dressed as human hair, wreathed in a red, evil light. The mouth opened. Razors framed a tongue instead of teeth. The mouth opened wide, the grey tongue shook, wretched. And then it came pouring out. The vomit. A red river of it. And he stood over her, her mother, heaved over her and she was grey and did not move, and then he would come for her too.

She opened her mouth to scream but she could not. She could not breathe. She could not wake but she was awake for she could not be asleep. Her lips were parted but silent and though her lips were silent a question lay upon them and that question was: *why*.

Thirty

There was an elephant in the room and it was Rosie's breasts. They could no longer be ignored. They just kept on growing. Rosie worried they were inhibiting her breath. At breakfast one morning, after he had left, Sandra finally addressed the issue.

'Honey I'm sorry but they're actually almost indecent to look at. I'm afraid it's time.'

'Time for what?'

'To get you fitted up.'

They made a day of it. Sandra drove the little red car into the city centre. They sung along to the radio together and their singing and the makeup Sandra wore was almost clever enough to hide everything else. They parked up and Rosie followed her mother's echoing footsteps towards a small shop off the main street.

Only ladies worked there. It felt like a secret. Rosie ran her fingers through the hidden things, shaped and soft to the touch, festooned with boning and strings and ribbons and lace.

'Your first is it?' said the lady in the shop.

'It is,' Sandra said, looking at her daughter from the feet to the hair as though trying to memorise her.

'And Jesus, the size of them already - I suppose you didn't want to accept it did you?'

'I suppose I didn't.'

'I was the same with my two. Sometimes I wish I had been blessed with boys. They're far less hassle.'

Sandra nodded. Rosie pretended not to notice.

'Well you,' the lady said to Rosie. 'Come here 'til we size you up.'

She was led into a small changing room with a mirror, behind a curtain.

'Take your things off for me love,' said the lady.

Rosie took off her jumper and the vest beneath.

'Well you didn't get them from your mother that's for sure,' the lady muttered. She unravelled a measuring tape and circled it around the hot spots of Rosie's body. It all seemed very complicated, but the lady seemed to know what she was doing.

After Rosie had dressed, she was led out to a selection that was thought would suit her taste. It was very pink. It felt wrong. She turned away from it, instead choosing something plain and white. A new beginning. A pale silk ribbon between the cups its only adornment. Perfect. When she came out of the changing room, Sandra almost cried.

'Oh you look gorgeous,' she said. 'They're even bigger than I thought.'

'She's already a C you know,' the lady said, with a deep sharp breath as though she was trying to avoid drowning.

Sandra's mouth dropped open in shock.

'How old are you love?' the lady asked.

'Nearly twelve.'

'Jesus Christ.'

Sandra and the lady shared a private look.

'She's starting secondary school this September,' Sandra said darkly.

'Is she? Jesus. Well. I hope she has a big strong Daddy to look after her.'

Rosie and Sandra went silent, their heads went in opposite directions. The mischief on the lady's face fell away and coolness crept into her voice.

'Here, I'll help you out of it now if you're happy,' she said.

When Rosie was back in her own clothes again Sandra passed her the money and let her pay. Rosie watched as the lady wrapped her choice in crinkling paper and tied more ribbon around it in a neat interlacing pattern. She took the bag with reverence and left the shop with her mother feeling at last her equal.

They went for coffee after. Sandra chose for them a famous old-fashioned place where everything was made out of wood and gold and the coppery surfaces gleamed, just like in her grandmother's house. Rosie ordered a Cafe au Lait because it sounded nice, but spent the drinking of it with gritted teeth. It was awful. Sandra laughed as she enjoyed her normal cup of tea.

It had been a wonderful day. Just her mother and her, the way it used to be, before. Rosie wished she could make her coffee stretch on for hours. She would have drunk a bucket of it if it meant they could stay. In the car on the way home the music played and she watched the trees sprinting past, counting counting.

It was dinnertime when they arrived back. Steak again. The smell of it wafted down the hall to greet them, along with Dog. As soon as they were in the door Rosie went straight to her room to try it on for real.

She unwrapped it taking care not to rip the paper, living with her grandmother through Christmases and birthdays had instilled in her the virtues of thrift. Out it came, satin-sheen and brilliant, with the matching pants. She slipped off her clothes and put on her new things, remembering the easy way she had been taught in the shop to fasten the bra. She looked at herself in the mirror. She felt beautiful. She pulled back on her jeans and shirt, leaving one extra button undone at the chest.

She followed the smell of dinner into the kitchen. Sandra and Mr. – were already seated. He looked up as Rosie walked in. Sandra stared down at her plate. The dinner was served before them, untouched. The chair at the third place setting was empty. Sandra's hands were in her lap, pressed together as if in prayer.

'Do you enjoy making us wait?' he asked as she took her seat.

'Sorry. I was just –'

'Never mind. It's going cold.'

Knives and forks were seized. Sandra was eating at breakneck speed. Rosie watched her and pushed the vegetables around her plate. After all the excitement of the day she found she had no desire for food. He watched her. Rosie felt his growing impatience like a cloud pressing around her. She looked at the food. Three lumps, three colours. She sliced the knife through the slab of beef. It cut through easily, like butter left out overnight. She put the piece in her mouth. It tasted like warm blood. She tried to chew but was aware of the bit of flesh revolving as her tongue and teeth moved. She could be eating a piece of herself. She would have to get rid of it, but how without being seen?

'Something wrong with your steak?'

He had marked her.

Rosie felt the meat on her tongue, an obstinate mass. But his eyes were on her. She forced herself to swallow. The meat slid down her throat. She arranged the food on her plate to look eaten. It piled up on the outside like piecrust.

'I'm finished.'

She rose and took the other plates, piling them quickly on top of her uneaten one. She put them on the counter top and scraped the rinds of fat and leftover potato off each one into Dog's bowl. She put them in the sink and let the hot water run over them. There were eyes everywhere. She felt them burning into her back as the muscles of her shoulders worked beneath her shirt.

Sandra coughed gently. She heard the scratching of a match being lit, the burst of the flame lighting. A deep inhale. Pause. Long exhale. Smoke gathered under the light bulb.

'Outside Sandra for God's sake,' he snapped. 'Have I to remind you of your own daughter's lungs?'

Rosie felt her mother pass behind her and go out the back. She scrubbed the dishes furiously. She stacked them up on the counter. The water streaked its way into the sinkhole. She unplugged the sink and turned to make her excuses, but he was standing in the doorway watching her. Sandra's back was to the window. She was staring out into the navy night, seeing nothing, her smoking breath escaping in dense intestinal folds.

Rosie would just ask him to step aside. It would be easy. But when she approached, he stood his ground. Behind her Sandra could have been carved in ice. Rosie tried to push past but he resisted.

'Excuse me,' she said, her eyes on his shoes. They were gleaming as always.

With one hand he guided her face upwards by the chin so she had no choice but to look at him. His irises - had she ever seen them so closely? - were a strange yellow colour. And even the whites of his eyes were not white, but straw, like the hair on his face and head.

'What is it?' he said.

'What?'

She wished she could just find it in herself to push past through the door.

'What is what?' she asked.

'Something's different.'

His eyes went all over her. They saw everything.

'I'm tired. I want to go to bed,' she said.

She looked down the long dark of the hallway. Her bedroom was so close and yet not at all close enough.

'I know what it is,' he said. 'You're getting fat.'

Sandra's sharp intake of breath behind her turned into a phlegmatic cough. Rosie felt heat spreading over her cheeks. She had to leave the room, but her feet were stuck to the linoleum with superglue.

His one hand freed her face and it joined the other as both hands moved to her shirt buttons. They shook slightly as they reached the opening at her chest. Her breath caught in her throat with a stab. The kitchen had never before been so quiet. Even the clock held its ticking. His fingers caught both lapels and held them, his tips barely brushing off the silken underwear. He exhaled. Rosie smelt the meatiness on his breath.

He refastened the buttons, slowly, up to her neck collar. Each time the button went through the slit, his skin caressed hers. Her lips were together tight like a purse clasp.

'Cover yourself up,' he said.

His hands fell \away. He brushed past her, walked to the sink. Water gushed out from the nozzle and contained itself in a glass, the vowel sound changing from broad to slender. He gulped loudly as he drank. Sandra remained in stone at the window. Her cigarette had drawn down to the butt. All was ash. A gust came and dispersed it, littering her shoulder with a fine, grey powder. Rosie stood and looked at her for some time but she didn't turn. He stayed hunched over the sink. Rosie left the room.

Back in her bedroom, she undid the shirt buttons. She pulled off her jeans. The underwear looked grey in the cold dull light. She ripped it off and threw it into a pile in the corner. She put on her soft flannel pyjamas. They had pictures of stars and moons on them. She lay down on the bed, but couldn't get comfortable. Something pricked at her side. She felt under her cotton shirt and her hand fell upon a small, boned thing. She pulled it out and observed it quietly. It was a black feather.

Rosie got up and went to the door. She listened at it for a moment, but heard no sound from the other side. She turned the key in the lock and waited for the click. She tried the handle. The door was shut fast. She took the key and lay back on the bed, kicking the duvet over her body.

She turned on her side and drew her knees into her stomach, forming a small ball. She slid the key under her pillow and kept her hand clamped shut around it. It didn't take long for the cool metal to warm in her palm.

Once it did, she closed her eyes.

Thirty (a)

'Come and find me again,' he said.

'But how will I?' she asked. 'I never know where you'll be.'

'You know,' he said, and he pointed a feathered arm at her chest: 'You know in here.'

Thirty-one

'Rosie!'

Clear as the ringing of bells the voice that called her name acted like a summoning and she followed it through her bedroom door. The hallway was pitch black, the stillness absolute. She tiptoed down the hallway and came to rest at the ancient wooden staircase. It twisted and curved out of sight. Only the gleaming gilded frame of the portrait on the upper landing lit the way upwards. The way appeared to her infinite.

'Rosie. Ro. Sie.'

The image separated and recombined and stretched out of all possibility. She blinked, and when she opened her eyes again she found herself shrunken impossibly to the height of a mouse. To the height of something that hides behind sofas and scurries across floors and makes elephants and grown men fear for their lives. The steps towered above her. A winged yellow-eyed creature flew· overhead, and she pressed herself against the step hoping it could not see her, would not swoop down and snatch. There was this awful wailing sound: a continuous wavering note coming from beyond the top of the stairs where she could not go. Even if she reached into the very limits of herself she would not even touch the lip of that first step, and there were hundreds upon thousands to climb.

'Why won't you help me?' the voice called.

'I am sorry,' Rosie cried out, and though her mouth moved nothing came out.

'You should have helped me.'

'You should have helped her.'

'Why won't you help me?'

'Help her. Help her!'

But what use was she and her the size of nothing with that cruel-beaked thing patrolling the ceiling? The foundations beneath the floorboards trembled beneath her and the walls shook with mocking laughter. They mushroomed around her and lifted up into the night. Rosie stood, alone, under the apex of what was now an enormous cathedral. She was insignificant as a bit of dust. The sky is falling, the chicken said. The sky was falling in. A new voice shook the ground beneath. A warm rolling sound that held her in its grasp.

'You're so far away. Come here. Come here to me.'

'But I am so small,' said Rosie. 'And the stairs are so high and so many.'

A dash of light - a gem-bright spark danced from wall to wall, little more than air. But she could not see how such delicacy could travel or what anatomy it was bound to for she could not see her own nose.

Time is running out.

A gentle clicking stood beside her, like a friend. But now everything was too loud and the ringing of clocks shook the walls and she put her hands over her ears and they were twice the size of her head and did not block the sound. Time was running out, but she was stuck in the ridge between the floor and first step where the dirt collected. The man at the top of stairs swelled in his portrait. His neck strained against the canvas. He was laughing, his teeth chattering in the dark.

Then - a voice that offered comfort, but that she knew not to trust:

'I will lift you up. Remember, I have wings enough to fly across an ocean.'

And then she was in the air, in the clutches of some powerful flying beast. The claws clung to her shoulders and her feet dangled giddily beneath her. The drop was far, and she felt safe. They rose up to the ceiling and were suspended there, tempting the yawning mouths and yellow eyes beneath. Up the staircase they flew. The portrait snapped at her ankles, missed. As they reached the top, she felt herself lengthen. Her feet stretched away from her hips and her arms grew long. She was herself again.

She was back on her feet, full-grown. All had settled around her. The portrait was flat and lifeless. The staircase an average length and height. No creature held her at the shoulders, she was alone. In her hand was a single black feather. She slipped it in her pocket.

A weak beam of light ran around the doorframe. Voices could be heard, a dry sob. She advanced toward them. A familiar, dragging sound dogged her footsteps. The patient came to life again, roused by her scent. Her gaze did not waver. She did not look left or right.

She pushed open the door and there, on the bed, lay her mother. Her dress was up around her waist and beneath she was naked. Her shoulders fell out of her sleeves. She was pale, her neck was bruised. She was very still. He lay astride her and obscured her face, sucking on her neck and jigging up and down in a fit. His trousers fell to his ankles. His yellow socks, bobbling now, stood up to mid-calf ahead of his belt. It was all wrong.

'No.'

She spoke only for herself, as though a screen divided the room and what passed before her existed somewhere else, no more substance than what was played out on a stage. The boards shook beneath her and Rosie felt the power transfer through her feet. It burned through her ankles and up her shins, it slopped into the bowl of her pelvis and shot along the curve of her spine into her throat, it filled her head and surged out of her mouth in a long piercing scream. She had his attention then. In the scramble to cover up he fell from the bed. His thing stood out from his hips like an injury: inflamed, purpled, gasping for air. It was an alien thing, sewn on and pointless, with a shiny film of moisture anointing the rosy tip. It drew her eyes and she could not look away. How it challenged her for so small a thing.

'I didn't do it,' he said.

The words were repeated as her mother lay still, her face turned to the wall, her skin ashen and her eyes seeping blood. The bed sheets were badly stained. They would need a good soak. Marie would not be happy.

234

'I didn't do it,' he said.

'Then who did?'

'You did. You should have helped her.'

And something was in her hand. A little thing. A toy. It lay like a dead weight in her palm. A small black bird. The Raven. Its sharp beak stung her palm. It was not The Raven's beak, but a razor. Just there, no physics for it: just there. It cut into her. A thin red line was drawn as though by a pencil. Images flashed before her at speed: a single red head staring out a window in an empty room; a woman watching a door; a wall on fire; plates vaulting through the air defying gravity; the thousand glittering eyes of a dark creature; night-ghosts with sharp nails and probing hands; a beeping phone; a rattling doorknob and whispered, obscene words.

'Rosie help me.'

Sandra was grey. She did not move. She was herself and she was Rosie and she was someone else entirely.

And the feathered face of the Raven appeared, fully grown at last, large and black in the shape of a man with brilliant blue eyes. The voice that had spoken to her for so long was united with form and substance, after all that time. How long had it been?

'It's been too long,' he said.

Black feathers fell from the ceiling like snowflakes, blocking out the light. The razor glinted in her hand.

'Do it Rosie. Do it now. Then come back to me, across the sea.'

And he stood babbling in the corner, a shock of matted straw for hair and razors for teeth, a red wet worm in his hand, his trousers still undone. And Rosie was charging at him like a madness and he hadn't time to draw breath before the sting hit his side. But once was not enough. It was repeated again in his neck, again in the stomach, and lastly, in the heart.

Thirty-two

The sun rose and filled the room with blinding light.

Rosie was first to stir. The room stank. The blood had crusted and congealed, the whole place was a sight. And his body was there still. It lay on the carpet, shrunken and stiff as frozen hands. It had not miraculously disappeared in the night as she had hoped. It would have to be moved.

Rosie gave her mother a shake. There were things to be done. Sandra blinked and rolled around to her smiling. Then her face fell into horror as time caught up. The body came into her sight and she hid her face behind her hands as though it could reshape the facts, reanimate blood and bone.

'I'll go wash,' she whispered.

She slid off the bed. The body was seen through and past. Her eyes danced beyond to the bright day outside the window.

'It's beautiful out.'

'It is,' said Rosie.

'Great drying weather.'

Rosie stared at her mother. Sandra's silent back did not respond. Then she turned away from the sunlight and her face was grey again.

'But what are we to do?'

'I don't know.'

'What have you done?'

Sandra watched her with sadness and left the room, moving slowly. She was still unsteady on her feet.

'I did it for you,' Rosie said, but Sandra had already left.

The immersion went on. Rosie stripped the bed. As she turned to leave the room, a change in the normal lie of things was observed. A new portrait hung on the wall above his heavy head. The face within was not bold enough to move but his smiling lips said plainly, *I have seen it all.* Rosie gathered up the soiled sheets in her arms and observed the shallow impression her feet made in the carpet. She left the room. A

236

naked patch of wall now existed at the top of the staircase as though it had been scrubbed clean.

She brought the pile downstairs. She shoved it into the washing machine and added her soiled bits to the mix. She stood in her own skin while she piled an amount of powder into the drawer and pressed one of the many buttons and nozzles at random. She hoped she was doing it right.

Dog was whining at the back door to get out. She opened it. Peter was standing there with his arm raised, about to knock. She was about to invite him when she realised she was naked. She shut the door.

'Just a minute!'

She crawled along the kitchen floor under the window and prayed she could not be seen. She found a clean towel in the utility room and secured it and opened the door. There was nobody there. Dog streaked past her shins again and settled under the kitchen table, spooked. From what? The front doorbell rang. Rosie recoiled from its clear command, afraid that its sudden vigour could raise more than the sleeping dust. She answered the door quickly.

He could hardly look at her clad only in the towel and stole glances from the safety of his fringe.

'Can I come in?' he asked.

'You could have just knocked.'

'I'm sorry.'

'It's alright. Come in then.'

'Did I wake anyone?'

Rosie turned away from the question and knelt to pat Dog. She whined softly as she licked the congealed matter from Rosie's open palms.

'What is that on your hands?'

Peter faltered before her as her own mother had. She could think of no falsehood, no safe little lie, to fill the silence. A nosebleed or a tumble down the stairs, perhaps. These things happened, didn't they? Accidents always happened. She was

237

sure he would believe whatever she chose to tell him, but could she risk being branded a liar when the truth came spilling out?

'I have to show you something,' she said.

He lay in the same position. Some part of her had believed wildly that he might walk again, or somehow have moved in her absence. He was resolutely dead. There he lay: flat, eyes wide, mouth parted, with the edge of the blade sticking out iceberg-like above the surface of his skin. She had readjusted his trousers. Its absence drew her the more and she wondered if it turned into the same heavy thud as the rest of the body when it died. It had seemed so separate, something that could easily be snipped off and freed. She wondered if it released itself after death and ran away to live its own life, a self-governing body no longer subject to the whims and commands of its owner.

'You're going to have to get a new carpet,' Peter said.

He had taken it all in his stride. The killing the most natural act. He moved past her to examine the corpse and his fingers brushed lightly against her own. He crouched at the head and began an examination. His magnifying glass had appeared beside him.

'Did these feathers come from inside the pillows?' he asked.

'Rosie?'

Sandra was calling from the bathroom.

She was still pale, her eyes shot through and veiny, turned inside out. She held the door ajar as though shielding herself from a sudden attack.

'Could you get me some things? I don't want to go back in there.'

Rosie went back to the wardrobe, watching the image of Peter crouched over what appeared to be a gaping wound slide away as she moved the mirrored door across. She took some clothes and layered them on top of one another on her arm. She herself had not washed.

'I'm going to get clean.'

'Sure,' Peter replied, not looking up.

'Please don't scare my mother.'

'Ok.'

'I'll be down in the kitchen in a few minutes.'

'Ok.'

She passed by him and he briefly took her hand in his. His hand was warm, hers cold like rubber. She looked down at him. He was already back at work, deep in experiment.

The bath was warm, viscous as honey. The water ran pink. She scrubbed her hands, arms and face, and shampooed, repeating three times. She dug her nails into her scalp. The sponge touched every inch of skin. She unplugged the stopper and stepped out weak, as though part of her had been sucked down the plughole along with the dirty water. She dried herself, dressed and went downstairs.

Peter and Sandra were already at the table, as though it was any day. Peter was scribbling. Sandra had her hands curled around a mug of tea.

'You're up,' she said.

'Yes I'm ...' Rosie began.

'Did you sleep well?'

Rosie just looked at her. The cup she was holding would break if it was held any tighter. Dog's head lay on Sandra's lap, her muzzle soaked in blood. Sandra stroked her absentmindedly. Rosie took a seat. She was about to speak, but Peter was first.

'We have to call the police,' he said.

It was said with an impractical simplicity, as though life could be marked by colour and numbers.

'You've decided that.'

'Yes. It's the best thing to do for everyone.'

'Is it?'

'Yes. It's the right thing.'

'Is that so,' Rosie snapped.

'Don't fight - I can't stand any more fighting,' Sandra moaned, tracing the outline of her face with her fingertips.

'I'm trying to help you,' said Peter.

'You are?'

'But why didn't you help me?' Sandra cried.

Dog began to growl.

'Yes, Rosie. Why didn't you help her?'

As one, they turned to her. Their eyes held a sudden savageness. Dog barked ferociously and snapped at her heels. She fell back to the floor, her chair clattering behind her. The milk jug rocked, disturbed, and a slop of milk spilled over the edge. It snaked in a straight line to the wooden surface of the table, where it pooled around the base. It all happened so curiously slowly. Rosie scrambled to her feet and ran to the door, but found it shut. The three advanced on her and she was sure to be eaten alive, ripped asunder by those she loved. Just as their hands, anointed with sharp nails like little teeth, were close enough to take her, the door unlocked, and she was away.

Her feet led her. The long grass rustled, disturbed by her running thighs. She climbed the backyard wall. It was the only way out. The climb was not hard. She landed easily on the other side. She crawled through the dirt on her hands and knees. There she took refuge, returned to the quiet of that forgotten graveyard. There she sat and wept. Centipedes and woodlice surfaced in the earth, disturbed by the strange presence on their territory. Innumerable spiders ran up the tree bark. They watched her, scouring the terrain of her face. Rosie sat and still she wept.

She had blood on her hands. Her skin stank: the meaty smell of it. She was a common butcher, she was full of slaughter, an evil thing. She had taken a life and she was to be cast out. They would send her to jail. She would be stuck behind the bars, the iron cage with food like slop out of a can and going in her cell in the corner like a beast and she deserved no better, for to be a murderer, to kill, one must first be a monster and that's what she was. She knew it now. To be stuck inside her skin was the most awful curse, the most perfect punishment. She raked her nails down the naked skin of her arms and watched the thin red stripes appear, stippled with little bloodspots like money spiders, those little legged dots. They were all over her on every scrap of skin. Oh! To shake off her skin and walk away!

Shake it off Rosie. Wake up.

But what was done was done. The pain of the knowledge - oh, to erase the past, to be washed clean, sanctified and holy!

'Give me peace!' she cried out to the sky.

'Only with death does that come. The long, dreamless sleep,' the voice replied.

'Is that all there is?'

Life was time spent trying to remember the best of it, but failing and forget the worst of it, yet failing still and then, there was death. Murderous wasps and murderous girls: was there a difference? Death did not judge. Rosie had always been a killer. A wasp and a grown man were not so different.

'Come out, come out wherever you are.'

Rosie retreated further into the nook behind the tree and drew herself into a knot.

You're going to have to come back eventually my dear.

'Not after what I've done.'

And what did you do?

'You know.'

I do?

'We killed him!'

Time passed, who could tell how much. All clocks had stopped in the forgotten graveyard.

'We?' the voice asked: 'I, who have no form?'

But he was before her, the bird. The black feathered Raven with the body of a man sitting atop a blank-faced tombstone.

'Even you don't know if I truly exist. You said it yourself, inside your head. I heard it.'

'What are you?'

Rosie needed something: reason, explanations, meaning. Anything.

A silver pin came out from behind The Raven's ear like a magic trick. It hovered in the air and gleamed. It pierced the corner of his beak with savage precision. It disappeared inside his mouth, the glittering tip returned, poked through again. Over and back it weaved through the upper and lower parts of the beak and drew them together, a scarecrow's mouth. Meaning was close.

And then her father stood before her in the bird's place featherless, his mouth sewn up, his gaze strong. The man she longed for, the man she dreamed of, the man she wished she could piece together and fix with sellotape and glue. And then, he could speak. He was whole.

'I am everything you've ever wanted me to be.'

He spread his wings wide and beckoned her close. It felt good: warm water on gooseflesh, silk against a burn, a drink of water on a rough day. He was man, he was bird, he was all. He wrapped his feathered arms about her. Such closeness she had never known. She was folded into the smell of him and it was a thing she would remember always. She breathed deep and felt strength return to her. Very lightly, it began to rain, a soft summer fall. His voice was warm and rolling and thrilled like the first warning of thunder.

'You know what you must do,' he said.

Thirty-three

It was time to go home. Rosie climbed back up the wall. At the top, she looked back. He was gone. Again. It was a sensation she would never grow used to. But there were things to be done and no time for tears. In that moment of longing for him she lost her handling. Her balance went, she grasped at twigs, but it was no use. Before she could stop herself, she was falling.

She hit the ground. She sat up gasping with fright, but she wasn't hurt. The ground, soft with rain, had broken her fall. It was strangely unreal, surrounded by all that grass. No one had ever gotten around to cutting it. How it shot up in the summer, shimmering around her in fine green spears. She felt dog tired. She lay there hidden, her backside damp against the doughy earth. But there was something to be done.

She entered through the back door. She was wet with the fine rain, the worst kind for getting soaked through. Muddy footsteps followed her as though her shadow had form. She would have to change her clothes before she left.

Through a crack in the dining room door she watched them. They were as she had left them. More teacups littered the table top. Dog had curled up by the stove. It was midsummer, and it was bright, but the rain had brought with it a peculiarly cool breeze that ran through her and ruffled the hair on her mother's head. She shrunk back from the gap in the door.

It was just as though someone had died. It was that empty time upon hearing the news of a passing when hours glide by and the mind is full of thought, full of the whys and whats and hows. There was no real action. The making of tea, perhaps the preparation of a sandwich, anything to keep one busy for only in activity can life be real. *I am alive*, thought Rosie. Through her mother and the bond that bound them, she was filling the kettle, taking out the cups. She heard them clink. She cut through the butter, its yielding yellowness. She took a corner, spread it on a slice, watched it melt and sink. The water came to boil, the steam burned her skin and she knew she was not lifeless. She felt the cool water from the tap caress the burn and there was a sort of pride in it.

In those moments, watching from the crack in the door, the absurdity of life was grasped, however fleetingly. The survivors pushed themselves into industry to prove they were worth life. Death had made a claim and the living felt his presence. He was hidden, near, watching for a weakening spirit and all were on their best behaviour. But it was different for Rosie. Death had not chosen her. She had chosen it. She had killed another. Would it enslave her as it did those who once they had tasted such power could not stop? She had taken another, and still she lived. She was invincible, and that invulnerability was the most moreish drug, the most fatal dose. She had got a taste for it on the playground. The first killing of the wasp had been painful, the second had brought relief. Would the next bring pleasure?

She would not go to them, the living. Sandra was at the counter making breakfast as if it was any other day. Peter was quietly drinking his tea and Dog was lying sideways on the floor beside the stove. It was all so wonderfully mundane. Rosie had no part in it anymore. What business had murderers with eating breakfast and sitting at tables? She had turned her back on life, and such normalcy would always be tainted with the unnatural act she had committed. Sandra, Peter, Dog. How she loved them in their innocence. They did not deserve to be involved. It had been her choice.

They had not yet seen her. She took care to be quiet. She walked through the dining room, into the living room and through to the hall where the table was. And the telephone.

She picked it up. The bell rang faintly when she lifted it off the hook. The clattering from the kitchen masked it. She dialled the numbers. They were simple, readily remembered. She did not need to get out the phonebook. Only two rings before they answered.

'I want to report a murder,' she said.

Any moment now the doorbell would ring, and it would be them, come for her. She had given herself up, surely that would count for something? She did not want to go to jail. She wasn't even thirteen. She would be going to secondary school after the summer. She and Peter had convinced their parents to send them to a mixed school so they could be in the same one. It would have been nice. They said they would cycle together there and back, take classes together, sit beside one another writing notes. That was a thing to fight for if anything. She did not know what would happen now.

They would come and take her into questioning, that much she knew from watching the television. Then, there was no other thing for it, she would be put away. The body lay up there cold and stiff, waiting to be discovered. She had told them all. She couldn't go back on her word.

What if Peter forgot her and tired of waiting? Was one kiss under the lamp post one time never again talked about enough to hold him? That was what was said about men. They lost interest. She'd heard her mother talking about it with Jennifer, with Marie, on the phone to faceless others with names she couldn't remember. Men were fickle, they needed variety. Her father had been like that. She'd heard Mrs. No. 4 and 5 say he liked them easy from behind the settee. It was one of those memories that had stuck in her mind resisting the erosive power of time. But he was also waiting out there, in the graveyard, for her. Perhaps he would wait for her however long it took.

Who would look after Dog? Rosie was the only one who did. How could life go on in the house without her? But she must go. She had called. She had been brave. She had done the right thing. It would be better for all this way.

The doorbell rang and Rosie felt her stomach leap, the way it did when she drove over ramps with her mother in the little red car. This was it. She left her bedroom and walked down the hall.

'You're finally with us,' Sandra said as she walked out from the kitchen.

They stopped, facing one another in front of the door. Marbled shadows warped and shifted in the glass.

'Peter's here,' she said.

'I know,' Rosie replied.

Sandra looked at her with a squinted eye. She was on the point of speech when the doorbell went again.

'I'm coming!' she called.

The brightness was back in her cheeks. Tea had revived her. Peter appeared.

'Hi.'

He looked at her. He remembered it too. He looked down at his shoes. This could be the last time she ever saw him: the red-tipped ears, the wildly primitive hair that today was hiding the little patch of psoriasis, the thin cool lips. Could she kiss him goodbye in front of her mother? She hoped they allowed visitors where she was headed.

Sandra looked from her to Peter and back again. Peter was looking at her clothes.

'Why are you so wet?'

She had forgotten to change after the rain. The doorbell rang again. The knocking began.

'Where have you been?' he demanded.

'Open up. Police.'

Sandra and Peter's faces set in shock. Rosie could ignore this no longer, she had chosen. She opened the door.

'Miss Rosie Cotton?' The officer asked.

Rosie nodded. Peter and Sandra exchanged a swift, laden look.

'Come with us please.'

Thirty-four

They were remarkably prompt. On with the cufflinks and the speech. An image of her father came to her again through his shadow The Raven, who would not leave her side now. He had been with her all along in his way. He had grown wings and sprouted feathers to be close to her. And now she stepped into his outline as the cold metal tightened around her wrists. She was her father's daughter after all.

'This way please.'

'What is going on? Could someone please explain to me what the hell is going on?'

Rosie was led into the car while another officer removed his hat and stepped into the house firmly leading Sandra away. She had started to shout. Peter stayed in the driveway framed by the garage door. Rosie watched him diminish as the car drove out. His expression told her nothing.

The journey was silent, broken only by the static and unfathomable mumblings coming from the radio. The officers kept their eyes ahead. Not once did they swivel in curiosity or ask even the plainest of questions. At the station they opened the car door.

'Out you get now.'

They led her through the busy reception area where civilians sat and read magazines as though waiting for the dentist. Down brightly lit corridors they marched, down echoing stairs and yet more corridors. It was impossible to remember the way back out. Finally, they stopped. A plain black door was opened. Inside was a simple, sparsely furnished space. The door was closed. Rosie was instructed to take a seat. She sat. One of them, the older of the two, pressed play on a tape recorder and spoke.

'July the eighteenth, twelve thirty-one pm, Nineteen Eighty-Three. Gardas Fennel and Hague interviewing Rosie

Cotton of The Lodge, Shanvanagh Vale, Wicklow, aged twelve.'

'Twelve and a half,' Rosie corrected.

The officers' eyes met quickly before continuing.

'Aged twelve *and a half*,' he repeated. 'Miss Cotton called emergency services this morning to report a murder committed at the aforementioned address.'

He stopped there and took a breath. He reached into his pocket and took out a packet of cigarettes. Blue Lights. The same brand her mother pretended not to smoke.

'Do you mind?' he asked.

'I have asthma,' she said.

'I'll open a window so.'

He lit it up and inhaled deeply. He blew the smoke away from Rosie. The other officer stood up and cracked open a sticky frame. He sat down. He spoke.

'My name is Garda Fennel, Rosie. You don't mind me calling you by your first name, do you?'

She shook her head.

'Well, Rosie. At ten forty-five am this morning, emergency services received a call from you reporting a murder that took place in the early hours of this morning at your home. Do you remember making this call?'

'Yes,' she said.

'Do you remember the details of the call?'

'Yes.'

'What were they?'

'I said I want to report a murder.'

The Garda nodded.

'The lady on the phone said where and I told her. She asked when it happened, and I said last night, very late in the night. She asked me who was murdered and who did it and I told her it was Mr. - and that it was me. I killed him. And now he's dead. She asked me my name then and I told her that as well.'

Fennel looked down at his notes.

'You are responsible for the murder of your stepfather?' he said.

'Yes,' she replied stoutly. Then she smiled. The officers looked at one another again.

'Am I going to jail for a very long time?'

Garda Hague's mouth was poised to issue sound when there was a knock at the door.

'Come in,' he called.

Another officer opened the door. She was pale and her hair line had a slick of sweat running across it. She was slightly out of breath.

'I've been looking all over for you,' she gasped, hovering on the threshold. She caught Rosie's curious gaze and held it intently.

'Yes?' the man called Hague prompted.

The officer's body stiffened, and she was suddenly alert.

'Yes,' she replied. She glanced at Rosie quickly again. 'We have ... a problem.'

She jerked her head to indicate that the officers should follow her out. Hague placed his cigarette in the ashtray. They both stood. Hague restrained Fennel.

'Stay here,' he said.

The Garda cast back once more as Hague joined her. The door closed behind them. Her bright face was shut out.

The officer and the young girl sat quietly. Rosie drummed her fingernails on the table between them. The Garda folded his hands upon it and took a deep breath. Then quickly with his eyes on the door he stubbed out the still smoking cigarette with controlled violence.

'I hate it when he smokes in here,' he said.

'I have the same problem at home,' Rosie replied.

His face stood still. The door opened again, his hands disappeared under the table top.

Hague came through, his hand on the doorknob. The other officer floated behind and looked over his shoulder into the room. Red patches had flared up on her cheekbones.

'Well,' he said, looking directly at Rosie. 'I'm afraid we need to have a little change of scenery. This is Garda Coles,' he said indicating the officer behind him, who stepped forward on cue. 'She will go ahead with you, Miss Cotton, and we will follow.'

She beckoned her forward and Rosie went to her. The older Garda looked down at her sternly from under his bushy eyebrows and above his flabby paunch.

'On with you then,' he said.

Rosie fell into a quickstep with Garda Coles, who held her by the crook of the arm and sped her along. Where was she taking her? She had confessed, but surely it couldn't be over all that quickly? They must have thought her too monstrous to be worth a full interview. It was straight to jail with her and she hadn't even said goodbye to her mother. Or Peter. Not properly.

They jogged back up the concrete stairs. They passed uniformed men and women, some holding clipboards, some adjusting their hats or walking in and out of doors. Styrofoam cups were everywhere. There was a constant hum of chatter and activity. A phone was always ringing somewhere and every now and again a voice came through the loudspeakers. They passed through reception. She'd only been there minutes before. They walked out into the car park and stopped beside another car, as plain and unmemorable as the last.

She stooped into the back seat and Garda Coles started up the engine. Rosie laid her head back and closed her eyes. She really needed to sleep. She couldn't remember the last time she'd had a good rest. Her dreams had commanded her nights for so long.

'You look tired,' the Garda said. She had been watching her in the rear-view mirror. 'Are you tired?'

'Yes,' said Rosie. A hard yawn overcame her.

The Garda nodded once. She did not smile.

'You can rest soon,' she said.

The car jolted to a halt. Rosie's eyes snapped open; she'd been dozing. The light rain from earlier had gained weight and the windows had fogged. The driver's seat was empty. She was alone. She tried the door. It was locked. She was stuck. That familiar sense of déjà vu swept over her again, along with a wave of heat. She felt weak. Something rapped against the window. Then the door opened.

'We're here,' said Garda Coles.

Rosie wriggled out as best she could. The cuffs pinched at her wrists. She had forgotten she was wearing them.

'Sorry about these.'

Coles unlocked the cufflinks. Thin red lines encircled the skin where they had been. Rosie caressed the marks remembering others like them, their cousins. She looked up. She was ready to accept her fate.

They were back at her house.

'But,' she started, 'but ... I thought you were taking me to prison?'

Coles did not respond. She took her by the crook of the elbow again and led her up the driveway. There were more cars there: two white police cars and another, a long navy one she did not know.

Coles rang the bell. Garda Fennel, the policeman from the questioning room, answered it. How had they got there so quickly? His expression was unreadable as he looked from Rosie to Coles and back again.

'They're in there.' With his head he knocked towards the kitchen.

They walked down the hallway. The kitchen was very full. Sandra and Peter sat at the table. There were teacups, papers, tissues everywhere. They sat in the same chairs. They did not look up as she entered. Hague was there with them. His forearm was on the board and his hat was on his lap. He swelled as she entered. His face was red and sodden.

251

'Here she is,' he said.

He mopped at his brow with a handkerchief. The officer who had restrained Sandra earlier was there still, shadowing her behind her chair. He held his hat between clasped hands. Two other men were there that she did not know. One stood near the back door observing her quietly. She did not know him and yet he was familiar. The other was facing away from her with his head bowed by the sink. All the faces except this one turned toward her: expectant, waiting. It seemed as though the whole room was holding its breath. The clock was silent. Even the fridge did not hum.

Garda Hague cleared his throat and broke the silence.

'Do you ... know this person, Miss Cotton?' he asked, pointing with his hat at the man who faced away from her at the sink.

Peter caught her eye. The corners of his mouth turned up ever so slightly in the tiniest of smiles. She looked back toward the tall frame at the sink. Slowly and deliberately he turned to face her. It took just a split second for her to know him. Her knees went from under her and she fell sideways into Garda Coles, who caught her and held her in her arms. There he stood, flesh and blood and full of life.

Mr. - walked again.

(b)

'And five, four, three, two, one, and come back.'

Rosie opened her eyes. It took a moment for her to adjust to where she was. She gathered herself in. Previously hostile objects softened and became familiar again: the scuffed wooden desk with the dancing medicine balls, the groaning bookshelves, its excess stacked on the floor in towering piles, the very last of the afternoon's wintry sunlight coming through the shuttered windows, the steady nasal rhythm of Dr. Waters' breathing.

'Good progress today, Rosie. You barely left the couch.'

She discovered herself curled up on the carpet, wrapped around the corner of the sofa.

'Went nowhere near the window.'

Rosie shook her head gently and sat up knees folded under, hands on lap. She caught her breath and felt that odd shrinking sensation as she returned. Dr. Waters halted the swaying metronome and for a brief moment a deep, throbbing silence spread throughout the room. He took a full breath.

'Yes. Today. Yes, yes, yes,' he said. 'Well. Where do I start?'

Rosie waited. He observed her without expression and continued in low tones, as though speaking only for himself.

'Physicality almost wholly repressed, less verbal prolificacy. And your previous fixation on the raven/father symbol has lessened some. In fact, by your usual standards, it was all fairly mundane. Your glass doors seem to be mending.'

It was difficult to tell whether the latest developments depressed or pleased him. His enthusiasm for the symptoms of her condition - as it was now referred to - had become subdued. The months had passed since they'd first met in her kitchen. A new revelation on the couch would set his heartbeat off at a pace, reminiscent of those dewy first sessions in the psychiatric ward and the observation tests that followed. But for Rosie, mundanity was good news. It meant she could go home again, which, considering everything, was her best option now. She sat tight as he took the minutes and waited for the moment that she would be required to speak. The ticking clock kept her company. Dr. Waters pursed his lips as he pored over his notes.

'How have you been sleeping in the last week?'

'Fine.'

'No midnight wanderings?'

'None.'

'The drugs are doing their job.'

Rosie shrugged: 'Suppose.'

'So we won't have to take you back in?'

'I'm sleeping fine,' she urged.

Dr. Waters made a low noise in his throat. 'How are they making you feel at the moment?'

Rosie shrugged again. 'Stiff. I can't really even touch my toes any more. Tired, too.'

'Well you'll have to keep up your stretching. You've callisthenics at school, don't you?'

Rosie nodded. Dr. Waters smiled.

'Yes, yes, yes that all seems normal. Fatigue is usual with any sleep disorder. Your mother's got that electric heater in, I hope?'

'Yes.'

'And she's keeping you away from the matches still.'

Rosie gave a smart nod.

'I'm amazed it was only the once you did your mischief.'

'Yeah.'

'Because you're borderline there, too.' Rosie kept her face cold. 'But then you were a prisoner for a while.'

She didn't want to let her mind wander back that far. Not again.

'I'm always fascinated by the ways different families create normality out of anything but. It really is fascinating. But then again, what is normality?'

Rosie traced shapes on her knees. Letters. Letters that formed words. Dr. Waters watched her closely.

'Did you remember the diary?'

'It's in my bag.'

Shaking his hand, he commanded Rosie to retrieve it. She obliged.

'Thanking you.'

He skimmed through it, humming Mozart. Rosie was by now well acquainted with his taste in music and his theories on its rehabilitative power. A tape of his had taken the place of the ones she had made herself. She listened to it every night now, after she'd taken her medicine.

'No change, then?' he asked.

'None.'

'Good good. We're progressing nicely.'

He handed the diary back to her and she slid it into her bag.

'How is your stepfather?'

Rosie cringed briefly at the phrase.

'Still alive?' Dr. Waters allowed himself an indulgent chuckle. Rosie was unamused.

'Don't mind me.' He lifted his hands, a supplication. 'I forgot. You're at that age. My Timmy's the same. Can't say boo to a ghost. '

He cast his gaze out the window briefly, recalling something to mind. The light was failing fast. He switched on the desk lamp.

'You're getting along better? I am referring to your stepfather, naturally.'

Rosie looked down at her hands.

'Has the counselling group been improving things? Have you talked ... about anything?'

The tassels at the edge of the carpet beckoned. Rosie began plaiting them together in groups of three.

'Rosie,' he spoke her name gently. 'I've asked you before.'

Her hands returned to her lap.

'Good girl. So, tell me. Have you spoken about any of your issues?'

Rosie sighed. This was still her least favourite part.

'So the atmosphere hasn't been, shall we say, the most convivial?'

'Convivival?'

'Friendly.'

'Oh.'

'Well?'

'Granny's been staying over a lot. Mum was saying she might move in.'

'Is that so.'

He exhaled slowly, and it was clear he had tired of her evasiveness.

'Well it's not my area, but as I've said, if you're happy, we can make arrangements for him to come in with you some day. And Sandra. And even your grandmother if you like. It may help you all make sense of things a little more.'

Rosie turned her head and looked out the window.

'I can't force you to do anything, Rosie, I can only impress on you how beneficial to you all I believe it could be. Ok? You're in control here.'

Rosie swallowed loudly. Dr. Waters followed her gaze out the window. The sky had already darkened.

'How these evenings close in on us.'

He stood up and navigated the desk and the towers of books to get to the overhead light switch. The sudden brightness took the strain off Rosie's eyes. He returned to the desk.

'Well,' he said, clapping his hands together, 'if all you say is true, the medication seems to be working. We do not need to increase the dosage at this moment in time. I will have to discuss it with Sandra first, of course. Not that I don't trust you Rosie - but we all of us can fall into a trap when we are left to self-assess.'

'But –'

'Yes?'

'You said things were better.'

'That's right, and they are. But it is still very early days yet, cognitively speaking. Who knows, your body could develop immunity to the medication in the coming months and it will cease to work. You may relapse.'

He peered at Rosie over the rims of his glasses. She wondered why he wore them at all if he had no need of looking through them.

'This is all very new. The drugs themselves are relatively new. I don't need to tell you again that you're one of the very first documented cases of this in Ireland. You're a gift to us, but it will make your road to recovery that bit harder, I'm afraid. We're feeling our way through the dark with this.'

'But I never dream at all anymore.'

'Yes. That is an unfortunate side effect ... or perhaps, in your case, fortunate?'

He smiled, and it was meant with kindness.

'The medication is a necessary evil. You could be a danger to yourself and your loved ones if you don't continue with it. I'm amazed you've had so many lucky escapes - why it had to go as far as it did before your mother called me in is beyond me. But there you go now. She had her reasons, I know. The scrutiny of the world can be tough. Not everyone is as enlightened as you and I.'

He smiled benignly and presented an impartial façade propped up as a veil against his reproach. Rosie tried to think of another argument, but Dr. Waters was already absorbed in the musical symmetry of the row of medicine balls before him.

'Seen your bird friend in daylight at all recently?' he asked from behind the swing of their chiming dance.

Rosie lowered her head and picked at her nails.

'The odd feather every now and again. But I –'

'Yes?'

'I wish I could hold him again at night, just for a little while.'

257

'Ah.'

Dr. Waters looked down at his desk and his right hand strayed towards one of the drawers within it. Then he looked back at Rosie and his eyes were kind but stern.

'I'm afraid I can't give him back to you, Rosie, not yet.'

Rosie looked down at her nails, willed herself to hold it together.

'I don't believe you're ready for it,' he continued softly. 'It's better that I keep him, and we use him only to help you find a way in there.' He pointed at the space between her eyebrows. 'You need to find your own strength. No little crutch can ever compare to that.'

Rosie nodded bleakly. 'Ok,' she whispered.

'Good good,' he said, clearing his throat and hardening his tone. 'Well, you've come a long way in a relatively short stretch.'

It felt like a very long way indeed. Time had sped on for Rosie since those first tests, the earliest sessions, the first discovery. Hours had turned into days and weeks and months. A cold white room in a place filled with strangers became her new home. Time had filtered away and she had grown. She wore new clothes and new shoes now, a new bra. She had to wear one these days. It could not be avoided any longer. Without it, they hurt. The natural bouncing rhythm of a walk was agony. They were soft and malleable, Sandra had said, and she demanded the thing be worn lest they begin to droop. 'You'll regret it when you're older,' she'd said. 'With everything else going on the last thing you need is a saggy chest!' Simple actions became a nuisance. Every morning it seemed some new body part had swollen or shrunk or begun to perform abnormally. And all the while she was being quizzed and pressed and drawn out by the doctor and his team and she felt as exhausted and beaten as a wrung sponge. She was weighed down by the heaviness of her own insanity and her impossible cups. She felt she had become a character in her own life, a puppet without visible strings, bound by the commands of those around her. If ever she protested against being subjected to another test or a new round of medication or a particular style of clothing, she would be met with a wall of pained, stoical patience and the words: It's For The Best. And finally, after tests upon tests, months of observation and sessions of talking talking talking, it came. The diagnosis. REM behaviour disorder. A rare and unusual affliction only just coming to medical attention. That had been the first thing. If it had just been that alone it would have been almost bearable, but after further round-the-clock examination it was discovered that Rosie's case was more complicated still. Her condition had another dimension. The doors between her conscious, subconscious and unconscious appeared to never fully close. Her waking experiences spilled into her dreams and vice versa. And That. Explained. It. All.

'They are the invisible doors between the compartments of the mind –' Dr. Waters had said on the day of the discovery, '- or, as I like to see them, doors made of glass, for they are as fragile and easily broken. And in your case, you seem to have spent your life thus far crashing through them over and over again. There's a lot of broken glass in your psyche, my dear Rosie.'

When at last she was let out of the ward, each week became punctuated by the circular hour on the clock face and each day regulated by the circular unscrewing of a pill bottle lid. Circles ran her life and she was running in them. And almost every week there came a new discovery, a new connection, and a new layer of Rosie's reality was unceremoniously stripped away by the doctor's brilliance, leaving Rosie naked, unclothed, scrambling for modesty. She was no longer an almost thirteen-year-old girl with wants and feelings and desires of her own, she was an idea, a specimen, a lab rat, a vessel of others' thoughts, others with clipboards and biros and curiously interested frowns. And each time Dr. Waters took a deep breath she knew she must prepare to let go of some previously held truth of hers, things that most people -

she was just short of calling them 'normal' - took for granted as simple memories of the past, of a childhood once lived, always vague and indistinct but irrefutably theirs. Rosie was no longer in control of her memories. They were now the property of her doctor and by extension the medical community at large, all those immigrants who came to poke and assess, who lifted layers of her thought as though lifting the petticoats of an eighteenth-century whore. And she knew she ought to feel grateful for each revelatory moment. It was another door shut, more broken glass swept away. It brought her closer to a cure, closer to the end of the reedy shake of a thirty gram jar in her rucksack and the tyranny of the dream diary. Each day the same word after the same night: *fog*. But it had happened. She was what she was, and she had been found out. The clock could not be rewound. And she was there as usual on a Thursday afternoon in the office, talking about her.

'Yes, it has to be said that you are doing well. Very well indeed,' Dr. Waters repeated. 'But remember Rosie - always - *en garde*.'

Rosie looked up at the clock. The minute hand had come to rest at ten past.

'Let me hear you say it,' he prompted softly.

'En garde.'

'That's it.'

The doctor cleared his throat and removed his glasses. He took a flannel from his pocket and cleaned them, then placed them back on the bridge of his nose. A dusty shaft of desk lamp light fell across his jaw leaving his bespectacled eyes in shadow. Before Rosie could think of some other line of argument, something else to hold him or prove to him, there was a knock on the office door.

'Come in!' he called.

The bright voice of the doctor's secretary Meredith floated in through the doorway over Rosie's shoulder. She was American and wore high heels. Rosie was fascinated by her.

'Your next patient has arrived,' she said.

'Why didn't you call through to me?'

'I've been doing that. There was no response.'

Dr. Waters began fidgeting about his desk, lifting books and diagrams and shifting papers, finally revealing a deeply buried blinking machine.

'Oh yes. Sorry about that. Do offer them my apologies, who is it again - Harriet?'

'Gerald.'

'Good old Gerald! I'll be ready right away.'

He stood, and Rosie knew she had been dismissed.

'Right, off you go. Your mother will be waiting.'

He took out the brown handkerchief from his breast pocket and dabbed at the pearly beads on his top lip. A good session made him sweat.

'She'll kill me one of these days if I don't start letting you out on time.'

Rosie walked out of the building at a distance from her surroundings, swallowed in what felt like an invisible shield. Thursday afternoons left her feeling as though she existed in another space that sat tight and hidden alongside the real. And she did. Passersby, trees, cars - all seemed impossible. They were shimmering mirages that passed and dispersed before her. She was the only true thing. She was weighed under with thought and her back ached, still too narrow for the monstrosities she carried out front. She was alive and true but was carried as a passenger by this alien brain and body that moved and grew and acted independent of her. Or perhaps the her she thought she knew as Rosie was the alien? She couldn't tell the difference anymore. Perhaps she never could.

Sandra was waiting across the road in the car park behind the DIY complex. The driver's window was open. Ribbons of smoke streamed out and up and melted into clouds.

'Hi.'

'Hello darling,' Sandra said, hastily stubbing out the butt.

She was supposed to have given up months ago, but Rosie kept her secrets.

'How did it go?'

Rosie flopped into the passenger seat beside her.

'Fine.'

Sandra started the ignition. They joined the main road and drove on in silence.

'He kept you late again today.'

'He always keeps me late.'

The street lamps were on. It was getting dark earlier and a definite chill was creeping up on them. Rosie watched the orange glow of the night streak past the car window.

'Did you talk about anything new today?'

'Not really.'

'Not really as in yes or no?'

They came to a halt at traffic lights. A group of teenagers were sitting at a bus stop laughing. They were holding brown paper bags of food and drinking from straws stuck in cardboard cups. They were alone. Unchaperoned. Free. They weren't much older than Rosie herself. Sandra tapped Rosie on the thigh.

'Well?'

'What?'

'Oh for Christ's sake Rosie.'

The light went green and Sandra moved into gear. Rosie watched the teenagers until they were out of sight.

'You're always like this.'

'Like what?'

'Like this! Every bloody week it's the same.'

'What's the same?'

'Oh don't start.'

'I was starting nothing.'

'Lord give me patience,' Sandra's nose flattened as she took a deep breath. 'All I asked, Rosie - all I asked - was a simple question. Is it so hard to just answer it?'

'What do you want me to say?'

'Just talk to me.'

'He tells you everything anyway. I hear you on the phone.'

Sandra pursed her lips. Her tongue darted out to wet them. Her lipstick was cracked and flaking from the cigarette.

'How else am I going to know what's going on with you these days.'

Silence filled the car like sand.

'Did you at least ask about the medication?'

'Yeah.'

'And?'

'Of course he said no.'

'Well –'

'Don't say it.'

Sandra made a clucking sound, but held her tongue otherwise.

'Can we stop talking about this now?'

They hit traffic. Ice was forming on the roads. Steam billowed from the engine exhausts. Rosie chewed her tongue and kept her arms firmly folded across her rapidly emerging chest, trying to squash them flat. It was a wonder to think that they could actually grow more and probably would.

'Are you hungry?' Sandra asked after a spell. Her voice was mild again.

'Suppose.'

Anything to put off going back to that house.

They pulled out of the queue and into another car park. The only light there came from the flashy signs of takeaway restaurants and the odd double-bright beam of a passing car. They walked into a familiar establishment and felt with appreciation the aromatic embrace of fat and salt. Rosie took a seat on a plastic chair while her mother made the order. Minutes later she was over with offerings. Rosie ate and punched holes in the styrofoam. Sandra did not touch the food, but watched her daughter's bowed and sullen head.

'Rosie.'

Rosie made the shape of a flower with the crescent of her fingernail.

'I know it's hard. But you have to talk to me.'

Rosie swallowed the last of her meal and kept her head down.

'It's not easy for any of us.'

The fading trees that lined the road across from the car park were like a fire dying in the wind. Rosie's eyes stung as she watched them dance and her mother's fingers found her hand.

'I know I should have done something sooner. I shouldn't have let it go on. But I ...' Sandra's voice faltered. She held tighter to Rosie's hand. The touch was enough. She squeezed her mother's hand back. Sandra ate her food one-handed until the last flake of salt was licked clean.

As they pulled into their drive, they saw a welcoming party of one waiting for them, hugging his knees against the cold. The person looked up at the approach of the headlamps. It was Peter.

'Back again.'

Rosie looked at her mother. She smiled softly but kept her gaze forward and spoke no more.

(ab)

Peter sat at the edge of her bed and traced symbols on the corner of the duvet. An equation. They had been sitting there for some time swapping irrelevancies, trying to find a way in to the conversation they both longed for but feared to start.

'You haven't answered your window since you've come home,' Peter said finally, putting to end the unusual silence. 'I've stood there throwing stones for ages and you never come out.'

Rosie tugged a few inches of quilt over her cold toes and settled back against the headboard. She sighed, wishing she didn't have to go over it all again.

'It's the stuff I'm on. I told you.'

'The medication?'

'Yeah.'

Peter looked away from the equation and stared past the empty grate to the glowing electric heater in the corner of the room. Apparently, the electricity bill had skyrocketed since its arrival. Mr. - had not been happy about it.

'Is it bad?'

'Yeah.'

'Can't you stop it?'

'No. I'm not allowed.'

He went quiet again and resumed the plucking of the linen.

'You're different,' he said softly.

Inside, Rosie curled up. 'I'm not ignoring you, if that's what you think. Even if I could hear you I wouldn't be able to get up and answer.'

'How come?'

'The stuff makes me seize up.'

'What do you mean?'

'Like I can't move.'

265

She mimed being a mummy and touched his face with her stiffened hands.

'Ugh, stop.'

Rosie shrugged, and her hands dropped into her lap.

'Can't you say you lost it or something?'

'I wish.'

His eyes flicked down to her chest and back up again. He looked toward the window and Rosie had the sensation he was considering hurling himself through it.

'You've never not answered before,' he said.

Exasperation was creeping up on her.

'Sorry but that's just the way it is,' she said with unusual hardness.

She had wounded him, but she didn't care. Did he not understand that she would have given anything to go back to ignorance? To the freedoms of tree-climbing, talking animals and drug-free days, when her fantastical visions were not to be feared, but enjoyed as a part of day-to-day life, of normality? If she could only find a way of turning back time, of proving that things were not as they now seemed but that she was right, and Dr. Waters was wrong. Those first memories of the winter of her birth were still vivid and true feeling, though she had fought him on them he had not been convinced. He had a counter-argument for everything: 'You could have overheard your mother and grandmother discussing it as a child and adopted their memories as your own. You could have read about it and planted those details in your mind. We still don't know the extent of your condition. But with a mind as powerful and complex as yours, Rosie, not much could surprise me ...'

If only someone else could see it the way she could. And then, it came. An idea, or the possibility of one.

There was a knock on the bedroom door and it sent her into action.

'Come and call for me tomorrow in the morning, at ten, no, nine –'

Peter moved back from her sudden change, his face troubled.

'Are you ok?' he asked.

'I'm fine!' she snapped. 'There's something important I want to –'

Sandra appeared around the door with a glass of water and the little jar. Rosie looked at the clock. It had hit nine-thirty. Time for the last pill of the day, and sleep. She could already feel her eyelids growing weary in anticipation.

'Time to say goodnight. Your mother's probably worrying about you Peter.'

Peter rose to leave.

Rosie took the offered pill and held it in her mouth. She took a sip from the glass.

'Night, Rosie.'

Her mother's wispy hair brushed against her cheek as she kissed her and gathered the duvet up. Peter hovered beside the fireplace.

'See you tomorrow at nine?'

His voice came from far above and far away, from the hallway by the door. But he was beside her. Also, he was not. His foot was already on the windowsill. The creak of the wood frame was muted as he leaned his weight upon it, but the curtains were undisturbed. The bedroom door closed. She felt a hand against her face. Something else was said, but it was sucked into the long slow sleep.

Rosie woke with a sense of purpose. For the first time since the treatment had begun. A sense that things could be put to rights if only her plan would succeed. At nine the doorbell sounded. Peter was always on time.

What would it mean for her should she fail? Her plan seemed to her the last chance to grasp at her former life, when she was herself and sane in spite of it. She could be taking a risk that would be likely to set her back far behind the progress her weekly sessions had made. But she had to at least try.

267

Peter was there beside her on the couch. His hand rested against hers but did not hold it. She had almost forgotten he had come. He had manifested at her side. But he must be real. If she could only touch his skin, surely she would know.

'So what is it you want to show me?' he asked.

But she was still salty from the heavy sleep. She needed time to gather herself. The fear of her quiet disobedience last night and the possible discovery of the soggy white pill hidden beneath her pillow was beginning to creep up on her.

'I'm going to get a glass of water.'

She walked into the kitchen. The house was like a twisting labyrinth, the rooms merged into one another, a kaleidoscope of shape and dimension. The metal of the tap was cool, a curving gooseneck, unyielding with its heartless gleam. The water soothed but would not satiate. Had she done the right thing last night? Surely one missed pill was nothing to worry about.

The doorbell went off again sending the previously silent house, dust-settled and ancient, into a flurry of life and activity. Footsteps thudded down the stairs and voices called above the residue of the bells. She was considering calling the whole thing off. There had been plenty of evidence to prove that she was mad after all. Mr. - lived and breathed. The portrait remained fixed at the top of the stairs. Her father had not set foot out of London since the late seventies. Knowledge could be dangerous.

And then she was in the hall and found herself at one side of a square facing Marie, who had just come in through the front door. Sandra was to her left and Peter, who had stepped out of the solitude of the living room, was on her right. There was a moment when nothing was said. Then Marie broke in:

'And how are you feeling, Rosie?'

It was the tone that did it. Never in her life had she been spoken to with such kindness by her grandmother, with such softness, such held tones. The moment was so weighted with absurdity that she stared at her mother wondering when she had mastered the art of ventriloquism. But Marie was now regarding her gently, or as gently as was possible for her and the words simply must have come out of her mouth. And in that moment all doubts disappeared. If the extent of her madness was such that her grandmother thought her so far gone she was worthy of her pity, or even - and she didn't know which was worse - that Rosie had imagined the exchange, then something had to be done. No matter how redundant a scheme it might be.

'Let's go.'

She took Peter by the hand and led him out the open front door.

'Where are you two off to?' Sandra cried.

Rosie did not stop or turn, only ran.

'Rosie would you ever ...! Come back here! Your grandmother's only arrived!'

'Well I did always say she was stone mad.'

Marie's voice came running behind them to tap them on the shoulder, but the figures of Rosie and Peter retreated into the distance and did not turn back.

They followed Rosie's first twisting route through the streets. The path her feet had trodden on that first undisturbed night. Some inner sense, a compass, led her. The place had a freshness as though a heavy rainfall had washed it clean and returned it to a new state.

'What are you looking for?'

Rosie was feeling her way along walls and bushes looking for the spot, for the way in to the place that would redeem her. She stopped.

'I think it's here.'

They stood facing a wildly overgrown thicket in a narrow quiet road. She hadn't come this way in some time.

'Here,' she said. 'Behind these branches.'

'Here?'

'Right here, behind all this, is the thing.'

'The thing.'

'The thing, yes. The ... thing. The place.'

'Is it a thing or a place?'

Rosie gave him a hard stare.

'Give me a hand will you.'

'So behind this bush is what you wanted to show me?'

'Yes.'

'If you wanted somewhere private there are plenty of other places.' His ears were red, and he gnawed at his lip through a shy smile. 'Like the secret laneway down the road.'

His ears went redder still.

'The thing I want to show you is something only I know about.'

'Oh.' His smile faded.

'It's really cool,' she insisted.

'Will you at least tell me what it is?'

'An old graveyard.'

'A graveyard?'

'Yes.'

'Really?'

Yes.'

'I've never seen a graveyard around here and I've lived here all my life.'

Peter had not grown out of that irritating habit he had of always needing to be right.

'Well maybe there was one thing I found myself that I didn't tell you about.'

They stared at each other hard, and there was a moment where it could have gone on far beyond how it had begun. But it passed. It was not the time for that now. She swallowed it down and turned back to the task at hand. The plan she had made. The very important plan. There was still the matter of the graveyard to attend to and the simple matter of her sanity.

'Help?' she asked again.

They hacked away. The branches were cold and stiff. It was tough going with just hands. She hadn't thought to bring gloves or tools. It had never been this difficult.

'There's nothing here,' he said.

'It's well hidden.'

'It's a wall,' he said.

It was just a wall. The bricks were staring back at her.

'Maybe this is the wrong spot,' she said.

But she felt - no, she knew - it couldn't have been anywhere else.

'They must have closed it up,' she said, with a finality that had Peter swallowing his unvoiced suggestion.

'There is another way in,' she said.

'Where is it?'

'In my garden.'

'Why didn't you bring me there in the first place? We were just there.'

'I don't know ... I didn't want my mother to see I suppose. I think.'

The sky was overcast with iridescent grey clouds. The air was sharp and clear. Their breath was a fine mist. They were inadequately dressed.

'Why don't we just stay here for a while then go up to my house for tea?'

'No!' she cried.

The sudden volume of her voice shot down the street like a marble in a pinball machine, echoing endlessly. The vehemence of it again took Peter by surprise.

'It's really important that I show you now,' she said, catching her breath and trying to weave her way back to balance. 'Will you come?'

He looked at her steadily.

'O-k,' he said.

She took to her heels immediately, but he hung back. Her run slowed to a stop.

'Are you coming or not?' she asked. Her chest rose and fell deeply, though she wasn't out of breath.

'I'm coming.'

As they got to the front door, it opened for them. Mr. - stood framed in it, scowling. Over his shoulder Marie's voice could be heard calling from the kitchen.

'I'm looking forward to the new situation,' she said in a voice built to carry: 'This place could do with more of a feminine touch, don't you think?'

Quiet power hid beneath her words. He gritted his teeth.

'I'll be back around five,' he called back, his gaze not wavering from Rosie's face. It had a note of defiance in it, but then he bowed his head and walked off to the car. Peter scuttled around him and Rosie marched ahead through to the kitchen. Marie and Sandra were talking quietly together but brightened as the two children walked in.

'Are you back at last? I was about to do some lunch. Peter you're welcome to stay.'

But Rosie was in no humour to chat. She walked straight to the back door and ran out into the long grass.

'Christ, she gets worse not better,' said Marie. 'That one is mad as a brush.'

Peter followed her out.

Rosie had come to a stop.

'Over there?' he asked. He followed her gaze to the top of the garden wall. 'But it's so high. Are you sure it's safe?'

'It's fine, I've done it loads.'

'But it's icy out.'

'As long as you're not scared.'

'I'm not.'

'Then what are you waiting for? I'll race you.'

They launched themselves at it. The grip was tough. It was a slippery climb. Footholds were scarce and narrow. The ivy had been cut back. It had never seemed so difficult. Rosie blamed the weather and her vast breasts. Peter got there before her. He had always been the faster, with less to weigh him down. He was already sitting comfortably when she looked up.

'Go carefully at the top,' he said. 'The drop to the other side is much further down.'

She struggled on, refusing to give in. When she reached him she was fighting for breath. He straddled the wall with one leg on either side, helped Rosie balance as she sat. His face was closed to her.

'A graveyard?' he asked.

She looked down into the graveyard. She felt dizzy. The ground stretched away from her, far away, much further than she remembered. It seemed wholly changed. There were no tombstones. It was overgrown with bramble and weeds. It was filled with rubbish. There were broken bottles everywhere. Everywhere was moulding packaging and yellow wet grass.

'It's just some empty land,' Peter said quietly. 'A dumping ground.'

'That can't be right.'

'You seemed very sure of yourself before.'

'It was here Peter, I swear. They must have gotten rid of it.'

'Why would anyone get rid of a graveyard?'

'It was very old.'

'That doesn't happen.'

'It grew over then.'

'In months? I can't even see any headstones. It's not possible.'

'It must be.'

'How would you even have gotten down there? You didn't climb.'

'I did climb. I know I did. I remember.'

'Down there? It's so high, no way. You'd break your neck if you fell and you'd never be able to get back out.'

'I don't know. It seemed so easy before. So simple. Just like ...'

'A dream?' Peter offered.

Rosie stared at him. He tried to shut the words back in his mouth, but they were already out there in the cold air between them. And then it came crashing down upon her. The unbearable weight of the truth.

'No. No! It was supposed to be here! It was here only months ago! I saw it from that window up there! And he was here too, he spoke to me. That morning. I was in here the morning of the –'

'That morning?'

Peter had spoken quietly, but he had spoken and been heard. Rosie had known her plan was dangerous, but she had wanted just once to be right, to at last find and keep something for herself. But she had proved herself wrong and Peter knew it too and the pain could not be taken in. She was surely insane. It was what was said about her, she knew. People did not need words to express it. Eyes, sighs, a pursing of lips, a pulse of a forefinger. It was all enough. Her breath galloped off and paid no heed to her. The skin on her arms was smooth and clean and blemish free. She dug her nails in to it. She was desperate for confirmation, for proof, that not everything was a lie. The skin tore and she felt it, but could not tell. Was she even human, even alive? She screamed. It came out wild and raw and her throat stung. She must feel. She must know.

'Rosie. Stop. It. Now. Stop it! You'll fall!'

Peter was beside her still. He held her at the waist and held her as she shook.

'You ... you won't let me fall?' she whispered.

'Never.'

She dropped her head against his shoulder. He held on, he wouldn't let her go. That was one thing she knew for certain. Her breath came back into her chest.

'I was so sure it was here,' she said.

'I know.'

'Do you think I'm mad too?' she asked.

The back door squeaked as it opened behind them, calling their attention back to the right side of the wall. Rosie's question went unanswered.

'Rosie, Peter. Lunch.'

274

Peter looked back at the house, bound by Sandra's command.

'We should go in. It's very cold.'

Rosie looked up at him. His lips were dry.

'Alright,' she said.

He let her go and swung his leg over to the garden side as though dismounting from a horse. He lowered himself and climbed slowly back to the cold grass.

'Are you coming?' he called from below.

She was about to turn and follow him. But she had to look back, just once.

Then: she saw from beneath a twisted tree's roots on the other side of the wall a sight like shining coal.

'There - can you see that?'

'What?'

'Just over there - at the foot of that oak tree.'

'I can't see anything from here,' said Peter. His voice had grown quiet.

The weeds that carpeted the earth floor on the other side began to shimmer. They breathed with a fresh and holy light, lit from within. They receded then, shrunk away. And the grave markers appeared again before her. Beloved Father. Beloved Daughter. Father and Child, together. And another that read: THE END. From beneath the twisted tree's roots, a figure rose up.

'I knew it. I knew it all along. I'm not mad!' She cried out, and she was laughing.

Voices called to her, but she could no longer distinguish the words. The figure rose up to his full height. The hair was black and brilliant like raven's feathers. The eyes a brilliant blue like the sea. There he stood. The man she longed for. The man she craved more than any other. He stood before her in plain view, solid and strong. His hands were large and rough and his hair was long and wild like a woman's. He was the most handsome man she had ever seen.

'Are you coming?' he called. His voice was warm and rolling and thrilled like the first warning of thunder.

'Where are we going?' she asked.

Words were said, other words, but not by him and they came to her as through a badly tuned radio. Her father smiled, and it was the brightest smile she'd ever known. It blocked out all other forms of light until nothing else existed.

'Across the sea,' he said.

'But how will I get down?'

'Jump.'

'But it's so high. I'll surely be hurt.'

'I'll catch you.'

He walked towards her and his scent, his powerful scent, drew her towards him.

'You won't let me fall?' she asked her father her dad her daddy her Joe. One hand lost grip with the wall.

'Never.'

A dog was barking. Voices cried out. They called to her. Rosie, they called. Rosie, Rosie.

And they were soft and hard and they were gentle and pleading and though she could not hear all they said she knew it was with love. Her father stood before her in his worn leather jacket and he widened his dark arms to receive her and she raised her arms to him, her fists opening and closing like a blinking light.

And she jumped.

Acknowledgements

This book has been a long time coming, almost a decade. It has gone on a winding road, a road that would certainly have come to an abrupt dead end were it not for the encouragement, assistance and support of many wonderful people. Thank you to the Dalkey Book Festival who have been supportive of *The Glass Door's* journey from the beginning, awarding it the 'Discovery' prize, and introducing me to Vanessa Fox O'Loughlin, a great champion of new Irish writing who urged me to keep going with this book through many twists and turns over the years. Thank you to Barbara for her encouragement to enter, and support since. Thank you to the judges and organisers of the Irish Writers Centre Greenbean Novel Fair, through which I met my lovely agent Paul Feldstein, who has been a steady, present support for me throughout the last few years. I wish to thank my first readers, Jean and Colm, for their great advice, and my unwavering advocates, Ruth, Kwamie, Laura (IQ), Natasha, Jean (again) and Trag for their constant support and kindness. I also want to thank Charlie Byrne's book club in Galway who chose *The Glass Door* as one of their books of the month before it was released into the world, with considered and kind reviews. Thank you to Nika and Cathy for the mutual holding up at crucial times and to the girls for supporting all my work. Thank you to Esther who has been a bright support across the years. Thank you to Jamie and Abi who back my work though they'll never read it, to Naomi, who might, and to Garreth, who does. Lastly, thank you to my mother, Grace, who has been there from the start and is a guiding force in many ways.